UNRAVELLING

UNRAVELLING

PREETHI NAIR

KTF

This edition first published in the
United Kingdom in 2024 by
Kiss The Frog Press

Copyright © Preethi Nair, 2024

The right of Preethi Nair to be identified as the author of the work has been asserted by her in accordance with the Copyright, Designs and Patents Act 1988.

All rights reserved. No part of this publication may be reproduced, stored in a retrieval system, copied or transmitted, in any form or by any means without the prior written permission from Kiss The Frog Press, nor be otherwise circulated in any form of binding or cover other than that in which it is published and without a similar condition being imposed on the subsequent purchaser.

Every effort has been made to trace copyright holders and to obtain their permission for the use of copyright material. The publisher apologises for any errors or omissions and would be grateful to be notified of any corrections that should be incorporated in future editions of this book.

A CIP catalogue record for this title
is available from the British Library.

ISBN 978-1-9989972-9-9

Typeset by Marsha Swan
Printed and bound by TJ Books Ltd, Padstow, UK

For you, reader – when you think that it's all over, may you find the courage to blossom.

the beginning of the end

The sari that I had chosen for my fortieth wedding anniversary was bought in Mumbai on one of our recent trips. The shopkeeper reiterated that it had taken the sweat of twenty women, and over a month, to handcraft. I didn't believe him. These days, I can spot a lie from a mile away. More so if it is delivered by a man with a thickset monobrow – the tension of a lie is held just above the eyebrow.

"For a forty-year wedding anniversary, ma'am, you deserve only the best. The colour is suiting you very much," he said, draping yet another sari against me. "Feel: Benares silk, perfect for your auspicious occasion."

It was a beautifully embroidered sky-blue sari. I shook my head.

"Ten women handstitched the work on this. See here." He briskly fanned out the sari's pallu to reveal a row of intricately stitched golden elephants.

"No brocades, please, and no blue."

"But such a good colour for your complexion, ma'am."

Let me explain. In the Indian skin colour chart, used mostly for matrimonial purposes, my complexion would be referred to as "wheatish". This terminology is for anyone who does not fall under the "fair" category but is slightly higher up than "dusky". For those unaccustomed to arranged marriages, Indians have a colour chart to match prospective partners; think of it as a Dulux colour chart – or indeed, for those who are more upmarket like my daughter, Farrow and Ball. The lighter the shade of skin tone, the better the marriage prospects. "Fair" trumps an MBA. You may read in a potential bio data (CV for getting married): "Dark but has MBA", and you can be sure that this candidate will unfortunately go to the bottom of the pile.

In spite of being "wheatish", I too would have gone to the bottom of the pile had I had an arranged marriage, or I would still be on the shelf with a sack of old chapati flour, as family background and social standing are very important when matching up prospective candidates. Compatible horoscopes are also taken into account. I would have fallen at this hurdle too: I have what is known as a Mars defect, the consequences of which are likely to cause your husband's premature death and untold destruction to the family. I bypassed the arranged system by opting for a hasty "love" marriage in a cold, damp registry office.

"No, not this sari," I insisted.

The seller speedily reached for another sari. "Abundant green, ma'am, for fertility."

"Do I look like I am at an age to have more children?"

I am fifty-nine. I look fifty-nine. I am not an age-defying celebrity who is about to have twins.

My husband laughed. I smiled at him laughing and was about to add a joke to the comment when the seller raced to the glass cabinet and back with the speed of Usain Bolt.

"For you," he said, trying not to wheeze as he ceremoniously held out an orange sari.

As soon as I saw it, I knew it was the one. The poet Rumi has a saying, "What you are seeking is also seeking you." And when I saw the sari, it was an immediate moment of recognition.

"Georgette," he stated as he draped it against me. "Made for you and you alone by the handiwork of twenty women." He skilfully unfolded more material. "See, like the rising sun. You are a rising sun, ma'am."

Ordinarily, I would have made a comment about me being a rising sun, but the sari was so breathtaking. It had crystal sequins that shimmered as they caught the light. But even more beautiful was the memory that the rising sun briefly evoked.

My grandmother and I were sitting on a red tiled floor in her bedroom as she delicately unpacked her wedding sari to show me. It was her second wedding sari; she had been widowed and as a widow was not allowed to marry again, but she defied custom and remarried.

"I defiantly chose red because the sun always rises. Always, my little one, no matter how dark the nights. Remember that."

Not long before she died, she handed me that wedding sari and asked me to wear it when I got married. Back then, I thought it would be worn when I married my first love, Deepak, but fate had other plans. Well, it wasn't really fate, it was my sister. People have the power to subvert your destiny if you allow them to. The red wedding sari was carefully packed away and later used by my daughter as a decorative tablecloth for her twenty-first birthday party.

Yes, this orange "sunrise" sari was definitely it. I gathered the fabric in my hands and smelled it, half expecting it to smell of my grandmother, but it smelled musty, as if it had been kept in a cabinet for far too long. It smelled as if it wanted to be transported to Harrow on the Hill and given a new history.

The seller raised one side of his furry eyebrow and tilted his head with great agility towards my husband, Hiten.

"The sari is your wife's second skin, sir, and for such an occasion money should not be an issue."

Before I had an opportunity to respond, Hiten took out his wallet. With lightning speed, the seller snatched my husband's money. "Thank you and wishing you forty more years together, sir."

That would make me almost one hundred. I don't want to live until a hundred. I don't want these lines to make even deeper tracks on my face; the left side is already lopsided like a stroke victim's. I haven't suffered a stroke, but it is from years of a slight, uneven smile that time has caught up with. My friend Pushpa says it is because I predominantly chew on the right side and she has sent me a YouTube channel link on facial yoga to correct it. I haven't opened the link yet. Pushpa also uses Crème de la Mer on her face. It costs around £200 a pot but if you look at Pushpa's face, it is not really worth it. Good old turmeric does the job, but even that is now being packaged up and being sold for hundreds. I tell you, the man in marketing will find any way to make you part with money. But I don't have to worry about ageing too much: long life doesn't run in my family. Everyone gets their one-way ticket by sixty-five.

Hiten's side is different. My mother-in-law is eighty, with no imminent signs of making it to the transit lounge. I certainly don't want to live to a hundred. Just give me ten, maybe fifteen more good years.

I slowly put on my sunrise sari ready to go to my "surprise" fortieth anniversary party/vow renewal. It was truly glorious, but I didn't feel glorious. I stared in the mirror again, not recognising the woman who was staring back at me. I looked more like a sunset, and was the bun in my hair too big, too ridiculous? Just as I was about to undo it, Hiten strode into the bedroom and presented me with a diamond necklace. It wasn't from one of his own jewellery shops but from Tiffany's.

"You look beautiful, Bhanu. Still so very beautiful."

No, I don't. I look like an ageing drag queen, I wanted to say. *And... I know about the wedding ceremony and the party. Can we not do this? I don't think I can go through with it.*

Instead, I smiled. "Is this really for me?"

"Who else?" he asked, undoing the clasp effortlessly. He placed the necklace around my neck, and we stood in front of the mirror.

"It's beautiful. Thank you," I said, touching his hand. It was beautiful.

"Like you," he repeated. "You're still hot."

"And not just with flushes," I added in an attempt to lift my mood.

Hiten laughed heartily. I wanted to top it off with, *And does my bun look big in this?* but he would not have got the reference and it would have killed the laughter; I know my husband's limits.

"Forty years! Remember the start. Now look at us. Not bad, eh, Bhanu?" he asked, still laughing.

The start... It was 1978 and Pushpa's twenty-first birthday party. She had arranged a gathering of her friends in a bowling alley. I was running late and turned up in a flowery, orange-and-green miniskirt. I also had cropped hair, so everyone turned and looked at me. Some of the girls gasped. Pushpa introduced me proudly as, "The Twiggy of the Asian community. Everyone, this is Bhanu. My friend from college."

I smiled awkwardly.

A few of her male friends gathered around me to offer me a bowling ball and to show me their techniques. One of the girls, Manju, kindly offered me the long scarf from her salwar kameez to wrap around my skirt.

I could sense his presence. He was watching me from a distance, and then I saw him out of the corner of my eye. He was the spitting image of John Travolta with his jet-black hair and freshly starched white collar – like Concorde wings, they were. He was definitely going places. He then got up, rolled the ball, knocked down all the pins and glanced at me.

"Three consecutive strikes are known as a 'turkey'," he stated.

I ignored him and picked up a small bowling ball. I could feel his eyes watching me and I did not hit a single pin because I couldn't bend very far in my outfit.

He strutted confidently past me and delivered two further strikes.

"I'm as good as my word. So, when I say I am going to marry you, it means I am going to marry you."

'You're The One That I Want' started playing and he began singing along. He didn't care what anyone thought, and when it came to the part about the power I was supplying, he made some thrusting motions towards me.

"Come on, Bhanu, do something," Pushpa encouraged.

I didn't know if I was supposed to sing Olivia Newton-John's part, but I felt it was time to leave.

I got my coat and went to exchange my shoes. He followed me. He apologised for the strange movement that he'd made and then gestured to the space between the two of us, saying, "You have to admit – it is electrifying."

I didn't say anything and continued putting my shoes on.

"At least let me take you home. It's late."

"No thank you." I rummaged in my handbag for a bunch of keys. I wasn't going to use them on him; I just liked to be prepared and feel secure, especially when I walked on my own.

"I am going to accompany you to the station," he insisted.

I liked that he used the word "accompany", and so I nodded at him.

"I saw it, I saw that look, so I know there is hope," he exclaimed excitedly.

"There was no look."

"There definitely was." He smiled.

Hiten has aged better than the real John Travolta, and with no plastic surgery required. He has got a very natural look: salt-and-pepper hair, and still that mischievous sparkle in his eyes. He and my daughter Anita have organised the surprise Hindu vow renewal and party at The Grove in Hertfordshire. Though technically, we never *had* a Hindu ceremony so it's not really a renewal. It is our Hindu wedding. The Grove was a wedding venue that I had spotted for Anita, but she didn't get married there so I had it in the back pocket for my son's wedding.

Anita, in spite of being "fair", possessing an MBA and working as an investment banker, did not do well in the traditional marriage system. Don't get me wrong, it was not for a lack of trying on my part; I was like Cilla Black, setting her up on dates every week, and there was a queue of men who were waiting to marry her. She rejected every one of them and then got married to white Hugh. Those unaccustomed could think, *Jackpot! That's white on the colour chart.* No, to marry a white, English person is still considered by many in the community worse than marrying someone who is dusky.

Anyway, I mentioned The Grove to Pushpa, saying that's where I would want my son Hari to get married to the wonderful Sarah (also white), and then lo and behold, that's where Pushpa organised her son's wedding last summer. It was arranged in the sense that Pushpa had introduced them both through the community network (which consists of nimble-fingered Indian women who can swipe left or right in an instant and who can recall the bio data of any individual in the community, including any anomalies, quicker than AI). I was more upset about the fact that Pushpa hadn't told me until I saw the invitation.

"What does it matter, Bhanu?" she asked me. "Your Hari is so laid-back he won't be getting married for another five years and anyway, English people like to do things their own way; they don't want our interfering. You saw that with Anita."

I didn't tell her that Sarah wanted to have a Hindu ceremony. Best to keep some things back.

Anyone would have thought it was Pushpa's wedding; she hurried along with the photographer and the happy couple to have pictures taken. Hiten and I strolled into the gardens and then Anita and our granddaughter Leyla joined us. We sat listening to the string quartet playing Bollywood themes and admired the water feature. Then I sighed, "I thought we would have ours here." What I meant was, I thought Anita would have had her wedding at The Grove and I knew that I should have corrected myself there and then, but I got distracted by Leyla, who was trying to jump into the water. Anita had misunderstood me, it turned out, thinking I was referring to the fact that my husband and I hadn't had the traditional Hindu wedding ceremony and that this was where I would have wanted it.

Anyway, before I knew it, Anita was secretly liaising with my husband, booking the venue, the catering, the Bollywood orchestra, the priest, and sorting out the guest list. That's my daughter: you give her a target and she will get the job done.

I accidentally heard her on speaker as she was talking to my husband.

"Daddy, Daddy. I thought of giving the tables names of all the places you and Mummy have been to the last couple of years: Costa Rica, Mauritius, Hawaii."

"Don't add the latest Caribbean cruise," he requested.

I put down my Bran Flakes. I don't normally listen in on conversations, but I just had to double-check what I was hearing.

"Of course I won't, Daddy."

He didn't have a good time on that Caribbean cruise.

"And Hari said he will put together the music."

My son Hari has a talent for rapping and mixing and is an all-round good entertainer. He's also in IT and good with PowerPoint.

"I have got the priest sorted and they will allow the fire," she added.

That's when I spat out the Bran Flakes. A priest? A bloody priest? Excuse my language.

"Mum is going to be beyond surprised! In fact, she'll be ecstatic; she's waited forty years for this."

Well, actually I haven't. I was quite relieved that we hadn't formalised our wedding as, technically, in the eyes of God or the gods, my husband and I are not married. A Hindu marriage is only valid when certain rites like Saptapadi or seven steps are performed. This ceremony is where the bride and groom take seven steps around the holy fire (Agni) and make seven vows that are roughly:

1. To nourish each other physically, mentally and spiritually
2. To grow together in strength and to be faithful
3. To preserve wealth and prosperity
4. To share joy and sorrow
5. To care for the children and parents
6. To be together forever
7. To remain lifelong friends

First of all, number five is the one I know I am unable to commit to; I don't want to take care of his mother. She is pretending she has Alzheimer's, and has forgotten or is pretending to forget the deal we made over thirty years ago that I would never have to look after her. Moreover, I think she is trolling me by leaving completed sudoku puzzles all over my house – puzzles that even Carol Vorderman would have trouble doing.

The vows, as I said, are a loose translation. For example, the literal translation for point three is, "to protect the cattle and the agricultural business". Speaking of livestock, on some of these vows (notably number two), one could say the horse has well and truly bolted. I'm referring to my husband's infidelities.

Not that I am without fault; for most of our married life, I have created a parallel imaginary existence with my first love, Deepak. It is the only way I have survived my marriage – talking to Deep as if it was him that I had married and sometimes, in difficult situations, pretending that he was by my side.

The thing is, I bumped into him yesterday and even though I was always imagining our re-encounter, I never actually truly believed that he would reappear in my life, and certainly not the day before the vow renewal ceremony. It wasn't how I'd imagined it would be; I had turmeric-stained hands, was wearing elasticated tracksuit bottoms and looking quite dishevelled. Deep didn't seem to care.

"Come away with me," Deep whispered as he took my hand in Starbucks.

Imagine, me running off at fifty-nine! What would other people think? What about my family? Anyway, I love my husband, I do. I really do. I am not some naïve twenty-year-old with fantasies of what love might be like; those days have definitely gone, like the aforementioned horse. No, I am happy in my marriage. Of course we have had our ups and downs like any other marriage, but I am happy. I'm not running off with anyone. Unfortunately, I am unable to lie in front of the holy fire and this is the part of the ceremony that is making me feel incredibly nervous. Or perhaps "nervous" is not the right word – shit-scared would probably describe it better. The fire god Agni has never let me get away with anything other than being truthful. On the other hand, the fire symbolises burning all the impurities between the couple, leaving truth to unite them and this, symbolically, is possibly worth doing.

The Saptapadi ceremony concludes with a prayer that the union be everlasting. I think that means eternity (reinforcing point six) and that's also been keeping me up at night. When I am reincarnated, will my husband find me like a homing pigeon? I have wondered whether to speak to my daughter and tell her I know about the ceremony and ask if we could skip this part of the proceedings and just get to the party. However, the choice is between offending her and spending an eternity with my husband. After much deliberation, I have decided on spending an eternity with him.

"Bhanu, I am going to have to get Mummy," my husband said as he kissed me.

The mummy. Had I met her before the wedding, I don't think I would have married him. She has caused me heartache. I will save you a lot of trouble by telling you that if you don't like the potential in-laws, run!

Last week, my husband announced that she was coming to live with us; her other son can't have her – he said his wife is suffering with depression. My instinct was to scream, *No bloody way! I don't want my twilight years to be stolen by her.* But I contained myself since she had come for a visit and was sitting at the kitchen table when he announced it.

"I was thinking Mummy could move in next month. We can clear downstairs for her by then."

I couldn't think straight and, so it appeared, neither could she.

"Do I like tea or coffee, son?" she asked my husband, glancing at me cunningly as she clutched her handbag; it had a sudoku book in it.

"Coffee, Mummy," my husband replied. "You like coffee."

I gathered my thoughts and was about to say something when my son came down.

"It will be fun to have you here, Nanima," he said, bending down to her level and then he kissed her. She grabbed him tightly, reached into her handbag, pulled out a £50 note and handed it to him.

"Take it, *beta*. Please. I will always look after you." She shot another glance at me.

My son protested but took it. Her sudoku book fell out of her bag. I picked it up and flicked through it to show them both what an agile mind she still had but in this particular book, she had scrawled on the pages in big writing, *Who am I?*, *What is my name?*

"Mummy needs us now more than ever," my husband whispered, peering over my shoulder.

His mother smiled slyly at me.

"Any coffee going, Mum?" my son asked as he headed towards the fridge. My son is currently in between jobs and is home a lot during the day.

Back to Saptapadi step five: after thirty-four years, I don't really want to look after my son any more either.

"Bhanu, Bhanu, did you hear me? I said I'm just going to pick up Mummy," my husband repeated. His mother will know that I know that she knows that I know all about the surprise vow renewal and that we are really not going to the Taste of Taj for brunch (used as the foil for The Grove).

"Yes," I replied.

"I will be back in an hour and a half, hopefully sooner if there is no traffic."

It was the perfect moment for me to escape. To open the door and keep walking. I reminded myself how very lucky I am. I have a good husband, great kids, a lovely granddaughter and an amazing home. What more is there? I picked up my phone, caught a glimpse of all the missed calls and messages from Deep. All our friends and family would be arriving at The Grove in two hours. I placed the phone face down and slowly reapplied the blusher and focused on the event.

The car park at The Grove would be taken over and filled with personalised number plates – KI5H, VI5H, NI5H. A personalised number plate with an Indian name basically says that we came off a boat or a plane, spent months or years sleeping in any available confined space, have at some point swindled, or have been swindled but eventually triumphed. And now, look, look how far we have come! A party at The Grove is an amplified version of this, an announcement to the community that we have made it. Yes, we certainly made it.

My adopted sister Gauri (or Goggles as I call her behind her back) will drive up to The Grove in her dirty blue Datsun, symbol of her martyrdom, and will park awkwardly in one of the bays. She has the money to upgrade but doesn't want to; she likes everyone to know that she has made sacrifices, that she never married or had children but looked after and cared for our parents instead. Gauri did inherit an amazing family sweet shop that she ran into the ground, but my parents probably knew that she would do this, and made sure she was well cared for.

After I applied the blusher, I went to the bathroom and took two aspirins. I have got a dodgy back. I don't want to be dressed up all nicely and then the back goes showing that there is some problem. No doubt, one of the eagle eyes from the community will spot the anomaly.

Community Member A's detector process: "Hmm. Nice hair, nice nails, nice sari, but wait… something is wrong. Give me a second."

She will run a search with her own internal search engine.

"Yes! I have pinpointed it. Back. Back problem!"

She will swoop down upon me: "*Hare* Bhanu! Back problem, *che*?"

No, no, there is no problem. I just love dragging myself around for fun. Of course, I won't say this; I will smile politely and point her in the direction of the food, which will be getting cold.

As soon as we got back from our Caribbean cruise about a month ago, my daughter Anita organised an appointment for me to see a physiotherapist for my back. I had driven to Kew to deliver food parcels for her. She greeted me by kissing me like a French woman on both cheeks. Anita can be quite reserved when expressing emotions, but she likes this form of greeting. She did her MBA in Paris.

"Listen, Mum, I can't watch you struggling on. I have booked an appointment in Harley Street." My daughter can be really very thoughtful.

"Just to warn you, the therapist might be a bit alternative," she added.

Anita is like the Indian version of Gwyneth Paltrow. Chakra balancing, this balancing, that balancing and don't get me started on food – gluten free, dairy free, ghee free. Try making a chapatti for her and you will see the level of skilful conflict management required.

"Thanks, Mum," she said as I handed her the food parcels. "You are sure you made it with buckwheat?"

"Yes."

"Mum, the therapist believes that all pain is based on repressed emotions."

"Anita, what emotions do I have that are repressed?" I said, trying to avoid eye contact because the chapattis were made from wheat. "I am an open book. What you see is what you get."

This is not the truth. I have told myself so many stories that I don't know what the truth is any more. Even this is a lie. If I tell myself the truth, or my version of the truth, then... everything must change.

yard one

THE GUEST HOUSE
This being human is a guest house.
Every morning a new arrival.
A joy, a depression, a meanness,
some momentary awareness comes
as an unexpected visitor.
Welcome and entertain them all!
Even if they are a crowd of sorrows,
who violently sweep your house
empty of its furniture,
still, treat each guest honourably.
He may be clearing you out
for some new delight.
The dark thought, the shame, the malice.
meet them at the door laughing and invite them in.
Be grateful for whatever comes.
because each has been sent
as a guide from beyond.

— Jalāl ad-Dīn Rumi,
translation by Coleman Barks

"Bhanu, it all sounds very matter-of-fact. Disconnected. So, what I want you to do is to go back to being that seven-year-old little girl. Imagine her, imagine holding her hand. She is safe now. What does she feel when she is told that her mother has died?" The therapist tilted her head forward and her half-moon spectacles balanced precariously on her nose. With her round face and red flushed cheeks, she had the appearance of a cuddly grandmother from one of my granddaughter's fairy tales. I was expecting a back therapist but this one was a talker.

I couldn't go back to being a child, so I pretended. "I was very sad." I quickly corrected myself. "I am very sad."

She leaned forward. "It was a tragic way for her to die. I am very sorry."

I nodded.

She nodded back and made a note in her book. I sat there uncomfortably, trying to find something I could make a joke about. Nothing came to me except the sight of her cosy, green velvet armchair. So I imagined her with a knitted patchwork blanket on her lap, waiting eagerly for her granddaughter, bearing a picnic basket.

"Where did you go, Bhanu? You went somewhere."

I couldn't tell her about the picnic basket. "Nowhere," I said, sitting uneasily.

"When you get emotionally overwhelmed, do you find you escape, disassociate with reality?"

"Not really," I replied. She didn't need to know about my imaginary conversations with Deep and my parallel existence with him for the last thirty-five years. That would take me months to explain and, in the process, make her a small fortune.

"You hide your true emotions. Your emotions are not heard or seen..." She paused. "Do you feel unseen?"

I shook my head and then a tight lump began to form in my throat. I tried my best to swallow it and bit my lip to stop the tears from falling, but they began to flow and I could not control them.

"Don't hold them in," she said gently, passing me a box of tissues.

"Niagara Falls," I joked as the tears finally came to an end.

The therapist did not laugh. Her kind round face was very still.

Looking at the snowy white pile of tissues that had amassed on my lap, "Everest," I said.

She still did not laugh.

"Sit with it. Don't distract with humour. Your physical pain is the subconscious's way of protecting you from dealing with the emotional pain. It is a protection mechanism because it thinks you won't be able to cope. Just sit with your emotions. Feel them." She took a deep breath.

I wiped my face. "I can't, not now. I have a wedding ceremony that I need to prepare for mentally. It's my fortieth anniversary in less than a month and I'm getting married."

"To stop the pain, you need to feel it."

That's exactly what the poet Rumi says, I thought. *"The cure for pain is in the pain."*

"Not now," I said, gathering up the avalanche of tissues. "Maybe after the ceremony. I need to get through it. You don't understand what this means to me."

"Tell me."

"I need to show everyone that it has all been worth it. That we made it, that we have had, *have* a great life."

"And have you?" she asked.

"That is irrelevant. I want to explain to you something that you might not understand. What other people think is so important in our culture. Even before you think what you think, you think, what will other people think? I have to show them that it has been worth it."

"I find that very sad." She looked at me.

I tried my hardest not to cry again and dug my fingernail into my thumb.

"Who is 'them'?" she asked calmly.

"People. The community. They are judging me."

"Maybe it is you judging yourself?"

"No. They are definitely judging me." She had clearly never encountered community members – tongues sharper than Cuisine Pro kitchen knives.

"Do you have anyone who supports you in your life – cheerleaders who could counter this judgemental voice?"

I thought about it briefly. There was, of course, Deep. His voice in my head was always encouraging, always reassuring; but I couldn't bring him up. Lovely Sarah. But she was gone. Anita – not really; Pushpa – no; Goggles – definite no; mother-in-law or MIL as they now say – definite no. "I need to think about it," I replied.

"We have time," she answered, glancing up at the clock.

I had said too much; it was uncomfortable. I wanted to get out of there; I got up.

"Stay." She invited me to sit back down.

"I will do this properly after the wedding ceremony. I really have to go. My daughter and granddaughter will be waiting for me." I put the tissues in the bin.

"You are suffering from childhood PTSD, Bhanu, and it is not going to be an easy few weeks ahead. Things will come to the surface. The external world has a strange way of reflecting the internal one." She put her notebook down and readjusted her glasses. "I suggest you come in next week."

I considered it momentarily but decided against it; four weeks before my wedding was not the time to unravel.

"I will make another appointment," I lied.

She stood up and touched my arm. "In the meantime, I'd like you to think of a supporter – a cheerleading voice that you can hear in times of doubt or judgement. Will you do that?"

I nodded.

"The other important thing I would like you to do is to be present with your emotions. When your back hurts, ask it to show you the pain. When emotional pain rises, do not disconnect."

"I will certainly do that." I grabbed my coat. She didn't need to know that it would be after a month, after the ceremony was all over and I was officially married to my husband and our family unit was intact.

As I was leaving, I saw a sign on her wall.

These pains you feel are messengers. Listen to them.

I stopped. "Rumi. He is my favourite poet," I said, staring at the quote.

I had thought of Rumi and here he was on her wall. If I were a romantic, I would have taken this as a sign – the pull of the universe leading me to exactly where I needed to be – and perhaps, once, I would have done this, but there was a wedding ceremony to prepare for.

I have trained myself so skilfully that I don't know what my honest response is any more. Or I do know, but I assess the situation and override it. So, when I saw my granddaughter Leyla sitting in her high chair and Anita playing with her, my first instinct was to run up to them both, beat my chest and fall to the ground howling. But we were in a coffee shop off Harley Street.

Anita looked at me and asked me how it had gone. All I could say was, "She was not a physiotherapist." Then, despite me trying to push them down, tears began to form uncontrollably. Anita looked uncomfortable. She is not very good with emotion, especially mine.

"Oh, Mum, I know how it can be." She touched my hand. I put my hand on top of hers.

She jerked slightly.

"Where did it go wrong with us?" I asked.

She didn't say anything.

I filled the silence. "Good business for the therapists: blame everything on the mother."

Anita ignored the comment and reached for the wet wipes. I dried my tears.

Anita and my son Hari don't know about my family history. I killed my parents off in a rickshaw accident. I have told myself I did this to protect them, to give them a secure upbringing; perhaps I did this because of the shame I carry?

"Are you still okay to take Leyla to the park? I just need to run a few errands while we are here." Anita stood up and began cleaning the table with the wet wipe.

Nothing could ever stop me from taking Leyla anywhere. I could have been in the invented rickshaw accident with my arms hanging off, but I would still manage to push her stroller with my foot.

"We haven't talked about your cruise." She took out another wet wipe.

"Daddy was sick for most of it," I informed her.

She would know this. My husband and daughter speak every day.

"Yes. Daddy said." She cleaned the tray on Leyla's high chair.

"I met an amazing German lady. Her name was Helga and…"

Helga! That was it! Helga could be my cheerleader. Just as the expensive therapist suggested.

"You'll have to tell me about it later," she said, leaving the tray immaculate. "Remember, don't give her any biscuits and if you really have to, make sure that they are the organic ones here and not the ones from your handbag."

I keep digestive biscuits in my handbag.

"And don't let her fall asleep." Anita took Leyla out of the high chair, adding, "It will ruin her sleep later. Be back here in two hours?"

"Take your time," I replied.

"No, Mum. Please be back in two hours. I have a meeting." She handed Leyla to me, kissed her on the head, gathered her things, kissed me like a French woman and left.

I held Leyla tightly in my arms and started to cry again. Leyla touched my face. I said, "Silly Nanima. I don't know what's happened to Nanima today. She is feeling a little bit frightened, not sure about what exactly, but it's nothing for you to worry about. Where's your favourite Humpty book? Humpty? Let's look in this bag."

We took the book out and sat back down like Humpty on his wall – precarious, vulnerable. Unlike us, he had a great fall, and no one could put him back together again. Well, perhaps the therapist could, especially if she delved into his childhood and found his mother. Leyla laughed as I read Humpty to her over and over again in an attempt to distract myself from a very uncomfortable feeling.

"See, Leyla, that's an iambic pentameter, like Shakespeare. When you're a bit older I am going to read you Shakespeare and Rumi. Rumi is Nanima's favourite poet. Someone very special introduced me to him. I think it's time Nanima let go of that someone very special because she is getting married soon. Maybe I could do it symbolically with the holy fire? Yes, perhaps that's the way to say goodbye?"

"Bye, bye," Leyla repeated.

"Yes, bye, bye, Deep. It is the right thing to do. Anyway, do you know what Rumi would say about

Humpty? Who cares if you're broken, Humpty – 'The wound is the place where the light enters you'. That's so true, Leyla, but you have to be ready to feel the wound. I think Nanima applied too much glue when she put herself back together again."

I put Leyla in the pushchair and took her to Regent's Park, remembering how I would take my daughter to the park and feed the ducks with her. Anita would scream with laughter and my heart would be full with the love I felt for her. Everything was worth it, every bad decision that I'd made was worth it because I had Anita and then my son. When Hari came along, I thought my heart was unable to expand any further but it did; it made room for him. It was then the three of us feeding the ducks. Afraid of them, Hari would cling to his sister, or hide behind me. Time goes very quickly, love changes, it evolves. Leyla had fallen asleep.

Now, the question was whether to wake her. It wasn't sleep time but Leyla looked so peaceful. What to do? Tell my daughter that she had fallen asleep or lie as I usually did and face the consequences later? It was then that Helga popped into my head again. Helga wouldn't care what anyone thought and would let her sleep and then tell her daughter that she had let her sleep. So, I decided not to wake Leyla and tell the truth.

Just as we got to the pond, I got a call from Anita saying that there was a change of plan and Hugh was on his way to collect Leyla, so I headed back to the café where he was waiting for me. The interaction was quick and polite, as if I had handed him the latte that he had requested.

"Thank you very much, Bhanu."

"No problem. Any time. She fell asleep. I'm sorry."

"Ah. Slight problem. Can sort out later. Off we go, Leyla."

He too kissed me like a French person before he left with Leyla.

It's all very formal with Hugh. Truthfully, he would not have been my first choice for Anita. We never pressured either of our children to get married. I might have set up a few dates for them through our network, but it was totally their choice if they wanted to take it further. Of course, all the applicants we selected were rejected and I have to say when my children reached their thirties, I started to get worried.

"Bring home anyone," I encouraged. I am generally not very religious, but I might have done a few pujas and fasts to speed things along.

So, when your children hit thirty-five and you have given up all hope, you thank God for whoever they bring home. We met Hugh for the first time at a restaurant. My husband went over the top. I thought he was going to fling himself at Hugh's feet. Instead, he kissed Hugh's hand as if he were the Pope and had blessed him and he kept saying, "Thank you, thank you." He suddenly remembered that I was standing behind him.

"Hugh, this is my wife, Bhanu."

We are not desperate people and I didn't want Hugh

to think he was getting some second-hand goods. To be honest, I also felt slightly uneasy at his cursory glance at my sari (only worn for special occasions). He didn't know that I had changed five times for him. I felt as if I had chosen the wrong outfit and needed to show him that I was educated and not just some middle-aged woman in a sari. In fairness to Hugh, his look could have been because he found the electric green and pink combination distasteful.

I held out my hand. "Pleased to meet you, Hugh." And then I continued, "'Nature's first green is gold. Her hardest hue to hold... nothing gold can stay'."

There was silence. It was difficult to read his reaction. Confused more than impressed, I would say.

"Mummy's really into poetry," Anita added quickly.

"How charming," Hugh responded.

And why I said it, I don't know. Well, I do. Anyway, it just came flying out of my mouth.

"Anita is gold to us. Do you think you are hard to hold on to, Hugh?"

Anita stared wide-eyed at Hiten. Hiten rescues her from all uncomfortable situations.

"Any plans for the wedding?" Hiten asked.

"Actually, Daddy, we are going to do something very low-key. Just a few friends and family."

Low-key? Low-key? I wanted to shout. *No way low-key. WWOPT (what will other people think)? We have waited years for this marriage.* I was upset but I didn't say anything.

Anita and Hugh got married in a magnificent castle in Tuscany; it was just their close friends and family. They didn't want us to pay for the wedding so we didn't get a say in who was coming. Our friends and extended family members were of course very disappointed and Pushpa has never let me forget it. The wedding was the first time we met Hugh's parents; we generally don't have much contact with them.

Malcolm, Hugh's father, is florid due to excessive alcohol consumption. He knows a lot about high-speed trains and his hobby is trainspotting. Hugh knows a lot about trains too. Anita probably still finds this endearing. In a few years, depending on many variable factors (help with childcare, work, hormonal changes, extended family relationships), she will ask him to shut up about the 6.40 from Brighton or 18.13 to Bristol Parkway, or perhaps want to put him on one of those trains and send him off.

Hugh's mother, Margaret, is inoffensive and very polite and puts up with her husband, Malcolm, who doesn't really speak to her. The only interaction I have seen between them is when she reaches for a napkin and puts it around his neck when he is about to eat. It is like a bib. There is no reason for this – he has no apparent signs of the onset of dementia or anything like that. It is just a habit. She takes care of his every need and he reads his papers and ignores her.

This is their deal. Every marriage/relationship has a deal – an unspoken code of conduct that keeps the dynamic and status quo held neatly bound together. This part of the deal was left over from the time when Malcolm was a stockbroker bringing home the money and her job was to take care of him, the family, the house and organise his social calendar. He is now retired, the children left a long time ago, the big house is crumbling, and she doesn't even question whether to renegotiate the deal.

Well, that was until a few weeks ago; while we were on our Caribbean cruise, their daughter, Cynthia, died suddenly after an aneurysm. She was only forty. Unmarried. No children.

We got off the cruise and I wanted to go and see Margaret immediately, but we were told that we could not just turn up. Of course, when someone dies in our culture, we land on their doorstep with food and we just leave our finger on the bell until somebody opens the front door but on this occasion, our visit needed to be planned and just as he left with Leyla, Hugh confirmed it would be okay to see them in the afternoon.

Although I was totally disorientated by the visit to the therapist, I thought it was only right that we pay our respects, so I went back home, collected a few food items for Margaret, and we drove to Cobham.

I extended my arms to hug Malcolm, but he held out his hand. "So very sorry, Malcolm," I said, shaking it.

"These things happen," he said, matter-of-fact.

The space between him and Margaret was so vast that you could have got lost and never found your way back.

"I am so sorry for your loss, Margaret," I said, clinging to her.

"I have shed a tear, Ban-oo," she replied steadily, disentangling herself. "Let me show you the rhododendrons that have bloomed in the garden."

I didn't know if this was some code for loss but if that were my loss, I would have grabbed her, beaten my chest, beaten her, wailed uncontrollably and then fallen to the ground. Instead she showed us around the garden, and we drank tea and ate scones. Malcolm had his bib on. It was all very polite. I noted I felt deeply sad for her, for them, and I had to pinch myself to stop myself from crying yet again.

We navigated around safe subjects like the weather. I imagined her in that big crumbling house on her own, barely making eye contact with her husband except to put on his bib, and I wanted her to know that I was really there for her, that she could express her emotion and I would hold her safely. So, I decided to step directly on the landmine and talk about death. I was about to ask if Cynthia went peacefully but my husband, sensing this, did a course correction and told them about our holiday and how much he had enjoyed the Caribbean cruise and proceeded to go into great detail about it – docking at each port as if he were the captain of the ship.

It was, of course, utter rubbish. He was seasick, and for the entire time he was either in the cabin asleep or throwing up in the toilet, so I made friends with

Helga. I don't have many European friends but, since Brexit, I wanted to show unity.

I met Helga in the sauna. I don't normally go to the sauna as I have my own – it's called the ongoing menopause and you can't control the thermostat. But I read a magazine article that said that the sauna could help with my back pain. I have to say at this point that it was an out-of-character, spontaneous decision to go into the sauna – I just wanted to check it out as I was on my way to the ship's cocktail party dressed in a sari. I wasn't sure if I would actually make it there as I really don't go anywhere on my own, but I was bored of being in the cabin watching my husband throw up, and I thought the likelihood of me actually going to the party would be higher if I got dressed up. I had a peep through the little glass window of the sauna just to double-check nobody was in there and I didn't see anyone, so I went in.

Imagine my surprise when I saw this figure sitting there on the top bench. Naked. Yes, naked – and she wasn't small either. She was just letting everything hang out and the hair... you could have knitted a pashmina with all that hair. It was awkward as I wanted to head straight back out but I thought, *What will she think if I just leave?* She could think I was a pervert, or that I was offended by her body. So I froze for a second before taking a seat on the bench opposite her.

"You must be hot," she said, in her strong German accent, wiping the sweat off her thighs.

I was in my sari and my cardigan. Of course, I was bloody boiling. I wrapped my cardigan tighter.

"No, I am fine, thank you," I replied, very worried about what the heat was doing to my Kanchipuram silk sari, but unable to escape.

"Take off your cardigan and sari and breathe. Breathe," she instructed, inhaling deeply.

No way, German lady, I thought, but I just smiled at her politely.

"I'm Helga."

"I'm Bhanu. Pleased to meet you." I was unsure of where to look.

Then she started having a conversation with me. She was waving her arms, moving her legs and at one point, she stood up, planting her feet on the bench beneath her. She just got up and displayed all her naked goods; her post box was right in my eyeline. At first, I was slightly alarmed but then I thought, *How brave, not to care what anyone thinks of you. You go for it, German lady!* How amazing to feel totally at home and alive in your body. My spirit has always felt that it was an Airbnb guest as opposed to a homeowner, and a respectful guest at that, fearing that it would be rated for its stay – and so it has not always done what it has wanted.

Helga was travelling on her own; she was widowed.

This is what the community would focus on.

Community Member A would look her up and down, distracted momentarily by the size of her thighs and then pronounce, "*Hare!* Her husband is dead."

Members B and C would make suggestions as to the cause of death.

Member C: "Heart attack?"

Member B: "Brain haemorrhage?"

Back to Member A: "No. It was cancer."

Post-mortem carried out and cause of death established, they would apportion blame on her.

Member B: "She fed him too much ghee."

I had a quick glance at all the flaps and folds of her body and had complete admiration for her as I wished I could stand naked. Be free. Really free, and not care what other people think. She commented on the beauty and elegance of the sari – not mine, as it was getting crumpled – but mine had probably triggered her thoughts. Helga had been to Kerala and seen "many beautiful women" wrapped so elegantly. She smiled at the memories this brought back, telling me how she had worn one. I told her that the sari I was wearing was from South India and went into great detail about the silk used to weave the material, at which point I think I lost her.

She had gone to Kerala on her own to an ayurvedic spa without a care in the world and had spent a month there. I told her that though I had always wanted to go I hadn't made it further than Mumbai, but it was certainly on my list of places to visit. We hadn't gone as my husband wasn't keen due to "too many communists" there. My husband is all about conformity – when it suits him. I told her that if she ever wanted to try a sari on again, that I had packed a few and she would be most welcome to wear one of mine. It was then she looked like she would burst with happiness and told me that she had brought her sari with her, just in case there was an occasion to wear it.

"It's destiny. Meeting you is destiny." Helga beamed.

"What you are seeking is also seeking you," I quoted Rumi.

She appeared to be confused.

"You wanted to wear your sari again, so you brought it with you, and I want to dress you."

After the sauna, I went back to the cabin, got changed quickly. There was no lasting damage to my sari, and I hung it out to dry. I checked on my husband (who was asleep), took out some of the methi parathas I had packed for the journey and rushed back to her. I gave them to her. She was so grateful.

"What is this?"

"Vegetarian food. No piggy eating for me. No lamb."

Even though her English was very good, I made the sound of a pig and a lamb.

"And certainly, no beef and no eggs." I did the chicken motion. "I am a vegetarian." I wanted to add that I was a vegetarian long before it was fashionable and I took pride in my food, long before what you ate was photographed and put on social media, but she interrupted me with her hearty laugh.

"Ah, yah. No vegetarian food on ship?" she asked, looking at the parathas.

"Yes, but very bad food." I did the motion of being sick.

She took a bite from the paratha – actually, she ripped it with her carnivorous teeth.

"*Wunderbar.*"

"Made with methi – I grow herbs in my garden."

We then had a conversation about gardening, and she suggested we go to the ship's cocktail party together and from there, we were inseparable, meeting every day for the next ten days.

There was of course a slight language barrier, but this just added to the laughter and we understood each other perfectly. Helga had two grown-up children and grandchildren but was not an active babysitter; instead she pursued her own interests, more so after her husband's death (heart attack) two years ago. I asked her how it had affected her.

"Happy. I was very happy."

There was probably some misunderstanding in the translation, so I asked her again.

"He was difficult. Difficult marriage but you know – stay together for children and then because of routine."

I looked around, seeing if anyone was overhearing this conversation. In the Indian community, no one really spoke of these things. Perhaps in the early years of marriage, you speak of some difficulties with your mother-in-law but when you get to our age, you don't even allow yourself to think, *Am I happy, could I be happier?* I mean why would you? Marriage is a lifetime contract. If you are unhappy in your marriage, you maintain an outward focus and pick yourself up with a nice sari and put on some jewellery; perhaps you get a new car and a personalised number plate and you demonstrate to the world how happy you are.

Helga continued, "When he died, I say, 'Helga, now time for you. Time to enjoy life'. Only one life, *nicht wahr?*"

Well not really, not if you are a Hindu and believe in reincarnation and that this is your karma. Moksha, or liberation, for us only comes after inhabiting endless homes, or Airbnbs in my case.

By the end of the ten days, Helga had managed to get me into the sauna with just the sari's petticoat tied around my chest. She even taught me to swim – something that I had resisted for over fifty years.

"Don't put the slip on over your costume. Take it off," Helga instructed. She was referring to the sari petticoat I put over my swimming costume. "Come on, Bhanu. Nobody is caring what you look like."

And it was true. Nobody cared about my deflated breasts, that my upper thighs looked like shrivelled mango skin and that my round stomach was like a sweet ball of gulabjam tucked into my swimming costume, not floating but sinking in the water.

During the week, Helga coaxed me gently into the pool, making me feel confident that I was in control of my body's movement and breath. After a week, when I got the hang of swimming, I would only remain in the shallow end where I could firmly plant both feet down and feel the safety of the ground.

"Come into the deep end, Bhanu; you have come this far. I will not let anything happen to you. Come on." I resisted for days and on the last day, I thought, *Fuck it, if I die, I haven't felt so alive in a long time*, so I swam the length of the pool where she was waiting for me. I could hear her call out my name like a cheerleader, encouraging me. She didn't even care that there were other people in the pool. "Just breathe, Bhanu, breathe, good work, *sehr schön...*" When I got to the other end safely, she held out her arms. I wanted to cry and then she pulled me towards her and hugged me. This is what I wanted to do for Margaret: to hold her and become a container for all the unsafe emotions.

This is how it was with Helga. In her company, I thought momentarily about being free and what I would do. Imagine going on a flight somewhere on your own? In my imagination, I got as far as searching on the internet for destinations – perhaps I could pay her a visit or perhaps go to an ayurvedic spa in Kerala – but I didn't get any further than that as the automatic self-correction took hold and I thought about what other people would think if they knew I was thinking such thoughts.

I ran back to the cabin to tell my husband that I had finally learned to swim.

"I did it!" I cried. "I did it!"

He looked out from the sheet covering him, motioned a thumbs up and turned around to go back to sleep.

I WhatsApped my son and daughter. They texted back a thumbs up and high five respectively. Pushpa texted back an emoji of an ethnic minority swimmer with the words, *Next stop, the Olympics. LOL*. I would have automatically responded to Pushpa's text with a smiley face but this time, I didn't feel like it. She had recently been on a family skiing holiday to Val d'Isère but she hadn't bothered to go skiing and instead spent the entire holiday in the spa. I sent back an emoji of an ethnic minority skier with the words, *Pushpa the Eagle*.

She did not respond.

"I learned how to swim on our cruise," I said to Margaret. The image of water must have triggered her as she responded by saying that she had to water her rhododendrons. My husband took this as a cue to leave and got up.

"Come, Bhanu, before we hit traffic."

"There is still time before rush hour," I replied, looking at my watch.

I recognised that look Margaret had: she had vacated her body; she was somewhere else. I wanted to stay with her, to bring her back. Because if someone did not bring her back, she would be lost in the rhododendrons forever — that's what growing older does, it makes things harder, it makes you invisible and nobody sends out a search party for invisible people.

If I had listened to my instinct, I would have grabbed her, taken her to the bottom of the garden and built her a huge fire pit. We would have lit a big bonfire and invoked Agni, the god of fire and asked him to witness and then take her pain. *Scream, Margaret, scream loudly, scream it all out, it's safe.* But Margaret got up swiftly.

"They really do need some water."

I hugged her. Margaret stood immobile like an iceberg.

"Thank you so much for coming, Ban-oo."

"I am here for you. I understand," I whispered.

She did not melt into my arms or allow herself to be held. Instead, she uncurled herself from the hug and turned to my husband and extended her arm. "Hit-en. Thank you."

I reached into my handbag and handed her some methi parathas wrapped in tinfoil.

"Last thing you want to be thinking about is cooking. They are not spicy."

Margaret has IBS and cannot eat too much spicy food. She accepted them politely.

Malcolm got up from behind his newspaper and shook our hands. I went back to hug her again.

"The cure for pain is in the pain, Margaret." Reiterating what the therapist had said. I am generally good at giving people advice and not very good at taking it myself.

There was silence.

"It is a quote from the poet Rumi."

"Right," she replied stoically.

I asked her to call me if she needed anything – anything at all, knowing that she would not.

We got back into the Mercedes-Benz and drove through Cobham.

"So quiet, Bhanu?" My husband gets unnerved when I am silent. He normally turns on the radio to drown the silence out.

I was thinking about what the therapist had said and for the first time in a long time, I paid attention to my feelings. At first, all I could feel was Margaret's grief and then by feeling her grief, I could feel my own. The accumulated losses, big and small, hers and mine. She held it together because if she cracked, she would probably be lost at sea and nobody would ever notice, not even her husband. Nobody notices you after a certain age, no matter how much facial yoga you do or how much Crème de la Mer you put on your face.

A tear rolled down my face for her, for us.

I wanted to say to my husband, *I wish someone would really listen to her, without judging or saying one word, or being afraid of silence.*

Instead, I said, "You should not have recommended that cruise to her."

"Oh... Right. I was trying to lift the mood."

"And anyway, you hated the cruise. We should try to be more honest with other people."

He didn't say anything.

"With each other also."

Silence.

"And ourselves."

Yes. Come on, Bhanu, be honest with him. It was Helga's voice, encouraging me.

"That's what the therapist said," I continued.

We hadn't talked about the therapist. My daughter had probably told Hiten about the appointment. "What do you think?" I attempted to open up the conversation.

"Yes. Very good idea."

He turned the radio on.

Ordinarily, at this point, I would have closed my eyes and had a conversation in my head with my imaginary Deep. Deep would be listening attentively, both hands on the steering wheel. When we stopped at the lights, he would turn to look at me, taking my hand and pressing it reassuringly. We would have talked about the therapy session in some depth and then what we could do for Margaret.

Stay present, I heard the therapist say. Yes, I had to stop this; Deep had to go, preferably before the ceremony. I turned the radio's volume down and tried again. "I have things that I haven't told you about."

Hiten tapped his fingers on the steering wheel to the sound of the background music. "It doesn't matter, Bhanu. Past is past."

Try harder, Bhanu, Helga's voice encouraged.

"But it does," I replied.

"It's always better not to think too much." He began humming to the radio.

Now, do it now. Tell him, urged Helga.

"I think that—"

"Let's get a coffee machine," Hiten interrupted.

I couldn't continue so we discussed the purchase of a coffee machine. Hiten likes the latest domestic appliances.

Just as we were arriving home, Pushpa texted.

So sorry – clash in schedule can't come to the big day.

I regretted divulging the news to Pushpa that I knew about the vow renewal but when I found out, I was desperate, even knowing that she was the wrong person to share it with.

"Shit! I can't imagine a ceremony at our age. Sitting there under the mandir, being witnessed by everyone! Some would say mutton dressed as lamb, or in your case, Bhanu, tofu dressed as soya bean. No wonder you sound shit-scared."

I glanced at her text message and knew that another would come seconds later and what it would say. True to form, another appeared.

Coming. Only joking, LOL.

Pushpa is always texting me with *LOL*. It will be minus five outside and she will write, *The weather is nice today. LOL* or *I am drinking coffee, but coffee is not my cup of tea. LOL.*

For months I didn't know what it was until Hari told me. Then he showed me where all the emojis were on the phone and the way to respond. He's good with things like that because he's in IT.

Hari was getting the music ready for the party. I knew this because I heard it when I was hanging out the washing. He was working in the garage which we converted into his studio, mixing Hindi tracks from the late 70s and 80s with a hip-hop beat. I was hanging out my husband's Y-fronts when I first heard the music, and it made me smile. I reminisced about some of the times my husband and I had, dancing with each other; he could make me laugh with his moves, he still can. Hiten has his own version of a flash mob – it's just him but he will begin dancing in the most unexpected places: when he is filling up petrol or waiting to pay at the supermarket. Leyla loves it when he jumps out in front of her stroller and begins singing and when the three of us dance together, she doesn't stop laughing. Laughter counts for a lot in a marriage.

I think Hari might have a PowerPoint presentation up his sleeve; he asked where the family albums were kept. The presentation might run in the background as the music is playing and could be very similar to *The March of Progress* – how we, as a family, have evolved in the last forty years:

Slide one: a hazy Polaroid of our wedding – only four people; two of those are strangers. Slide two: outside a terraced house, one child, one red Ford Cortina. Then outside a semi-detached property: two kids and a blue Volvo. Outside a detached home, with a grandchild and a black Mercedes. Followed by the most recent picture of us at Leyla's first birthday party. Anita had a marquee erected in her garden. We were all laughing, dressed as clowns except for Anita and Hugh, who were ringmasters. Margaret would be in that photo too, smiling with her daughter Cynthia.

Yes, it's important to hold on to your children, your family.

There might be pictures of Hari and Anita growing up: messy, happy faces. Their first day at school. No, probably not Hari's. "Please don't leave me. Please don't go, Mummy," he screamed. "I want you. I want to stay home with you," he cried. It was heartbreaking. I knew it was for the best not to look back, otherwise I would have taken him home. He had always been with me. When I was cooking or cleaning, I couldn't put him down – attached to me at the hip. That was until he found hip-hop. He nearly married Sarah last year... Sarah. I was truly grateful and jubilant that Hari had finally met someone.

Sarah walked gracefully into our living room like a gazelle; she had dark, wavy brown hair that seemed to bounce with her inquisitive large blue eyes and very long lashes. This was the first girl Hari had brought home. Out of the blue, he called me up from work. "Mum, Mum, Mum, listen, we're just going out. Do you know what that means?"

Of course I bloody know what that means; I'm not stupid. You think you invented sex? I have had sex before marriage and it wasn't with your father. I didn't say this.

"That's when you see how things go. Am I right?"

"Yep. Exactly. So, we are not getting married, yeah? She wants to meet you and none of that stuff like when you first met Hugh. So no pressure, okay, Mum?"

I was elated. As soon as he put the phone down, I called up Pushpa. "Get ready for the wedding."

"Civil partnership?" she enquired.

I tell you sometimes your friends can be so stupid.

"It was a joke, Bhanu. LOL. Why are you taking everything so seriously these days? Since your volunteering job was cut you have become very serious."

"It wasn't volunteering. It was a proper job. I was an assistant librarian."

"Anyway, to be invited this time, or not to be? That is the question," Pushpa continued.

Hari, despite being thirty-three and still living at home, was asked to ring the doorbell so it would give me a few seconds to gather myself. I told my husband to act natural, no show. There was no need to impress her. We did, however, set up the dining table in the conservatory so she could admire the two-hundred-foot garden.

Sarah was very elegant in her green wrap dress. She handed me some yellow roses. "Hari said they were your favourite."

Peonies are my favourite. Hari winked at me.

"Thank you, Sarah. They are very beautiful."

"It's so lovely to meet you, Banoo."

I wanted to say, *It's Bhanu. My name is Bhanu*, but there was a marriage proposal at stake, and it could have been hinging on whether she liked us, so I turned to my husband and introduced him in my poshest accent.

"This is my husband, Hit-en."

My husband held out his hand. "Hit and run. Hit and run."

Sarah looked confused. My son shook his head. Hari had nothing to worry about. We had done a dress rehearsal of this dinner so we could welcome Sarah nicely and seal the deal.

My husband took her coat. Dinner went very well. It was hard, though, because when someone asks you not to say the marriage word, that's all you want to say: *What is the marriage forecast for tomorrow? Could you please pass the marriage paratha? I mean methi paratha.*

And then I said it. I was momentarily distracted, imagining her in a red wedding sari, looking stunningly beautiful and it was as if I were trying out the word for the first time; I just said it: "Marriage?" Unfortunately, it came just after my husband asked Sarah if she would like anything else.

Hari looked horrified. Hiten saved me. He was quick. He held out his hand. "*Mari jaan*, Bhanu."

My son acted swiftly. "Yes. Das right, Sarah. *Mari jaan* means beloved in Hindi. She was just adding 'love' to my dad's comment, you know – what else would you like with that, love?"

We left Sarah somewhat mystified, but she was polite about it and added that she had eaten the most wonderful meal and was fine.

Sarah was in no hurry to have children. *What? I wanted to shout. Just go for it, otherwise you will spend thousands on IVF.* I pretended not to be concerned and told myself that I already have a granddaughter and I don't want to take instructions from another set of parents. Well, I really do, but I have to admit that I find some of Anita's instructions hard to digest, just like the non-organic digestive biscuits that Leyla is not allowed to eat. Sometimes, I want to ask her, *Who raised you both, wolves?* Of course, I don't, but this is what I am thinking. Anita has recently hired a Spanish nanny, Concetta, to take care of Leyla as I was apparently not up to the job.

Yes, great idea, give the child two languages and always speak to the child in Spanish so nobody can understand what the hell the child is saying.

"*Agua, agua. Pan. Pan.*"

And then, tell me to speak to the child in Gujarati.

"Mum, firstly, it would stop you from signing. Leyla is fourteen months old and she's not really talking." It was true; I occasionally sign. "And," she continued, "to tell you the truth, your accent isn't that great and it would be good to give Leyla another language. You know they can learn up to seven languages."

She had just thrown a grenade at me and didn't even notice me injured by the blast. My English accent isn't great? It's not great? It was good enough to bring you up, International MBA Kew Banker.

Anita was five years old when I started reading poetry properly to her. These things they forget: the spellings, running lines for play rehearsals, reading books at bedtime, explaining poetry.

She was colouring her picture, sitting at the dining room table as I sat reading to her.

"Mummy, Mummy, how do you know so much about poetry?"

"It was my first love. Let me read you this one."

I opened my book of Auden's selected poetry and was transported back to Tanzania, looking up at the stars with Deep.

"Tara." That's what he used to call me. "Tara, 'How should we like it were stars to burn / With a passion for us we could not return? If equal affection cannot be, Let the more loving one be me'."

"Blake?" I replied eagerly.

Deep's love for poetry was infectious so I had begun studying, first the Romantics, and we would play this game where he would give me a line and I would tell him who the poet was.

"No, Auden." He smiled.

"But he's not a Romantic!"

"Just testing. I want to give you my copy of his poems. It's signed by him. Look, Tara! It's a shooting star."

It wasn't a shooting star. I didn't want to disappoint him but then I could never disappoint him.

"No, it isn't. It's a plane," I laughed.

He began laughing and he turned to look at me. "You know, one day we will travel the world together. I will take you to England to see Auden's birthplace in York."

I imagined travelling the world with him, looking up at the night sky as we grew old together. Knowing that this constellation, the Southern Cross, were the same stars under which we had made plans together.

"Forget York. I'd better go home now before they ask questions," I replied.

"We can tell them soon. After you've met Ma."

"I'm nervous, Deep."

"You, nervous?"

"What if she doesn't like me? What if I am not good enough for her – what will happen to us?"

"Tara. She will love you as I love you."

"But what if she doesn't?"

"I don't think that that possibility even exists, so it doesn't exist. That wrist is looking empty. Come here, wrist." He pulled out a golden thread.

"Deep, it's so beautiful!"

"'A thing of beauty is a joy forever: its loveliness increases; it will never / Pass into nothingness'."

"Auden?"

"Keats." He smiled.

"I give up, Deep." I rolled into his arms.

He kissed me and we made love, under Auden's stars.

"Tara," Deep whispered. "You will never turn into nothingness."

But I did. Marriage was not in our stars.

"Mummy, this is a picture I did of me and Daddy," my daughter said, pulling at my sleeve.

"Wow, that's nice," I said, looking at her drawing.

"What does your poem mean, Mummy?"

"See, little one," I said, lifting her on to my lap, "the stars shine so brightly with love for us and sometimes we might feel that we can't return their love, but they don't mind; they will shine brightly anyway as they don't need us to return their love."

Little do our children know of the sacrifices we make for them, both large and small, conceding small defeats for peace. My adult daughter was standing in front of me while I was sitting at her dining room table.

"So, Mum, do you think you can try to speak to Leyla in Gujarati?"

I acted as if her words had just sailed past me and not caused a major collision.

"I will do my best," I replied.

"If you could also stop feeding Leyla digestive biscuits, that would be great too. You know I got these from the health food shop." She took out a packet of coated baobab fruit. "Leyla loves them. You know they—"

"Ah, the baobab fruit. Bapa used to make this in his sweet shop. They used to be your favourites. Bapa..."

"They are so rich in antioxidants. Try."

If she had wanted to listen, I could have told her the history of the baobab fruit and the legend surrounding the tree and the various combinations of sweets that could be made from it and how she used to make them with my father in the sweet shop as I had done as a child. But she was busy. Your children think they have heard it all before. They have no idea of the life you have lived well before they came along.

The coffee maker purchase had been decided upon en route from Cobham. It was a joint decision. I broached the subject of denying my mother-in-law permanent residency at our home, but my husband was having none of it. He is flexible on most issues except his mother; after all these years, her grip over him has not loosened and there was no way around it.

"She needs us now more than ever, Bhanu. She is old and frail and if we are not there for her, who will be?"

There was his older brother and sister-in-law, but they were claiming that the space downstairs was not good enough for her and how would she manage the Mount Everest stair-climbing? My mother-in-law's legs are like Mo Farah's – built for distance. A stairlift? We could offer to pay for a stairlift!

"Absolutely not. It is our duty to look after her," Hiten replied resolutely.

As soon as we arrived back from Cobham, I went upstairs and opened up my airing cupboard. I have created a makeshift temple up there for the gods. It's also where I leave my home-made yogurt to set, so

I see the gods every other day unless there is something that is really troubling me. I am not especially religious but praying occasionally brings me peace. I addressed my first prayer to the goddess Parvati, asking that Margaret be given strength and that she be safely guided out of the rhododendrons. I then turned to the elephant god Ganesh, remover of obstacles, and asked that Hiten miraculously change his mind about the stairlift. I hesitated before uncomfortably getting on my knees: "If there is a way of finally letting go of Deep, please show me."

yard two

"Your task is not to seek for love, but merely to seek and find all the barriers within yourself that you have built against it."

— Rumi

My son gave me the letter yesterday. Yesterday, the day before the vow renewal. He jumped up at me from nowhere like the TV presenter Eamonn Andrews, *This Is Your Life*. I was blending a turmeric face pack to put on later that evening and was distracted as my husband had announced my mother-in-law's moving-in date. Hiten then promptly left to see her when Hari appeared from nowhere.

I thought it was an anniversary card. It was a bit early; Hari can be premature.

"Thank you so much, *beta*. Leave it on the table," I replied, washing my turmeric-stained hands.

"You need to read it, Mum." He sounded serious. Hari is serious when he doesn't get enough sleep and he was DJ-ing until very late.

"The nanny is sick again and Anita has sent me an Uber. The driver is waiting outside." I dried my hands. "Whatever you have chosen will be very nice, I'm sure," I said, trying to reassure him.

"Take it with you," he insisted.

"I will."

Hari has always had and continues to need a lot of attention and he doesn't like it when he feels his sister gets more, but I had to go.

Since Tescogate, Anita always sends me an Uber. It was quite an unfortunate series of events: I had gone to babysit Leyla and Pushpa had lent me a baby seat so I could take Leyla out shopping. I finished the shopping but before unloading it, put Leyla in the car seat and gave her the car keys to keep her distracted while I was unloading the shopping, and she locked the car doors.

Oh God(s), I can't tell you the level of perspiration trying to get Leyla to unlock the door. You can't even compare it to the heat of a sauna. I made faces at Leyla to click the button but nothing worked. A crowd gathered so I had to call the fire brigade and the police. The police of course had to go and inform Anita. She imposed a driving ban on me when out with Leyla and three more points against me were noted. She now sends me an Uber whenever there is babysitting.

The cab smelled of an overpowering lemon zest air freshener so despite it being cold, I wound down the window.

"Too hot in here?" the driver asked.

"Yes," I lied. Limited progress had been made in communicating honestly and in other areas, but everything would be revisited after the vow renewal.

I put the seat belt on and carefully opened Hari's envelope.

"Anniversary card from my son," I said to the driver proudly.

He glanced at me through the mirror and smiled. "Happy anniversary."

"Forty years," I replied.

"Congratulations."

"Thank you."

I was mistaken. It wasn't a card; it was a letter:

Dear Mum,
The therapist thinks it's a good idea to write out my feelings.

Ah, Anita at work again. She had also sent him to a therapist.

I'm a gambler and an addict and sorry for the damage I've caused with my gambling.

I felt relief, huge relief as if a truck had momentarily been lifted off me. Then, I read the next line and it came crashing back down.

You might have done your best, but you messed up. Big time. Everything was and continues to be controlled by you. Sarah would've

*stayed if you hadn't got involved. You didn't
have to tell her about the ring, but you can't help
yourself. You probably know about tomorrow;
you've probably also micro-managed that and
then you'll act like, all innocent, cos that's what
you do, Mum.*

My heart began racing.

*What has Dad ever done? Why stay with him
if he's made you so unhappy? I don't get it. Look
at your own stuff.*

I wanted to put the letter down, pretend that I had never opened it but I carried on. Why was he doing this now?

*Yeah and you were probably right about Sarah
being too good for me, but I was never good
enough for you, was I?*

I couldn't read on; my eyes just fixated on the last line.

I'm not pretending any more.

A lump began to form in my throat and then, involuntarily, I let out a guttural cry and if I wasn't strapped in, I would have recoiled like an animal and hidden away, but there was nowhere to hide.

The driver stopped the car. He looked at me awkwardly from his rear-view mirror, not sure what to say. I wanted to show him the letter, to tell him that it wasn't true, none of it was true. He handed me a tissue and turned the radio on to a classical station. I sat crying in the back seat and as I thought about it, I started to get angry. Why would anyone do this the day before a wedding ceremony? For maximum damage? Why not wait until after? What does the therapist know, anyway? Yes, you sit and judge me from your couch; I might not have breastfed him or I might have thrown away his finger paintings without sticking them on the fridge, but before you judge me, let me tell you, if I could have done a finger painting, it would have been black and there wouldn't have been a bloody fridge to stick it on.

"We are here," the driver announced, relieved, as we pulled into my daughter's drive.

Anita was waiting for me on her porch with the front door wide open.

"I'm sorry," I mumbled to the driver, ashamed. I rummaged through my handbag for some change.

"No need." He seemed eager to get going.

Anita came running over. "What's happened, Mum?"

"Hari wrote me a letter. Look!"

"What, he gave it to you? The idiot."

"You knew about it?"

"The therapist told him to express his feelings. He wasn't meant to give it to you. You know, Mum, it is going to sound worse than it is."

"But read what it says. Did I make you not feel enough, Anita? Was I controlling?"

Sensing the terrain was filled with landmines that she could have helped defuse, she glanced at me briefly. Her look said it all.

"Mum, I have really got to go, it's an important meeting. We'll sort it out later, I promise. It will all be fine, you'll see. Will you be okay with Leyla?"

I nodded and she hurried off.

I went upstairs to check on Leyla. Her little stomach was rising and falling without a care in the world. When she is older and things don't work out the way she wants them to, she will blame my daughter. That is how it works. I watched Leyla sleeping, I touched her little fingers and I started to cry. I closed my eyes. *Come,* I heard Deep whisper, *come, my Tara.* He held out his hand and I was so desperate to take it and escape into our imaginary world where Deep and I could sit down and figure this out. I shook my head, desperate to grab his hand, trying my hardest to resist and take control of my thoughts. I took a deep breath and imagined Helga and what she would say. *This is not the way,* she proclaimed, standing like a gatekeeper at the doorway to my imaginary world. *That's right, Bhanu, breathe, come on, breathe deeper.* Helga accompanied me downstairs. *This part you have to do by yourself. No more of this nonsense escaping, Bhanu.*

I went into the living room and sat on the white sofa of my daughter's white, pristine house. Almost everything is white. The one anomaly in the sitting room is a "shabby chic" cupboard, which she paid a fortune for. On top of this cupboard, she has placed three vintage brown suitcases, recreating the look we had when we first came to the UK as immigrants in 1978. I always found it an odd thing to do.

"It looks dirty, Anita. I don't understand why you have got it. We spent years getting rid of this look. And the sofa is going to get very dirty with a child. Why don't you leave the plastic cover on it?"

"I don't want Leyla to get an OCD habit and not let her play with her friends because they have dirty fingernails." It shot out of her mouth and at the time, I didn't quite understand what she meant.

"I know you mean well," she added quickly. "Both Hugh and I like it."

Perhaps that ugly cupboard is her letter to me; it's true she had a "dirty-fingernailed" friend who I stopped her from playing with, which, later in life, probably led to an obsession with order and cleanliness. *One day, I'd like to explain it all to you, Anita, to explain it to you, Hari. Buy your cupboards, write your letters, judge me and then sit on a therapist's couch and have someone else judge me but before you do, understand that most of my decisions were guided by the need for safety and then when I had you, they were about giving you security so you would never have to endure what I did. Whatever I did, I did for you.*

This is what I have told myself, because the alternative, that I have lived most of my life under the spell of this one misplaced belief, is unbearable.

My parents were dirt poor as my father used to drink away all the money.

"Stupid, idiot child. Nothing but a burden," he would shout, hitting me over and over with his chappal or any other implement that was close at hand.

They say that my parents' fortune changed when I came along. My mother lost her mind – it was probably postnatal depression. The village astrologer told them that it might be due to the fact that I was born under the heavy influence of the planet Mars, and suggested a course of remedial ceremonies. My father invested in them, but none seemed to work.

He then started drinking heavily and lost his shop. His temper flared even further. I never knew what kind of mood he would be in, what I would need to do not to make him angry, not to make him throw something at me. It was pointless; he would use any excuse and beat the shit out of me, drunk or otherwise. My mother tried her very best to shield me and then one day, she didn't have to as he upped and left. I was seven.

He left because of a red dress gifted to me by my mother's sister, Vidya. We didn't see her often as my father didn't like my mother's family. Vidya Masi's husband had opened his second sweet shop and she came to invite us, bearing gifts: a dress for me and a sari for my mother. My mother's sari was lime green and pink. It was a bandhani sari that had been tie-dyed and had teardrop-shaped dots with tiny mirrors sewn into them. The mirrors on the sari caught the sunlight and glistened on the chair upon which it had been carefully placed.

Vidya Masi made me try the dress on and it fitted perfectly. I looked at my mother to see if I could accept it and she smiled at me. Once I knew it was mine, I fully appreciated it and began feeling the soft fabric and twirled around, playing with the ruffles. My mother and aunt began to laugh. It was the first time in a long time that I had seen her laugh.

"You need to send her to school. She's a smart girl," Vidya Masi said to my mother. "I will help you."

They chatted for a while as I enjoyed my dress, believing myself to be an Indian warrior princess.

Vidya Masi didn't stay very long as my mother was afraid that my father would return shortly, which he did. When he saw my mother's new sari draped neatly on the chair, he picked it up and ripped it to shreds with his hands. "They think they are better than us, that we can't afford anything? Then they buy her a red dress, knowing that she is cursed with Mars?" The village astrologer had suggested against the colour red for me as it would further invoke the Mars defect. My father turned to me to tear off the dress and my mother intervened. He beat her very badly, so badly that I think he was shocked at the state in which he had left her. He packed his belongings and left.

I couldn't call anyone to help as it was strongly ingrained in me that whatever happens in the home, stays in the home and no matter how hard that is, you do not call for help or tell other people what is happening for fear of what they would think. Any form of scandal could also ruin the family name and future matrimonial prospects, so I didn't run to the neighbours as I wanted to but took care of my mother to the best of my ability, cleaning her wounds with salt and boiling up some rice water for her to drink. I was unaware that he had broken her spirit and there was no way of knowing that I couldn't fix this.

Calm descended in the house after he left, though she continued pulling out strands of her thick black hair. The earliest memory I have of my mother is her sitting by the window pulling out single strands of her long hair. She was waiting for someone or something. From a young age, I remember feeling that if I wasn't good and did everything I could, something bad would happen to her – so I was a good child. I don't think I am naturally a good person. In fact, I don't actually know who I am as I have learned to assess and adapt to most situations. I know how to pretend to be good, pretend to be whatever is needed of me in any given situation, and to contain the fiery influence of Mars that resides in me.

Things appeared to be getting better, apart from the fact that we were short of money and occasionally went hungry. My mother seemed to smile a little more and there was lots of peace in the house and we had a routine, something that we had never had due to my father's unpredictable behaviour.

I usually woke up to the smell of incense and would open my eyes to see my mother kneeling on the floor, praying. But that day, it was still dark when I suddenly woke from the sound of the rusty brown cupboard door creaking open. I was half asleep as I watched my mother take out a package and an old biscuit tin. She put the tin beside the mat on the floor where we slept and carefully untied the string of the package, unpacking it very slowly. My eyes were so heavy that they wanted to fall shut but I kept them open.

It was the most beautiful thing that I had ever seen – a neatly folded blue embroidered sari. Caught between the darkness and emerging light, the heavy silver brocade shimmered. She carefully unpacked it and picked up two ends and pressed them between her fingers. In one movement, she flicked the two ends and the sari flew like an enormous glistening wave. I wanted to get up and play with the wave, but I stopped myself. Something was different about this day; it was the first day that my mother looked like she was excited about something. She had some kind of event or function to get ready for. This was an odd occurrence as back then there were no festivities for us – and where had she got this sari from? There was no money for clothes. Perhaps someone had lent it to her?

A wedding! I thought. *Perhaps we are going to a wedding*, and I lay there excited as the sari momentarily shimmered and swirled in the air before landing heavily. When she took out my best dress – the red one – I thought my heart would explode. We were going to a wedding. A wedding – we were going to eat, not just eat, but have a feast.

I wanted to savour every moment, so I continued watching her, pretending to be asleep. She scrunched my red dress into a ball, held it to her nose and inhaled its scent and then held it against her chest. Even though she had probably just woken up, she looked beautiful with her thick, long, jet-black hair, yet to be brushed, and her magnificent green eyes.

They filled with tears; a lump formed in her throat. She swallowed hard, shook her head and whatever the thought was, she firmly pushed it away as there was a wedding to go to.

She laid my red dress out neatly on a chair, opened the biscuit tin and picked out a blue thread to match the sari, then took out a strong, sturdy needle. It took her a while to put the thread into the eye of the needle as the thread appeared to be very thick or the eye of the needle was not large enough; she moistened the thread with her lips, and it worked. Her long slender fingers had a lot of work to do as she forced the needle through the areas of heavy silver brocade, but she worked meticulously as she sewed what appeared to be a pocket. A pocket for the sari – would she be taking food from the wedding feast for us? I watched her sew another pocket and then another and then I fell asleep.

On the morning that I woke up and saw the shimmering blue sari, I felt a surge of happiness as something was definitely different about her. She handed me the red dress to put on and she quickly wrapped the blue sari around herself. I remembered thinking that she should have taken her time to put it on because a wedding was such an important occasion. In spite of this, she looked like a goddess.

"Whose wedding are we going to, Ma?"

She bent down to talk to me. "I want you to listen to me, my little one. Vidya Masi wants to send you to school and it is going to be so much fun. You will learn so much and one day, you will do important things. You will be a somebody."

I swallowed hard as I could sense she would not be coming. "What about you, Ma? Are you coming?"

"I can't come right now."

"Why?"

"I have things to sort out."

"Promise me you will come back for me, Ma?"

"I will always be with you, my little one."

That didn't sound like a promise back, to me. I wanted to cry but I knew not to.

She packed a few of my belongings and we walked to the corner of the road where the bus stopped. It was a rare occasion to go on a bus so I distracted myself by looking outside of the window, watching the hustle and bustle of the town; the vegetable sellers with their rusty axes and the peanut sellers did not seem to be bothered by the fact that their produce was covered by puffs of black smoke emitted by all the different vehicles. I wondered what the peanuts tasted like. Whether on this trip we would get some. I didn't ask my mother but she saw my look.

"Want some?" She smiled at me. This separation was just temporary, I told myself. I smiled back and she bought two cones from the seller. We ate peanuts together. I made sure not to finish them so we still had some for the rest of our trip.

"You're a really kind girl, Bhanu. At least I did something good," she said as we boarded the bus. I held her hand tightly as we sat down. We changed buses and after a few hours, we arrived at the big farm where my aunt lived.

As we were walking to the house, I could not take it any longer and I started to cry. "I don't want to go, Ma, please don't leave me. Please don't leave me with them. I promise I will be good. I will try harder." I cried, clinging to her sari. Just then, Gauri, came skipping out onto the large veranda; Vidya Masi followed closely behind her. She glanced at my mother and nodded.

My mother kneeled down to look at me. She was trying to hold back her tears.

"Please don't go, Ma. Please," I managed to whisper in between my sobs.

"Be good for Masi. Do whatever she tells you and study hard." Her voice cracked. "You are destined to do great things."

"Please, Ma. Come back for me. You will come back for me, won't you?" I cried.

Tears ran down her face. She squeezed my hand, kissed my forehead, got up and left. I wanted to run after her, but my aunt held on to my hand tightly. I watched my mother run back down the lane and when I could no longer see her, I fell to the ground and cried.

Vidya Masi picked me up, told me that she would do her best to look after me, and wiped away my tears with the end of her sari. Gauri began skipping around us and from the corner of my eye, I was aware of an older lady dressed in white, watching the scene unfold. She was shelling garden peas and ordering people around. My aunt glanced in her direction, hesitated and took me to meet her. Gauri came skipping behind us.

"This is Ba," Vidya Masi said nervously.

The lady spat out the betel leaves she was chewing, looked at me, nodded, and continued shelling her peas.

Gauri came running up to me. "Come, Bhanu. Let me show you my dolls."

Vidya Masi hurried us off.

"You are not allowed to speak to her until she speaks to you," Gauri instructed. "She's my grandmother but she isn't very nice. My cousins tell me that she killed two of her husbands and if you get too close to her, you will befall the same fate."

I looked back at the lady and I thought I saw her smile at me.

It turned out that Ba was the powerhouse of the family as her second husband had left her the farm and the sweet shops in town where my uncles worked. She had three sons. Two of them were from her first marriage and Vidya Masi was married to the third son, Chetan, who was from her second marriage.

Ba lived in the large house with my aunt and uncle and the other two brothers lived in their respective houses on the large estate. Apparently, Ba had the last word on everything, and nobody could disagree with her.

I was shown the bedroom where Gauri slept, though she didn't really sleep there as she slept with her parents. It smelled of sandalwood and there was a bed made up for me, which she pointed to. I had never slept in a bed. My mother and I would roll out our mats and sleep on the floor. Gauri opened the wooden cupboard door and took out her doll collection; they were all missing several limbs. If I had dolls, they would all have their body parts and be neatly kept with their clothes on.

"This one is my favourite..." she said.

I wasn't really listening. I wasn't really there.

Ever since I can remember, I have had this ability to pretend to be in my body but not really be there. I can be in two places at once. When my father used to beat me and swear at me, I imagined myself playing with the neighbour's children. In spite of the pain, I could disappear and be elsewhere.

While Gauri was showing me the cohort of semi-naked dolls, I was with my mother, making the journey back home after our visit, unpacking the shopping that we had got with the money Vidya Masi had secretly given her.

"And this doll is called Asha. She looks like me, doesn't she?"

I nodded. My mother would soon realise that she needed me more than she thought she did. I helped her cook, clean and did many other household chores. She would come back for me – perhaps even that very evening. If not, definitely in the morning.

Around the time I was thinking this, I was unaware that mother was walking into the depths of the sea and allowing herself to be taken by it. The sari pockets were not filled with items from the wedding feast but with rocks.

Vidya Masi had cooked an amazing dinner and the large table was full of all sorts of dishes that I had never seen. She delicately served some food on a plate for me. Her fingers were the same as my mother's, long and elegant. Then she placed the plate in front of me. I knew not to eat it as if I were hungry. I learned from my mother not to show greed. Just as I was thinking how I would take some of it and store it for later, just in case, my uncle, Chetan Masa, walked in and he came straight towards me and said, "Don't just look at the food, little one, eat. I have brought you some sweets from the store that I made especially for you."

"Did you bring me my favourites, Bapa?"

"Of course I did."

He handed Gauri a laddu and then laid out a colourful mountain of Indian sweets on the tray. There were jelabis, halva, penda, barfis, kaju katlis... It wasn't even a special occasion. The old lady watched but she didn't say anything.

It was strange to witness such a dynamic. If that were my house, my father would have removed his sandal and beaten me for asking such a question. Though I would never have thought to ask it in the first instance. My mother would have been on edge, serving him politely, hoping not to put a foot wrong.

I carefully watched the interaction between each of the family members. Vidya Masi seemed happy to serve her husband food and he appeared very appreciative; they touched each other's fingertips, or she touched his shoulder. Gauri kept interrupting their conversation while reaching for another sweet and then another and they allowed her to. The old woman was watching me watching them and gave very little away but when she caught me looking at her, she looked at the sweet tray as if to indicate that I was welcome to take another. I smiled at her and took another piece. I had eaten four almond barfis when the houseboy came running in and asked to speak to my uncle. My uncle went off to talk to him and then called for my aunt. She came back and tried to hide her distress, but I knew.

I continued eating the almond barfi, pretending that nothing had happened and that my mother would come for me the next day. I closed my eyes. She would come early. Having slept by herself, she would realise how much she missed me; I kept my eyes closed for as long as I could, savouring that sweet. It would be the last one that I would ever eat.

They took me to one side. Vidya Masi had tears in her eyes. Chetan Masa lifted me onto his lap as she held both my hands and told me that my mother had drowned. She had apparently tried to help a little boy who was caught in a wave. I knew this was untrue. My mother was a good swimmer. She was going to teach me how to swim. I sat there motionless as Vidya Masi told me and then I threw up. I couldn't find a place to escape to in my mind; I couldn't occupy it by thinking of something or someone else, so I got up and ran, ran out into the fields, into the night. I ran and I ran until I couldn't run any more and then I stumbled, fell to the ground and hit my hand against something. I felt blood pouring out and I began to scream. I screamed and I screamed and then I fell asleep.

When I awoke, I was in the old lady's arms. At first, I was startled but then I didn't care if she killed me as at least I would be with my mother. The old lady had covered me with the end of her white sari and a piece of it had been torn off and tied around my hand. She began stroking my hair. I clung to her. "She left me, Ba. She is never coming back for me. I don't have anyone."

"You have me."

"But I am cursed. I will bring you bad luck – that's what they say about me."

"That's what they say about me too, so we will both be cursed together."

She took the end of her sari and tenderly began wiping my tears away. I started to cry again.

"You let it out, my little one. Look, look at the stars in the night sky. They shine so brightly because of the darkness. You are a star; you were meant to shine. Sometimes in your life there will be darkness, but you will always find the light because you are the light and when you feel alone, look up; the stars will show you the way. Look up, little one, look up."

From that day, Ba began calling me Tara, which means "star". Sometimes, all we ever need is just one person who believes in us.

A few days later, Ba woke me up at 4 a.m. "Come, little Tara, I have something to show you."

Half asleep, I followed her. She held my hand as we walked out onto the veranda and along the farm track. Ba led the way with a paraffin lantern, and she had a shotgun slung on her back.

"Wild animals, but don't be scared. They can smell fear."

I was frightened by the dark, by the various noises the animals and insects made but she held on to my hand firmly. Suddenly, I became more alert as I smelled burning wood. Behind the cowsheds, some of the labourers had got an enormous fire going. To me it was huge, at least double my size. It crackled and gave off a heat that wrapped itself around my body.

"This is a fire I have lit for you, Tara. Agni is the god of fire. He is the fire that burns in your belly, the fire of the sun. He connects heaven and earth, humans to the gods above, so whatever you give to him, he will burn and purify. Tara, I want you to do something for me. I want you to think of everything you are unable to speak of and give it to Agni."

Ba held me.

"You trust me, don't you? Let the unspeakable go into the fire, little one."

I thought about my father's uncontrollable rage and not being able to protect my mother. All the murderous thoughts I had about killing him surfaced, then the feelings of being a bad person for having these thoughts. I thought about my mother not being able to stay, of her drowning all alone in the sea. I didn't get to hold her and say goodbye properly. Then I saw the rocks placed in the pockets of her sari. I had seen my mother test the size of the pockets with rocks and I did nothing. It was my fault. The pain in my stomach was so unbearable. "It's okay, my little one, we are removing all the obstacles so the fire in your stomach can return. Let it out; let it go into the big fire. Scream."

I began screaming and screaming. Ba held my hand even tighter. "It will be okay, my little one, trust me."

Tears streamed down my face.

Ba stood there with me. We stood there for a while until the tears finally stopped. Then a sense of calm descended as if the gods had received all the messages that I had sent them; we just watched the fire burn, the sun began to rise, and the earthy fresh smell of a new day absorbed the smell of the burning embers.

"There is one thing I want you to know and I want you to feel it in your bones, Tara. And it is this: after the darkest hour, the sun will always rise for you. Always. You believe me, don't you?"

I wrapped my arms around her.

"Now you can start again, my little one."

The farm was a magical place. It was set in a small valley where everything was green and fertile; in the distance, you could see the mountains. There were coconut trees and mango trees from which the monkeys would swing. We would run around barefoot and play with the workers' children who lived on the estate. If ever we wanted to eat mangoes, guavas, pineapples, coconuts... Pendakazi, one of the farm hands, would pick them for us.

I remember the smell of jaggery, which Ba would supervise the preparation of. The farm hands would cut the sugar cane, put it through a huge machine and boil up the cane until it solidified. The jaggery would then be poured into enormous containers and left to cool.

The farm hands could take what they wanted for their families, some of it went to the sweet shops and was turned into delicacies and the rest of it would be handed out at the Laxmi temple across the river as an offering to the goddess.

Ba would take me to the temple every week. Laxmi is the goddess of good fortune, love, prosperity – both material and spiritual. "She's always looking after us, Tara, and in return we must be generous. We must feed people when they are hungry, love them when they have no love. The universe loves flow; don't ever hold anything tightly. The moment you do, it means that you don't trust that it will always look after you." She made me believe that everything in the universe was engineered in my favour, that whole constellations of stars would reorganise themselves for me, that the trees whispered to me and that the breeze would blow in my direction. There were signs everywhere in nature that showed how I would always be taken care of and all I had to do was to observe.

Ba opened the doors to the world of myths and legends, so nothing ever seemed ordinary when I was around her; everything was infused with possibility. Every day, she read instalments of the *Mahabharata* to me until I could read, and then I read to her. I don't know what made her love the broken parts of me so much, but in loving me, she put me back together.

We spent a lot of time in each other's company, but she was very clever about it and did it under the guise of making me work so I would not upset the balance of any unspoken deals that had already been created. I watched her daughters-in-law run around her in exchange for her favour. She didn't want to show that it could all be given away freely, that it didn't have to be earned and so she did her best not to show me any favouritism in public that would arouse suspicion as to the gentleness of her character.

"Tara, there is planting to be done. Hurry up."

"Tara, come massage my feet."

"Tara, come help me prepare the sugar cane."

"Tara, don't just stand around. Do some work and help me milk the cows, collect the dung and clean the shed."

On one occasion, Gauri followed.

"It's a dirty job. Tara can do it."

Ba talked to her cows as if they were real people. There were eight of them and they seemed happy to see her. "They like sensitive people," she said. "Just be gentle with them and they will listen to you."

She patted an enormous brown cow. "Tara is learning. Is it okay to milk you today, Laxmi?"

The cow mooed loudly.

"No, not happy today." She turned to me. "You have to talk to them before you milk them. Tired today, Laxmi? This one," she said, moving on, "is Sri Devi; she likes it if you sing to her." Ba began singing.

I told her that I didn't know any songs.

"No songs?"

"No. There was no music in the house."

"No music?"

That was it; she made sure music was played every day on the farm and we would go to the cowsheds and Ba would teach me songs and tell me what they meant. She would show me how, when you put words together, they had the power to uplift and transport you somewhere else.

One day, she announced to the family that we were going into town to get supplies. Her sons insisted that they took us but she held firm. We took the bus into town and walked amongst the busy stalls.

"Why so quiet, little one?"

"I'm thinking of the last time I came here with my mother," I said to Ba.

"She would be very proud of you."

She stopped at the popcorn seller's stall and bought two bags and then we stood in front of the cinema.

"Come," she said, as we went in.

I had never been to a cinema.

The cinema was crowded, hot and sweaty. There was an air of anticipation. I was so scared, nervous and excited that I had to sit on Ba's lap. People clapped and cheered before the film came on. I can't quite remember what the film was about but there was a lot of emotion. During the fight scenes, the audience hissed and booed; I buried myself in Ba's chest. Then when a couple danced round and round a tree in their best Indian clothes, the audience clapped even louder and then when they were separated, there were sobs from some of the women around us. They stopped when the couple were reunited somewhere on a cold mountain in Europe, singing the songs that Ba had taught me.

We left the cinema and then hastily bought some provisions as we were meant to from the shops. Not a single word was mentioned about the cinema when we got home. Every few months, we would make our trip into town to get "provisions" and enter another world.

Then, back at the cowsheds, we sang and enacted scenes from the movies that we had seen; I could turn into all the different characters and make Ba laugh. A hearty laugh of appreciation that made me want to make her laugh even more. We were, however, unaware that from afar, Gauri was watching us and that the seeds of jealousy that were being planted would at some point in the future turn into something very ugly.

Unspoken deals with people are used to create security. I worked out that the stability of my own existence depended not only on Ba but also Gauri. Gauri was spoiled primarily due to the fact that her parents had trouble having children and she came after many years. She was annoying and demanding but I played with her as much as I could and gave in to all her demands and made her dependent on me. I also skilfully learned to navigate the dynamics of this complicated relationship between Gauri, Ba and myself.

"What do you do when you are with Ba?" Gauri asked.

I tried to make it sound as uninspiring and factual as I could.

"We plant herbs. You know, the betel leaves she likes to chew. She shows me how to plant them. Sometimes, I help her prepare the jaggery."

"And what about in the cowsheds?"

"Milking, getting hay, cleaning."

"Is she fun?"

"What?"

"Is she fun? Is being with her fun?"

"No, it's boring. It's hard work. Sometimes, she is like an evil witch who prods me with her pitchfork."

"Really, Didi?"

"Yes, and if I do not collect the dung properly, she pushes me into the pile and cackles."

"But I hear a lot of singing and laughter coming from the cowsheds."

"Yes, that's right. She also wants me to entertain her while I am working. I am her personal jester. She teaches me her old songs so I can sing them to her whenever she wants and then she demands that I make her laugh."

"But you don't seem to complain."

"You know what Ba is like," I replied. "I could never complain. She would probably stab me with the fork and leave me to be eaten by the crows."

Gauri gasped.

I couldn't sleep that night. So, I crept into Ba's room and crawled into her bed.

She cuddled me.

"Ba, I am so sorry. I have said some horrible things about you to Gauri. I didn't mean them but..."

"It's okay, my child," was all she said. That is how I learned about the equal deal, the parts of ourselves we compromise for the promise of safety or whatever else it is we think we need.

Even though Ba dressed in white, which was customary for a widow, she took time to air out the rest of her saris, which she did once a year. It was a ritual that took all day and was done behind closed doors. One year, when I was about ten, she allowed me to watch.

"You, Tara." She pointed at me as we sat with the rest of the family on the veranda. "You can help me as I am getting old and it's hard work."

Gauri's eyes widened fearfully, hoping that she would not be pointed at and so she looked down.

Ba unlocked the door of a khaki metallic cupboard to reveal a stack of neatly packed saris. The inside of the cupboard smelled of mothballs and sandalwood. We began with the very top shelf as she carefully took out the saris and unwrapped the long piece of muslin cloth that protected them. Sometimes, a smile would spread across her face.

"Each sari has a story. This one is the first sari I ever had. Given to me by my mother when I was sixteen, a year before I married."

It was purple with a simple gold embroidered pattern of shells. She smelled it and then opened it out, flicking it with her hands so the sari flew high in the air; I wanted to run under it and be engulfed by it but resisted the urge.

"Go on, run into it," she encouraged. "A sari is alive, and we must keep them alive."

She flicked it in the air once more and I allowed myself to be draped in it as it landed on me.

"How does it feel?"

"Like a house," I replied. "Very safe."

"Good. Now I am going to put it on properly for you." She uncovered me from what appeared to be yards and yards of purple and began to tie the sari on me.

"In the *Mahabharata*, Tara, there is a story of Draupadi. She is one of the most important female characters and wife of the five Pandavas. Draupadi had been forfeited in a game of dice and is dragged off into the royal court to be humiliated. The enemies, the Kauravas, try to disrobe her but instead a miracle occurs – an unending stream of cloth appears from nowhere to protect her." Ba worked like a magician, skilfully gathering up the pleats and the sari appeared to be tied in just minutes. "This is the power of a sari, my Tara. It will always protect you; it will hold you together when all else seems to be falling away."

"How did you do that?" I asked, amazed by her mastery.

"One day you will learn to dominate these yards and yards of material. It's important that you know how to gather these layers up, no matter what is happening, no matter how you are feeling and I will teach you. Tell me, how does it feel?"

"It makes me feel beautiful, Ba, like I matter."

"You do, Tara, and don't you forget that."

She let me stand there admiring my ten-year-old self and made me momentarily feel the woman she believed I would grow into.

"It's one of my favourite saris because it was for my transition into womanhood and it has helped me many times on that journey. It is a sari for journeying. When I came to Tanzania for the first time, this is the sari I chose. When we opened our first shop, I wore this. Yes, most definitely a sari for new adventures."

We carefully packed the sari away and took out another one. She opened it out. It was a silk green sari with heavy work on the pallu. "It was given to me by my in-laws as a gift when I first got married. The sari your in-laws give to you will say so much about what they wish for you. They chose green, green for fertility so we would be blessed with children. This part is the soul of the sari." She picked up the pallu. "If you look closely, it has a hundred and eight Lord Ganeshas embroidered, see here. He removes obstacles and brings good fortune and happiness."

I began counting them, desperate to ask her what happened to her first husband as I did not believe she was capable of murdering him and I also wanted to enquire about her second husband. Later that afternoon,

I found out that technically it was her second and third husband as her first marriage was to a banana tree.

This requires some explanation. According to Hindu astrology, someone born under the influence of Mars, like myself and Ba, is said to have the Mars defect or Mangala *dosha*, and as such are called Manglik. According to superstition, a Manglik will cause her husband's premature death and other disasters (like destroying the entire family, not giving birth to a boy, and generally being an all-round fiery, dangerous woman). To prevent this mark of impending death falling on the future groom, the bride can be married off to a tree (usually a banana or peepal tree) so the tree absorbs all her bad luck, thus freeing the bride from the effects of being Manglik, and the resulting marriage can be a happy one. The marriage to the tree did not seem to work in Ba's subsequent marriage as her husband died and she was blamed for his death; but she did have two boys, so there was some anomaly there.

Ba took the pallu of the green sari in her hands. "Feel here; it can take weavers months to get the geometrical patterns just right. It takes years and years of skill and if it is not right, the weavers do not get paid and they do not eat. Their love and dedication are stitched into each sari. This pallu was so difficult to clean." She smiled. "I shouldn't have, but how many times did I wipe the faces of my boys with this!"

"Ba, you once said I could ask you anything." I heard Gauri's voice in my head saying, *Murderer, yes, ask her why she killed her first (technically second) husband.* I pushed this thought aside and continued. "Why, Ba? Why did you love me so much and take me in when I wasn't even yours?"

We folded the sari.

"When a star collides with your path, it can create an explosion in your heart and that sends a surge so strong that the only thing you can do is love, love with no expectation that it will love you in return."

We put the sari back.

"I want to show you something very special and I want to tell you the story of what happened to me."

Part of me was a little bit scared. Would she suddenly reveal her murder story, and how would I feel about her afterwards?

She carefully unpacked her wedding sari, which was wrapped in a long piece of muslin. It was her second wedding sari. Defiant red, feminine red, that showed off her navel and her power and that she wore in an act of defiance against society.

Ba had had an arranged marriage when she was sixteen and married her first husband, a shopkeeper. Technically, astrologically, they were not well matched due to the Mars defect but the parents knew each other well and performed the above-mentioned tree ceremony. By twenty, she had two small boys and lived in an extended family unit consisting of her husband's parents and sisters and brothers. Later that year, her husband contracted tuberculosis and died, and she was left a widow and also blamed for his death.

As a widow in her early twenties, she was expected to give up her life, dress in a white sari, mourning her husband for the rest of her days. That meant eating separately from the rest of the household, not partaking in any celebrations and being almost invisible, except to tend to the needs of her household and her children.

The day after her husband's funeral, she dressed in a pink cotton sari, kept her bangles on and attended to household duties. The family members were horrified and asked her to change immediately: what would people think if they saw her? What was this blatant disrespect? Ba said it wasn't her husband's wish for her life to be drained of colour and she later went to her husband's shop to work, which was considered scandalous.

In age-old tradition, the rest of the family swindled her. They threw her out of her home, blaming her for the bad luck she had brought into the household and told her that they would keep her two boys if she did not sign over the shop. She consented and returned with her boys to her parents' house. Her parents would not take her back, fearing what the community would say. She sold all her jewellery and, with the money, she rented somewhere to live and began working all hours so she could support herself and her children. Often, for days, the children were left without their mother, but she always came back and she always managed to keep a roof over their heads and feed them.

"It was very hard and I am not proud of what I had to do to feed them but I would have done anything for them."

One of her brothers-in-law, ashamed at the way the family had treated her, began looking for Ba and found her a year later. He asked if he could marry her and at first she refused but after he persisted for a year, she agreed.

"Did you love him, Ba? Did you love him?"

"Not at first but I grew to love him very much," she replied. "He risked everything for me. I told him, 'I think I am cursed.' 'I will be cursed with you then,' he replied. I said yes because he was persistent, and he was full of curiosity about the world. Tara, if you marry a man with curiosity, your life will be filled with adventure."

The young family were ostracised from extended family and talked about by the community and so they decided to move to Tanzania where there was an opportunity to start again. They set up a bakery together and a few years later, she found herself pregnant with my Chetan masa. With his arrival, the family's fortune multiplied and in the years that followed, Ba and her husband opened a string of sweet shops, which her sons helped manage. The other two brothers were not so interested but my uncle was a natural and business thrived.

Shortly after Chetan Masa's wedding to my Vidya *masi*, Ba's husband became ill and Ba stayed at home to look after him until he died a few years later. Ba did not go back to the shops. They had been married for forty years, dispelling the myth of any curse. She chose to dress in white. A short while after, I came to the house.

Years later, when I was about sixteen and had learned to tie a sari in under four minutes, Ba handed me a muslin package.

"I want you to take it now and keep it somewhere safe."

I slowly unwrapped it and inside was her fiery red wedding sari.

"For when you get married, and don't ever believe anyone who tells you that you are cursed."

My tears began to fall. At first there were just a few drops and then they would not stop. I was overwhelmed by her fierce love for me, how worthy she made me feel and the realisation that one day, she would not be there.

"Ba, I want to ask you what makes one woman fight for her children and another give up?"

"Sometimes, Tara, the spirit gets very tired of all the battles it has to endure. My spirit was not broken and yours will never break."

My uncle and aunt were noble and kind. The first thing they did after my mother died was to sit me down and tell me that they were my new parents, that they would always be there for me no matter what, and if I wanted, I could call them Mama and Bapa. Shortly after, they enrolled me into school. I loved school, dressing up in clean uniforms and learning. I learned to read quickly and this opened up another world for me. I read everything that I could get my hands on and exasperated the school librarian.

After a year, when the teacher said I would have to move up a class, my uncle was so delighted that I knew if I studied hard and made them proud, they would keep me.

"See, Vidya," he said to his wife, "we have a brainbox in the family."

"Two of them now," she said, hugging both Gauri and me.

"Our girls will travel the world and become scientists or explorers or whatever they want to be," he encouraged.

To him, education was everything. He stopped going to school when he was sixteen because he wanted to help his father in the sweet business but it never stopped him from learning. He would sit and read Goethe or Faust to us on the veranda.

"Girls, don't ever make pacts and compromise your soul. That is not the road to happiness."

Gauri was uninterested but I hung on his every word.

There was nothing that my uncle did not appear to know. He was adventurous and curious and would travel far and wide looking for inspiration and new sweet recipes. He would come back with stories from remote villages and we would all gather together on the veranda and listen in anticipation.

"The baobab tree grew proudly by the lake. It thought it was absolutely beautiful standing beside the slender, graceful palm tree and the beautiful flame tree with its bright red flowers. One day, it caught sight of its reflection in the water."

He got up and acted out the scene.

"Who is that hideous tree?" he said, becoming the tree staring into the pretend lake. "The tree realised it was itself and began to wail, catching sight of its ugliness."

Ba tried not to laugh at his wailing.

"The tree asked God why it was so ugly. God did not reply. The tree cried and whined until one day, God had had enough of the tree's lack of gratitude. 'Take this,' he shouted. God pulled the tree up by its roots and planted it upside down. From then on, the tree was quiet."

We sat in awe listening to him and then my uncle pulled out a cotton bag. "Here, here is some dried fruit from the baobab tree. Taste it."

He passed the fruit around. They exploded in my mouth, tasting of fresh limes.

"Too sour," Gauri said, making a face.

"We can coat them with sugar or put them in biscuits for you. There are so many things to do with them," he said enthusiastically.

When he wasn't travelling, he was in the kitchen experimenting. I wanted to follow him to see him mixing his potions. Instead, I encouraged Gauri to see what he was doing but she said she wasn't interested.

So sometimes, I would watch him through the window. He was like a mad scientist and when he made a breakthrough, he would call his wife.

"Vidya, Vidya! Come and taste this."

She would taste and, irrespective of whether she liked it or not, her eyes would light up and a smile would spread across her face.

"You are so very clever, Chetan."

My uncle's brothers did not care for myths or legends or the healing properties of food; they were much more business-minded and focused on expanding the business. Sometimes at weekends or after school, they would ask us to come in and help.

In exchange, we were allowed to take home whatever sweets we wanted. I didn't like sweets so exchanged mine for hair accessories, stationery or books with the other girls at school. This was the only real interaction I had with them as I kept my head down and tried not to be noticed, escaping to the library whenever I could.

"Gauri, how is it you look nothing like your sister? She's pretty and has brains but you've definitely got more..."

"Personality," another girl would say.

"Yar, definitely more personality."

"Gauri told us that her parents rescued you. Like a pet."

Inside, I would feel a heat rising through my body, desperate for them not to say the next line.

"What happened to your parents?"

I feared them finding out what had really happened. My other fear was that my real father would come back for me and separate me from my family, even though I had covered all the bases to make sure this would not happen. The fear of insecurity was a constant companion.

"Gauri said that they died."

I said nothing, taking further refuge in my books. Excelling without meaning to – so much so that I was awarded a full scholarship by the school. I was proud not to be a burden to anyone. My parents and Ba were proud of me. Gauri was not.

I did everything I could to make her feel more important, to be invisible in her presence. The more I did this, the bigger she got. This was our deal that she frequently tested.

We were sixteen when our parents gifted us with our first saris for the festival of Navaratri. A big party and dance was organised in the town and instead of the traditional costumes they normally bought us, they handed us two majestic saris. They were both sunshine-yellow with different coloured borders. Gauri's was peacock-blue and mine was red. I helped Gauri tie her sari; she was disappointed: "They are so old-fashioned. I don't know why Mummy and Daddy didn't buy us the three-piece ghagra choli."

"A sari is far more elegant," I said, dressing her. "All our memories of this evening will be wrapped in them."

"Didi, you are such a romantic! How are we expected to dance in them?" she complained.

"Just imagine it as your second skin. The more you are aware of it, the more awkward it will feel," I replied.

I got her dressed and then I got dressed and we stood in the mirror admiring ourselves. All of a sudden, Gauri began to cry. "Yours looks much better. It's *much* better, Didi!"

"Gauri, they are exactly the same." I knew what she wanted me to do.

"You know the red suits me more and maybe Mummy made a mistake when she gave it to you as she would know it was meant for me."

I should have said no, I should have waited to see what drama was to unfold, but my response was almost automatic: I untied both saris and we swapped them.

"This one definitely looks much better on me. Thank you."

She complained the whole time when we were at the dance, unable to appreciate how everything outside the temple had been transformed with such detail and dedication: the enormous canopy that had been constructed and beautifully adorned, the drummers and dancers all assembled in an assortment of colour. Nothing was quite right: it was too noisy for her, she was tired, her sari was uncomfortable, she couldn't move properly.

"What was Mummy thinking? It looks like we are the only two here wearing saris and I can't dance with it on."

I had had enough of her whining and needed to get outside, and left her saying that I was just going to say hello to one of our aunts. Before Gauri could say that she was coming with me, I ran off. But as I got to my aunt, I got swept up in a big dance circle.

The sound of the percussion of the dhol and tabla was loud and entrancing. I began clapping my hands and dancing in time with all the women and children in the circle. We danced around the goddess Shakti and it was mesmerising. The darkness was lit with lamps and tea lights, and as I looked up, the sky was pitch black, the stars shone so brightly. It felt as if all the stars were aligned, that we were dancing below as the stars above; as if the moment that was about to pass had been meticulously orchestrated.

Another circle formed with just men and before I saw him, I felt his presence – the man that would change my life forever. I felt the magnetic pull of his body and when I looked in his direction, he was already looking at me. Neither of us looked away; I knew instantly that my destiny would be intertwined with his. I felt it in every part of my body. It was like a layer that had protected my heart chose that moment to dissolve and then this surge of love flowed into me. If I had died in that moment, I would have known that a love or an energy that does not have words to describe it, existed.

We circled each other, knowing that we would dance all night if we could. I could not stop smiling.

Suddenly, a hand grabbed my shoulder and pulled me out of the circle. I turned around; it was Gauri.

"What is it, Gauri?"

"I have asked Mummy and Daddy if we can go home now. They are waiting for you."

I looked back at the young man, but the circle had moved on. I wanted to turn back and be amongst that constellation.

"Come on, Didi. It's late, I'm tired and I want to go to sleep."

I looked behind me to see if I could see the young man, but he had disappeared into an even wider circle. I was angry at Gauri, at her inability to appreciate, that she had drawn me away.

"Did you have fun, girls?" Bapa asked.

"My feet hurt," Gauri replied.

"Yes, Bapa. It was enchanting."

I knew it would only be a matter of time before I bumped into the young man again. I felt the space between us was not empty but filled with energy and possibility and that we would be pulled together again. Whenever I was alone, I began thinking about him. I kept imagining his slender fingers, his jet-black hair, the strength of his lean body and the energy he exuded. My fingers would trace the shape of his face. His beautiful, intense brown eyes that felt like they could see right through me. His full lips.

"You can tell a lot by a man's lips," Ba once told me. "Don't trust a man with thin lips." I wondered what it would be like to kiss his lips.

Every time I went into the town, I searched for him. I even began finishing my homework quickly so I could help in the shop regularly, just in case he came in. Four months later, in he walked.

Gauri and I were helping Bapa in the back.

"Hello," said the voice. As soon as I heard it, I knew it was him. I hastily placed the tray of sweets on the kitchen counter, Gauri following swiftly behind me.

I smiled when I saw him and felt the urge to touch him.

Gauri looked at me, then looked back at him. She rushed over to serve him.

"The coconut barfis have just been made freshly. They are exceptionally good," she said, pointing at them.

"I'm sorry, I don't really like coconuts," he replied, still looking at me.

"How about pistachio?" she offered.

"What would you suggest?" he asked me.

"I don't eat sweets," I replied.

It was a trivial conversation; both of us were talking and it didn't really matter what the words meant.

"The almond ones are very good. They are my favourite," Gauri interrupted.

Instead of ignoring her, he bought one to try. I noted that it was a nice gesture.

"They are delicious. I will take two boxes of almond barfis."

Gauri lit up.

"I'm glad I found you," he mouthed, looking at me while Gauri searched for a box under the counter.

"Please come again soon," she said, as he left the shop.

Gauri was overcome with emotion. "Didi, did you see how he took the boxes from me? 'Thank you for your suggestion, miss,' he said, 'very much appreciated.' Oh my God, don't you think that he is just the most handsome man you have ever seen?" She clearly liked him and in the unspoken terms of our relationship, I was to give some indication that he liked her too but on this occasion, I did not.

"Didi, Didi," Gauri came rushing through the door to tell me, "the boy in the shop, I found out who he is. His name is Deepak. He is twenty-one and he is studying at the university. Deepak is a lovely name, isn't it?"

"Yes," I replied. "It means 'source of light'."

Of course he would have been named Deepak.

He came in a few days later when my sister and uncle weren't there. He was carrying a stack of engineering books and amongst them was a book of poems.

"I've been searching for you since we met at the dance and I knew I would find you," he said. "Quantum entanglement."

"I'm not sure what you mean?"

"When pairs of particles interact, the actions performed on one are still able to affect the other even when they are separated. So, I knew that you knew that I was looking for you."

I understood him completely.

"I have been watching you whenever I could since I came into the shop," he continued. "That sounds sinister, doesn't it? It's not, I'm not – I mean, I wanted to know when I could catch you on your own."

He made me laugh.

"You know that it is inevitable that we gravitate towards each other. Do you like poetry?"

"I'm not sure, I haven't read that much." I hadn't really read any.

"Take this," he said. "I will talk to you about it the next time I see you."

He handed me a copy of Byron's poetry.

"I have bookmarked one for you." He touched my hand as he gave me the book and then rushed towards the door. "I have to go but I am coming back next Tuesday."

I turned to the page he had marked.

> SHE WALKS IN BEAUTY
> She walks in beauty, like the night
> Of cloudless climes and starry skies;
> And all that's best of dark and bright
> Meet in her aspect and her eyes:
> Thus mellow'd to that tender light
> Which heaven to gaudy day denies.
>
> Had half impaired the nameless grace
> Which waves in every raven tress,
> Or softly lightens o'er her face;
> Where thoughts serenely sweet express

How pure, how dear their dwelling-place.
One shade the more, one ray the less,
And on that cheek, and o'er that brow,
So soft, so calm, yet eloquent,
The smiles that win, the tints that glow,
But tell of days in goodness spent,
A mind at peace with all below,
A heart whose love is innocent!

I read it and I smiled. My sister came in and asked what I was reading. I showed it to her, but she stopped at the first stanza.

"You and your books, Didi."

His poem opened up yet another world for me.

When I got home, I headed towards Ba's room. She was in bed. Diabetes had taken most of her sight and she remained mostly housebound.

"Tell me what happened in your universe today, Tara?" she asked, as she did every day. She never said "day", or "world", but "universe".

"A guest star has appeared in the night sky, Ba."

"What does it feel like?"

"Quite magical; like there is another universe to explore, one that is full of possibility. Today, I'm going to read you something different."

I opened the book and began reading the poem, translating the words for her.

"The ability to see a person as they are with all their light and darkness, is a precious gift," she whispered.

"I know, Ba."

I waited anxiously for the following Tuesday and he walked in at exactly a quarter past four.

"Did you read it?"

"Over and over," I replied.

"That poem was written for you. Imagine, a man existed a hundred and fifty years ago in another place, just to write that poem for you."

"He did not."

"He knew of your existence even before you existed, just like I did."

"Do you speak to all the girls like this?"

"Listen to me, that night when I danced with you was when the pieces of my universe did not fit any more. And I stood watching you from afar before I had the courage to walk into the shop because I knew things would never be the same. My name is Deepak."

"I know," I replied. "Mine is Tara. Everyone knows me as Bhanu but I am Tara."

"How could it not be?" He smiled.

I held out my hand and he didn't shake it but placed his on top of mine.

A customer walked in. I pulled my hand away.

"Let me give you your book back," I said hastily.

"Keep it and read the other poems."

"I have," I replied.

"I will collect it then next Tuesday."

"A box of laddus and some jelabis," the customer said impatiently.

"I will be with you right away."

"What would your father say if he saw you talking to a boy in this way?" the woman asked, looking at us.

I looked at Deep. "Thank you for the book."

"You are most welcome," he said. "Madam," he added before he left. "We were not doing anything inappropriate and I am sorry if I have caused any offence."

She huffed.

I turned to the customer. "I'm sorry. What is it that you would like?"

"Your reputation is all you have," the woman said rudely. "Look at everything your family has done for you. Don't forget your debt to them."

"I will not!" I replied defiantly.

"On this occasion, I will let it go but if I see anything like this happening again, I will be sure to tell your father."

The sentence required me to apologise even though I did not want to.

"I'm sorry," I replied reluctantly.

Deep came to see me every Tuesday. We kept our conversation short and secretly exchanged poetry and notes so we would not arouse any suspicion.

It was difficult to get away to meet as Gauri was always with me but one day, I pretended to be ill and stayed at home. By mid-afternoon, I told my mother I was feeling better and was going for a walk. Deep had arranged to pick me up about a kilometre away from the farm. He came in a rusty Land Rover that he had borrowed from one of his friends.

"I am going to take you to one of my favourite spots."

We drove up long windy roads. I was worried that the car might stall and we would be stranded in the middle of nowhere.

"We will be fine. I would never let anything happen to you," he reassured.

Half an hour later, we reached a vantage point on a clifftop. It was breathtakingly beautiful. It was as if every conceivable hue of green had been incorporated into the leaves, the grass, the trees, the mountains. I had a clear view of the river that ran through the land. The river that Ba and I crossed to get to the temple.

"Look, Tara, there's a martial eagle."

It swooped down and caught an otter.

"I have an uncle who moves just like that," I joked.

He laughed. "I think everyone has an uncle who moves like that."

We sat there holding hands, watching the wildlife – the elephants that drank from the river, the flamingos that had elegantly congregated for a chat, and appeared undisturbed by their presence, the monkeys swinging playfully in the trees above. There was no need to say anything, to fill the silence, as we understood each other perfectly. Deep leaned over to kiss me. It was our first kiss and it was sensual yet familiar. Like coming home.

"I don't think I could be any more grateful," he said.

"That young man who came into the shop... remember, what was his name?" my sister asked.

I pretended I didn't know who she was talking about.

"You know the one? What was his name...? Deepak. Has he been in the shop recently?"

"I'm not sure," I replied.

"It is just that I think I saw him coming out of the shop on Tuesday," Gauri said, glancing at me.

"Yes, he might have."

"He had the same poetry book that you have been reading," she continued.

"That's a coincidence." I should have just told her.

But people lie. People lie for all sorts of reasons or they tell themselves that they are unsure of what to do. In every situation, a person knows what they are supposed to do, but they tell themselves they don't because what they fear are the consequences of the truth.

Deep and I began to meet secretly whenever we could, even if it was just for a few stolen minutes.

"Tara, please try to get away again, even for a couple of hours. What would you like to do?"

"Cinema," I said without thinking.

It had been years since I had gone with Ba; she no longer ventured out of the compound.

"Let's go to the one in the city," he suggested. "Far from here."

I told my family I was going to study with a friend.
"Which friend, Didi?" Gauri asked in front of them.
"Rekha."
"Rekha, no, I don't think I know her. She is not at school."
"No. I met her in the shop. She is also going to be a teacher and we are going to be each other's study partners. I will be gone for the afternoon," I added casually.
"Introduce me to her next time she comes into the shop," my father said, peering from his newspaper. "It would be good to meet her."
"I would like to meet her too," Gauri added.

We planned it so I took the bus most of the way and then Deep met me on his motorbike at the main junction. It felt liberating as we rode at speed, weaving between the traffic and errant animals. I felt fearless, trusting my life in his hands knowing that he would take care of it.

As we walked into the cinema, the same feelings I'd had when I first walked in with Ba came flooding back. Awe, excitement, nervousness and fear that we might be spotted. We sat down but we did not hold hands.

The film was *Kabhi Kabhie*. It was a story about a young poet who is desperately in love with his girlfriend. They make plans to get married but fate has other ideas. Halfway through the film, I burst into tears and then sobbed so loudly that one of the cinemagoers made a sound for me to be quiet. Deep took hold of my hand. I quickly covered both our hands with my shawl and then I became too conscious that we were in a public place and could be spotted, so I pulled away.

After the film ended, tears streamed down my face. What if fate had other plans for us?

"Tara. Look at me. It's a film. That will never happen to us. I promise you. You believe me, don't you?"

I believed every word he said.

"We will watch this film again at some point in our future and we will look back at this moment and laugh." He paused. "'Love will find a way through paths where wolves fear to prey'."

"Keats," I said quickly.

"No. Byron," he replied. "I want to kiss you right now, but I can't, so close your eyes and imagine it. It will always work out for us, Tara. Always."

Back then I was a naïve young woman who believed only in possibility. I did not fully appreciate that the beliefs that we hold unconsciously have a way of dragging us down when we least expect. I was also complacent, forgetting that we are subjected to the laws of physics – two objects can be drawn together but they can equally be pulled apart by a denser mass.

When we got back, I went into Ba's room and I told her about the film, describing each scene in great detail and then I sang a song from the film to her. I sang the love song from the film over and over until she began to sing it with me.

"Thank you, my Tara. I saw it all."

On every fourth Tuesday afternoon, Deep and I would do something together. This was the only time we had as Deep's father, who apparently was a formidable character, had suffered a stroke, and along with studying, Deep had taken on a bookkeeping job to help his mother and brothers take care of the household.

The time we had together was about making memories. I have often wondered whether somewhere in our consciousness, we are able to sense our fate? Therefore, with Deep, I lived the present moment intensely, perhaps knowing that in my future, I would revisit every detail over and over. Or perhaps the past is rewritten depending on the future that unfolds for us, and that in actual fact, had we lived a life together, these details would have been forgotten or told in a different way.

Our favourite thing to do was to ride to the coast, walk to a remote area and just sit in a cove watching the sea, holding hands. I have since been to many beaches, but none have been as glorious as the white beaches and the crystal-blue waters on the east coast of Africa. And even though I couldn't swim, I would hold Deep's hand and run into the sea, believing securely that nothing would happen to us and that the stars would always work in our favour.

We would lie in the cove and allow the sea breeze to dry us as we talked or kissed each other.

"Deep, I often wonder how my mother surrendered to the sea, resisting the temptation to kick, fight and start swimming. Doesn't it go against instinct not to want to swim?"

"She must have been in a lot of pain."

"I couldn't make it better. I tried. The whole time I spent with her, I felt she would leave, and I couldn't stop it."

"It wasn't your responsibility, Tara. You are not responsible, do you hear me?"

"I saw those rocks, but I didn't know what they were for." I started to cry. "Do you think *that* trait is passed down? That's what other people think, that I am faulty goods."

"No," he said, clasping my hand. "I don't think you believe that either."

Perhaps deep down somewhere I did, but Deep and Ba had managed to fill the abandoned spaces with their words, their tenderness and their love. They made me feel like I was somebody who was worthy of their love.

"Will we travel the world together, Deep?"

"Without a doubt, Tara."

And I imagined my future with him because, back then, I did not fear dreaming. I believed in the universe, that it would guide us to wherever we wanted to go.

"When Papa is better and I complete my degree, I am going to come and ask Ba if I can marry you, or we can go right now and I can ask her, if you want to."

I began to laugh as he got up. "Always impatient. I want to finish my studies, and perhaps even go to university."

"I am going to marry you before then."

"Deep, is there such a thing as a word doctor?"

"What's that?"

"Someone who prescribes the right words to make another person better."

"I am not sure. Why?"

"That's what I want to do."

"Well, we will travel the world and find such a place where there are word doctors."

"Are you making fun of me?"

"No, I am being serious. The best place to start is the land of the poets – England," he said confidently.

"England," I repeated.

"Yes, I will take you to Auden's birthplace in York, and maybe if we like it, we will settle there?"

"York?"

"Yes. Imagine, when we are old and grey, telling our grandchildren the story of how we decided to come to York." He smiled at me. "We will tell them that we followed the path that the universe unravelled for us. So, my word doctor, what do you think are the most important words that people need to hear?"

I didn't even have to think about this. I thought he thought I was going to say, "I love you," but the words were, "You are enough."

He paused and then traced the outline of my heart. "You are more than enough, my Tara."

Tears just rolled down my cheeks because I believed him.

"Didi," my sister said, "it's okay, you know. I know about you and Deepak. I saw you get off the bus and ride his motorbike together. You should be more careful."

"I'm sorry I didn't tell you. I was scared because I could see that you also liked him."

"You know me; one day I like this boy, the next day it's that boy. Is it serious?"

I wanted to say yes but instead I hesitated and said I wasn't sure.

"Tell me, tell me all about it, about him."

I began from the beginning, leaving the poetry out: his curiosity for the world, his tenderness, and the fact that we could finish each other's sentences. I didn't want to dissipate the preciousness of what we had by talking about it to someone who I didn't fully trust so I made him sound quite boring.

"He loves eating banana chips all day long."

"What else?"

"Well, some of his sentences are very long. I have to stop and look up most of the words in the dictionary and he also talks a lot about physics, which I don't quite understand."

"Yes, that is boring, but he is so handsome, so I suppose you don't mind. Have you kissed him?"

"No, because I imagine the banana chips stuck to his teeth."

"Has he tried to kiss you?"

"Not at all."

"I imagined so. He is not like the other boys. You have to be more careful, Didi, because if Bapa found out, he would be heartbroken."

"He would like Deep," I replied.

"So, it is serious?"

"No. I'm just saying that I think he would understand."

"I don't think so. He wants us to study hard. Bapa would be very disappointed if he found out that we were mixing with boys and that you have been lying – but don't worry, your secret is safe with me."

I wanted to tell Ba. I could not have Gauri know and not tell Ba.

"Ba," I said later that evening as I crawled into her bed. The same familiar bed I would crawl into as a child in the middle of the night, returning early in the morning to my own bed so that nobody would know.

"The poems are from a young man called Deepak, and one day, I am going to marry him."

"I know, Tara," she said. "Finish your education first. You are a bright girl. He will wait for you if he loves you."

"Of course I will, Ba."

"Tell me about him."

I described his kindness, his warmth, the way he managed to make everything seem surmountable. "His energy is big, so bright and full of life. He's so expressive, not afraid of any feelings, and he has a great love for nature and for poetry – but above all, I can be myself. I am not pretending to be anyone else but myself. Listen to the words of this poem. It is called 'The More Loving One' by an English poet called Auden. 'How should we like it were stars to burn / With a passion for us we could not return? / If equal affection cannot be, Let the more loving one be me'. This is Deep's favourite poem and it is mine and do you know why? Because in these lines is the way I feel that you loved me. You gave me life, Ba; you made me shine, loving me, not knowing if I would love you back, but you didn't care, you just kept loving me. I want you to know how much I love you."

Six weeks later, Ba fell asleep and she never woke up and after that everything began to fall apart.

It was 1977 when Ba died. She had once asked me to make sure she was not sent off to the afterlife in the customary white sheet but wrapped in her purple journeying sari for her next adventure. She had told me that she had also instructed her eldest son to do this, but she wanted to make sure that this happened. Against all custom and tradition, Ba wanted me or any of the other women in the family to attend the cremation if we so wished.

In all the commotion, I think the eldest son must have forgotten.

"Uncle, Ba told me that she wanted to be wrapped in her purple sari."

"Why are you making up such a thing?" he shouted at me. "It is against custom, what will people think – and who are you, anyway, to tell me what to do?"

It pained me not to fulfil her wishes and so I told my father, who approached both his brothers. I'm not sure what happened but for the last rites, she remained wrapped in a white sheet and the tension was palpable. I was also instructed that I would not be present at the cremation of the body. In Hinduism, women are not allowed to attend for the following reasons: the deceased will only attain moksha, or liberation, if the ceremony is carried out by male relatives; women were supposedly unable to handle the grief of watching a body burn; and lastly, they were required to do the cooking and cleaning of the house while the men were away. It was overlooked that in earlier Vedic times, daughters could assume the role under special circumstances.

Ba never conformed and I cried that this feisty, rebellious woman who had sacrificed so much for her boys had not had her last wishes fulfilled. There was nothing I could do as I watched her body being laid out on a ladder made of bamboo sticks and carried away by her sons.

"I'm so sorry," I repeated over and over.

I never truly got to say goodbye to both Ba and my mother. I wish I could have because they have both remained in the corridors of my mind, wandering like hungry ghosts, leaving me with a feeling that I did not do enough for either of them.

Straight after the men had scattered her ashes, a huge tornado ripped through the family. As in age-old tradition, the two eldest brothers swindled my father, selling the property from under his feet. The cows were sold, the sheds were dismantled, the saris in her cupboard were raided and we were asked to leave.

"Please, Uncle, this is not what Ba would have wanted," I pleaded as the contents of her room were emptied.

"How do you know? You are not even part of this family," he replied coldly. He turned to my father. "I'd be careful with this one. She is getting quite a reputation. She will bring the family down."

My father hit him across the face. My father never raised his hand to anyone.

"You will regret that," my uncle shouted. "I will give you a day to take your stray and get out."

We gathered up our belongings, left our home and rented a small house in the town. My father stopped going to work and woke up later and later.

"Chetu, show us the latest invention you have made with the cocoa bean."

"Yes, Bapa. We can help you grind it?" Gauri added.

My father would shake his head and go back to the bedroom.

Sometimes, I would catch him sitting in front of the large, framed photograph of Ba, weeping.

"She will always be with us." He held me, like a small child.

"I'm so sorry," I said, "for speaking to Uncle like that. I will find a way to make it right."

"It's not your fault, Bhanu. Please understand that."

"And what he said about my reputation…" I wanted to tell him about Deep, that I wasn't some girl running around with men as my uncle had inferred, but Gauri walked in and it wasn't the right moment.

I was going to sit down with him and have a proper conversation about Deep. I knew he would understand, and he would like him because in some respects they were very similar, but then the postman brought news. My mother handed him the letter and he leaped out of bed as if all his prayers had been answered.

"Where are my girls? Girls, girls, we are going to England, to London!"

"London, Bapa? What's in London?" Gauri asked.

"A friend of mine is opening up a sweet shop and he wants me to help him. You can both continue your education there. England has some of the best universities. It's a blessing, I knew it would work."

He looked up at the framed photo of Ba and kissed the space between them.

I couldn't go to London, not without Deep.

"What do you say, Vidya? Is it a yes?" he asked my mother.

She nodded and then smiled at him.

"Something good always comes out of something bad. Always." He put his arms around her and lifted her in the air.

"What an adventure we will have." He paused, "Gauri, Bhanu – are you okay?"

I pretended to smile.

There are set points in our lives that change the trajectory of our destiny and you know when they come. I desperately wanted to say, "No, Bapa, I am not okay, I can't leave. I am in love with a boy called Deepak," but loyalty pulled me in the direction of my family and the debt that I owed to them was too big; I had to make things right.

"Tara, don't cry. I will follow you soon after I have finished my exams. It is only a year and by then, Papa will be much better," Deep consoled me.

"I don't think I can live a year without you."

"Think about it. We were going to live in England anyway. And think of your opportunity to study."

"I don't think I can go, not without you," I sobbed.

"Look at me. My destiny is to love you and spend my whole life with you. A year is like a parenthesis in the book of our life together. I will write to you every day."

"Promise me."

"Of course I promise you, and before you know it, I will be there. Tara, think of all the things we will do in England."

"But what if something happens."

"Nothing will happen, *mere* Tara. Our marriage is written in the stars. Take this."

He gave me his most treasured possession, the signed copy of Auden's book of poetry.

I began, "'How should we like it were the stars to burn / With a passion for us we could not return?'"

"'If equal affection cannot be, Let the more loving one be me'," he continued. "I want you to know that we are like stars, and that the depth of my feelings will always pull you towards me, always, and I will come and be with you soon, no matter what. Promise me that you will wait for me, no matter what?"

"Of course I will."

Our father went ahead to make the necessary arrangements and we followed shortly behind. My mother, sister and I packed our worldly goods into three suitcases, tied them up with string and boarded a plane for London. My sister talked excitedly non-stop. I was scared – what if the stars had guided me to a foreign land and what if, as Shakespeare said, "the fault is not in our stars but in ourselves"? That Deep would find me but somehow we would not manage to be together, not because of fate but because of the fault in me? Nothing I truly loved stayed.

The romantic England I had read about in books was cold and inhospitable and our saris were unravelled as my sister and I were strip-searched on our arrival. Both my mother and sister began to cry. I felt the seed of bitterness and disappointment planted in me and instead of getting angry I buried it with politeness and thanked the security guard as she looked disdainfully at Deep's bracelet and handed it back to me.

The vibrant, multicoloured sari that I was wearing seemed alien in this grey, foreign land. It didn't seem to be the garment of protection, confidence and mastery that it had always been. I felt the cold bitterly in it and wrapped my cardigan even tighter. It made me feel self-conscious and attracted eyes that would give me a cursory look of either curiosity or dismissal.

My father was delayed picking us up from the airport. My sister began to cry again. "I want to go back. I don't like it here."

"He will come," I said, trying to sound reassuring. "Please don't worry, it will all work out. We will be fine."

My father arrived an hour and a half later.

"Welcome to London, my girls." He hugged us, attempting to hide his look of despondency.

"Bapa," my sister sobbed. "It has been awful."

"I'm sorry, *beta*, there was lots of traffic and, and I had to finish my shift."

He looked dishevelled and tired.

"Are you okay, Bapa?" I asked.

"Yes, fine."

"You look tired. Are you eating properly?" my mother asked, cupping his face.

"I will explain everything later," he replied. "Let's go." He reached for her hand.

It transpired that his friend took most of his savings and swindled him in the good old-fashioned way that one does. My father debated whether to send for us under such precarious circumstances but the alternative of us staying in Tanzania, he deemed, was worse.

"But you could have come back home and told Uncle what had happened. I am sure Uncle would have allowed you back into the business," Gauri cried.

My sister, I thought, had a rudimentary understanding of family dynamics. Not quite grasping that if you hit someone across the face, the chances of them welcoming you with open arms are quite minimal.

"It doesn't matter now. I have found work and we will find a way."

He had found three different jobs: as a cleaner, a night porter and helping bake bread in a bakery. He had also managed to rent a room for us as paying guests, which we were to share with five other families. There would be a total of twenty-five people in a three-bedroomed semi-detached house.

We drove from the airport in a rusty car that he had borrowed, and we all attempted to sound more cheerful than we were. I just wanted to turn back and return to Deep.

"You will like England, girls. The people are very polite and everything is very green," my father said enthusiastically, trying to lift the mood.

"I am sure we will," my mother added.

I looked out onto the grey concrete buildings on a miserable day in September, wondering where the rolling hills were and the people promenading. That was the England I had in my imagination, that and the land of the Beatles, Rolling Stones and Cliff Richard. Creative people dancing in the streets wearing long kaftans with peace, love and flowers. Instead, it was orderly, house after house like grey shoeboxes. We parked outside one of them.

There were people pouring out of that house in Wembley, sleeping in whatever space they could find. Open up a cupboard, find an "uncle" sleeping; go to the bathroom, an "uncle" in the tub and one more sleeping on top of the kitchen counter. Indians invented the concept of "hot-desking" with "hot-bedding" – if you were not at home during the day or in your bed at night, someone else would take it.

"I know it is not much," my father said, showing us around the shabby bedroom with the damp and the paint peeling off the ceiling, "but it is a start and I promise you, we won't be here for long."

My sister's lower lip began to tremble. She was about to cry again and I glared at her.

"It's fine, Bapa," I lied, looking at the filthy mattress and the dirty stains on the carpet.

"I am so sorry I have let you down. It is not what I want for you."

My mother held his hand. "None of this matters.

We are all back together now and that is the most important thing."

There was shouting and screaming coming from the next room, Hindi music was blasting from another part of the house and the noise of children running around above us. My father said that he had to go back to work and gave us the list of instructions for the next day. He left us money for groceries and asked us to lock the kitchen cupboard.

"Please also lock the bedroom door when you are sleeping. I will see you tomorrow." He kissed us all and he left.

Gauri sobbed uncontrollably.

"Listen," I said. "This is not helping anyone. We need to do our best to help Bapa. Tomorrow, we will look for work so we need to get a good night's sleep. Do you understand me?"

She nodded.

We unpacked the suitcases and made up the bed with whatever we could find. Before I got changed, I said I needed to get some fresh air. Gauri wanted to follow me.

"I need five minutes to think – alone." I tried not to sound angry.

I left the room and the house and walked outside in the cold. One or two stars shone dimly in that corner of London, and it looked as if it were a huge effort to shine. I pretended that it was the Southern Cross and imagined the same constellation in Tanzania, under which Deep would be sleeping or studying into the night.

I sat on the wall, pulled out the pen, paper and envelope that I had taken from the airline and began writing to Deep. It was a letter written in haste firstly because I felt unsafe being outside on my own in the dark and secondly, I didn't want to go into too much description of my first impressions of London and the house that did not sleep; it was just to give him my address as promised. It would be ten days before a letter would come back and by then, things would have changed and I could write more truthfully about the situation. I ended my letter telling him how much I loved him and signed off with lines from Wordsworth, *Fill your paper with the breathings of your heart*, because I knew it was this that would get me through. I placed the letter into my handbag. As I walked back, people were pouring out of the pub, and some drunken men began shouting obscenities; I ran back home as quickly as I could.

The next morning, we were awoken by a loud hawking and coughing noise. It was the sound of someone doing their ablutions and then a man began banging on the bathroom door saying it was taking too long and that he needed to go to the toilet.

"Go outside," the perpetrator responded.

I went downstairs to the kitchen. It was full of children eating their breakfast, running around and getting ready to go to school. Someone was using the kitchen sink to shave and another child was brushing their teeth. I looked out of the window to see another queue in the back garden for the outside toilet. People were also using the garden hosepipe to wash themselves.

I unlocked the kitchen cupboard that had my father's name on it and found some old biscuits and teabags. I couldn't find any milk with his name on it but an old lady kindly offered me some of hers.

"Chetan's daughter?" she asked.

"Yes," I said.

"I am helping you. One day, you will be helping me," she mumbled as she gave me some of her milk. I took it, knowing that I shouldn't have, but I wanted my mother and sister to feel that there was some element of routine.

I placed the cups and the biscuits on a plastic tray that I found and took it up to my sister and mother.

"Better to wait a little while until the morning rush is over before using the bathroom or before you go downstairs," I suggested.

When the house grew quieter, we got ready and ventured outside. I'm not sure what I was expecting, perhaps people in hats tipping them as we walked by or hippies in flower power dresses, but this was not what we found. There were very few white people in the area and the ones we saw looked shabbily dressed in oversized coats. The dustbins were overflowing with litter, there was graffiti on the walls with various unwelcoming slogans and the pavements were uneven. Then there were lines and lines of colourful washing hanging in the backyards. I couldn't imagine how they would dry in the cold, grey, damp air. Even though it was only mid-September, it was cold, very, very cold and we were inadequately dressed in our saris and cardigans.

We walked and walked, not knowing how to navigate the buses, until we stumbled across a parade of Indian grocery stores. While my mother bought the provisions we needed, I began talking to the shopkeeper, asking whether he had any jobs we could do. He shook his head but suggested that we might try going to Ealing Road, a road with many more Indian shops. My sister wanted to walk back to the house with our mother to help prepare the food, so I set off to find the street he had mentioned.

In the ninth shop I enquired in, I found a grocer who was looking for someone to start right away as one of the men had not turned up to work that morning and he had a policy of firing people if they did not turn up, irrespective of whether they were sick. He looked me up and down and he said he would give me an unpaid trial session and pointed to the stock in his van.

"Unload it all, put it in the stock cupboard and put the prices on the tins."

I did as he instructed and in half the time that he had given me.

"The pay is £10 a week for six days a week, nine hours a day, start at 5 a.m. – take it or leave it. You can start properly tomorrow."

"Thank you," I replied and then I ran off excitedly to find a post office so I could send Deep's letter.

There was a queue ahead of me and a blind man was taking his time, requesting that someone read out his letter to him. The customers were growing impatient; the cashier asked him to come back later when it was less busy. I went over to him.

It was a letter from his sister in Australia and she had sent him a £20 postal order. I read out the letter and he began to cry.

"You have a lovely reading voice," he commented.

He cashed the postal order and wanted to give me some money to thank me for my time, but I refused as he had not realised what he had done for me. I took this as a sign from the universe that things would be okay and rejoined the queue.

A lady came up to me. She was the post office owner. "How would you like a job?"

I wanted to cry. It was true what Ba said, that fortune would follow me.

"Yes! Yes, thank you! Thank you!" And then for a split second, I thought of Gauri. Gauri, who would need work; Gauri, who would be unable to do the manual labour required at the grocer's. I didn't want to think of her. I wanted this job.

"Ma'am, I would really love to do this job but I know someone who would be much better at it," I lied. "She is patient, kind, organised and polite. Would you be willing to consider my sister?" The words came out begrudgingly.

"And you can't do it?"

"I really wish I could."

"Tell her to come in."

I posted Deep's letter and went home to get Gauri.

Gauri complained about having to leave her half-eaten lunch. I told her what to say. "Tell her about the years of experience working in the sweet shop, about many of the difficult customers, but that you were always patient and understanding. Oh, and you are good with numbers. You like order and you will go above and beyond."

"I've got it, Didi. I am smarter than you think I am."

Indeed, she charmed the post office owner with an exuberance I had never seen and she got the job. The pay was double mine for half the work. I felt deeply envious.

I began another letter to Deep, telling him how we had found work. I described the fruit and vegetable shop as if it were something out of Keats's poem "To Autumn", "full of bountiful fruit and promise", omitting the details of the dishevelled pale vegetables and the angry grocer. I told him about the experience of reading the letter to the blind man and how I may have added a quote or two about love and family.

My father came home.

"Bapa, Bapa, Didi and I found work. I am going to work in a post office and Didi, tell Bapa what you are going to do."

"Sell groceries."

My father shed a tear.

"Thank you, my girls. I promise you that it won't be for long. We will get our own home soon and you will both go to college. Jobs so quickly." He smiled and shook his head. "My clever, clever girls."

"It was Bhanu who arranged it," my mother added.

"My interview was very difficult," my sister interjected. "All sorts of questions, she asked me."

"Bhanu," Bapa said, looking at me. "You have always been our lucky star. Did I ever tell you that when you came to live with us, our fortunes changed?"

I felt those words land in my heart. I felt proud to be able to repay them and in the end, believed it would all work out.

"Thank you, Bapa. I can't even begin to tell you what those words mean to me."

Deep had not written back. It had been three weeks and I began worrying. I wrote irrespectively, chronicling my life, omitting all the details about the shop that I knew he would worry about: the grocer's deviant eye that would fixate on my breasts as I unloaded the van, his cheap tobacco breath that came a little too close while explaining how to short-change customers.

I ignored all this by pretending to be elsewhere with Deep or imagining him by my side, helping me. When the grocer was away, I would have full conversations with Deep and managed to beat off every doubt that crept into my mind that he would not write, and I continued my letters telling him that I had found a college where I could enrol for night school in the new year and that I was working on finding a better-paid job to be able to afford the fees. It was too expensive to send a letter every day, so I sent them at the end of ten days; this was probably what Deep was doing too. I checked with my sister that she was sending my letters as promised.

"Of course, Didi. There is probably a postal strike. You know what it is like."

One day, when I got back to the house, the old lady was sitting at the kitchen table holding four envelopes. They were from Deep.

"My letters." I gasped as I went to grab them.

She put her hand on top of mine. "£5 fee. Remember you owe me."

"But I don't have that money."

"You will find it, or I can read the contents to your parents."

I stared at her so I could remember the details of her twisted face.

"Please keep them," I responded as I got up. "If you need to read them to my parents then that is what you will have to do." I walked away.

I didn't need to know what was in those letters; all I knew was that Deep was true to his word, he had written, he loved me and I didn't care if my parents knew how much.

I gave Deep the post office address where my sister worked as a new address and I dedicated every spare hour to finding a better job so we could all move out of the house.

Had the internet or mobile phones been invented back then, I would be writing a different story. Perhaps love stories don't exist these days in the way they used to. Everything is delivered speedily with instant gratification so it can be thrown away or disregarded with the same ease. There is no longer any waiting, hoping, yearning for a lover's letter.

Fourteen blue airmail sheets of paper would arrive c/o the post office every fourteen days. I would post my letters every ten days.

For two months, the facts of our lives were set adrift on a sea of poetry and love: Deep's father's steady recovery, his exam preparations, saving diligently for the airfare to London. My new job, continuing my A levels at night school, meeting my first friend, Pushpa, Bapa finding work in an Indian sweet shop, us saving every penny to move to our own home, which would be very soon.

He would end each letter, *Hold on to your imagination, Tara; it is our imagination that will make this separation bearable. I am with you, Tara, in every heartbeat: listen, and you will hear me.*

The letters grew infrequent and then they stopped.

I continued writing every day. My Deep would not stop writing to me, not unless something was terribly wrong.

"Gauri, is there anything today?"

"No, Didi. Perhaps there is a postal strike there?"

"It's been over a month. I'm worried, really worried. What if something has happened to him?"

"No, please don't think that way. I can write to one of my friends and ask her to make enquiries and I can send him a telegram from the post office."

"Yes! A telegram."

She sent one the next morning.

One came back.

MARRIAGE ARRANGED BY FAMILY. HEARTBROKEN. MUST FULFIL WISHES.

I kept rereading the words.

"No, Gauri. It's not true. I know it is not true. If it were, he would have written to me, he would have explained and not sent eight words. I don't believe it. Send him another one."

I was there when she transmitted it. *WRITE AND EXPLAIN.*

He did not respond.

"Send another one, tell him to go to the post office on Tuesday 4 p.m. and I will call him."

It just didn't sound like him. He didn't go.

"But it doesn't make any sense to me. Deep is not a coward. He wouldn't be afraid to tell me anything."

"I don't know, Didi. I really don't know."

I sat in the abyss of the unknown, not eating, not sleeping, wondering what to do next. I looked at the stars and asked Ba to help if she could.

"I know in my heart that we are meant to be together, Ba, and if this isn't true, nothing is."

A week later, a letter arrived from Tanzania. It was from Shoba, my sister's friend.

"Didi," my sister said despondently. "It's true. She says his mother found out about you, and you know" – she hesitated – "with your history, she does not approve. They have arranged a marriage for him. She is from a wealthy family. He has reluctantly agreed, for the sake of the family."

"No!" I cried. "He would have explained. He would have found a way. He would have spoken to me."

"Maybe he had no choice?"

I snatched the letter out of her hands and read it.

"Don't do it to yourself, Didi."

Gauri had omitted the words *her mother's mental illness and suicide.*

Stupid, stupid me; why had I thought it would be okay? He'd made me believe that it would be okay. He had used me. Seduced me with his flowery words and then abandoned me. I ran down to the kitchen, took a pair of scissors from the drawer, went to the bathroom and locked the door.

Stupid, stupid me! To think someone would want to marry me? I began hacking at my thick black hair. I snipped and snipped to his pathetic heartbeat that he'd said was with me, his deceitful words conjured from an imagination that he begged me in each letter to believe in.

You are the most important thing I have and our separation will be made bearable with our imagination.

It was rubbish, all of it.

"Please keep this with you," he had said before we left Tanzania.

"Auden's book. I can't take it. It is the most important thing you have."

"You, Tara, are the most important thing I have. Promise me you will wait for me? We will go to York together."

"Of course I will wait for you, Deep."

"Write to me when you have an address. Write to me every day. Whatever you do, just wait for me."

I cut and I cut.

My sister knocked on the door. "Didi, I am worried. Open the door."

I kept cutting.

"I will start kicking it; I will make a scene and people will come to watch." She spoke calmly.

Even in the midst of turmoil, that voice about what other people would think still haunted me.

I unlocked it.

She took the scissors from me and dragged me off the dirty floor. I fell into her arms and cried huge, uncontrollable sobs.

"I can't live without him. I can't."

"Didi, you will see. It will be okay. It will all work out. You will see how it does. I promise it will. You have me and Mummy and Daddy. You will always have us."

I clung to her. Desperate for her not to leave me, desperate not to be consumed by a black hole from which I would never emerge.

Eight weeks later, she lent me her miniskirt, helped me with make-up and gave me some money so I could get Pushpa a present and go to her birthday celebrations.

I met Pushpa at night school. She seemed hugely popular, always dressed in the latest fashion, and had a Farrah Fawcett hairstyle; she was surrounded by boys who were willing to do anything for her. At first, I was unsure about her; she could be intimidating, loud and outrageous so I kept conversation to a minimum. Pushpa had come to England a decade before me when she was ten and helped me navigate British culture.

"Are you washing the milk bottles before you put them out? Because otherwise, people call us dirty immigrants and you don't want to give us all a bad name."

"Bhanu, let me show you how to use the cutlery properly. Try not to pick anything up with your fingers, even though it might be easier."

"When they call you 'Paki', it's not friendly. For months, I thought it was a term of endearment."

"If they call you 'smelly Paki', you need to sort your cooking situation out. Just light a tea light; it gets rid of the oily smell. Got it? Now what are you doing wasting your time here? Are your parents setting you up with someone?"

I told her that I had a job as a clerical assistant at an insurance firm but I wanted to go to university and study literature. She seemed uninterested. Pushpa was repeating her A levels. "I'm not going to university. Educated up to A level standard is fine on my bio data. If I didn't have the looks, it would be a problem. These days, they like you educated but not too educated. I'm going to marry someone rich. You could also stop at A levels too if you wanted."

I began to tell her about my career plans when she interrupted.

"You're not one of these feminist types, are you? I bet you've never had sex with anyone. You probably won't have sex until you're married. Right?"

She was direct and funny but I'm not sure if we would have become friends had I not hacked off my hair. I rushed to evening class with my hair in a total mess as I couldn't afford to miss the class. She sat next to me.

"Fuck me! What happened? Don't tell me: heart-break?"

I didn't say anything.

"They are not worth it, trust me. Don't ever get all intense about relationships but fuck, we need to sort that hair out. You can't go into work tomorrow like that. They'll think us Asians are raving mad and they won't hire another one. That or one of them will think you've stolen a bearskin off one of the Queen's guards. Don't worry, I've got a friend who's a barber."

It was late but we drove in her green Mini to her friend's house in Barnet.

"I was thinking Twiggy," she said to her Italian friend.

He cut my hair in a short bob and admired his work.

"She's a model, isn't she, Pushpa? You could do some modelling. I can get you a job."

"It's not her thing," Pushpa replied. "Bookworm."

It was a truly wonderful cut. "This is all I have to give you."

"It's okay, any friend of Pushpa's is a friend of mine." He kissed her. They kissed for a long time in front of me and I began to get nervous.

"Was he your boyfriend?" I asked her in the car.

"No. I don't really have boyfriends. Don't get attached. I'm just messing about until my parents fix me up with someone."

I was in admiration at her audacity. "What if someone in the community sees you?"

"I'd just deny it."

She dropped me off at home. "I would invite you in, but—"

"There are uncles pouring out of every available space and it wouldn't be safe," Pushpa continued.

I laughed. "We are moving to a bigger space with two rooms next week."

"Wow, two rooms – luxury," she joked. "Well, if you need a hand, all you need to do is ask."

Pushpa came to help us move and that's how we became good friends. She would bring bits of furniture for us that she said her parents didn't need and also clothes for my sister and me that she didn't wear any more; some of them still had the tags on. My parents loved her as she changed into a demure Indian girl who would eat their food with her hands, not care about the smell and converse fluently in Gujarati.

"They love that shit," she said, as we left them.

It was probably this chameleon character that held me back from trusting her totally and completely. This, and the fact that she lacked a certain amount of sensitivity.

We were planning to go to Brighton with her friend Manju and before she dropped me off home, she said, "Bring your swimming costume or shall I get you one?"

"I can't swim," I replied. "I don't really like getting into the water." There was a long pause. "My mother drowned."

For some people, that might be an opening for further connection: *How did that happen? Were you there? Oh right, so that's not your real mother?* Then depending how safe it felt, I might have ventured further and told her the truth.

Not Pushpa! Her response was, "Right. You should watch him off the telly. What's his name – Duncan Goodhew. Don't waste your money on lessons, just watch him. What do they say? Copy a pro and you'll be fine."

I laughed and I couldn't stop laughing.

It was Pushpa's twenty-first but I didn't want to go. I didn't mind hanging out with her but I didn't want to socialise with a group of her friends. When I told Gauri about Pushpa's invite, she kept pestering me.

"It has been two months now, Didi. I can't bear to watch you being so sad. Go, have fun and meet some new people. I will give you my money that I have been saving. You can get her something nice. Please, let me help you get dressed." Gauri lent me one of her miniskirts that Pushpa had given us.

It was a last-minute decision to go, primarily based on getting Deep out of my thoughts, even if it was just for a couple of hours. I took out the piece of paper that Pushpa had scribbled the address on and got on the Tube. It was late, I felt a bit nervous and I couldn't find the exact location. Pushpa had omitted to write that it was a bowling alley. Had she put this small detail down, I'm sure things would have turned out differently. I looked at my miniskirt and went in.

Everybody there stared at me and some of the girls gasped that I had the guts to wear a miniskirt to a bowling alley. That and my short haircut made the boys gather around me. My husband-to-be pretended that he hadn't seen me and was the last to greet me and only did this after he took his turn.

"Hiten." He stared at me intensely as all the pins fell down with one decisive strike. "Three consecutive strikes are known as a 'turkey'," he added.

He watched me as I awkwardly took my turn and then made sure I was paying attention when he delivered two further strikes. Then he walked up to me. There was no poetry, no flowery words, just directness.

"I'm as good as my word. So, when I say I am going to marry you, it means I am going to marry you."

I laughed. Maybe he thought I was easy in a miniskirt?

"Don't be so ridiculous," I replied.

The *Grease* song came on and he made some thrusting movements. Pushpa's friends began laughing. "Do something!" Pushpa jeered.

I didn't want to; it was all too much. I wasn't sure what I was doing there so I made an excuse to leave.

As I was leaving, he followed me, apologising, and insisted that he drop me home safely. I declined and he continued walking with me to the station, trying to make me laugh by singing. And then, spontaneously yet decisively, he hailed a black cab, gave the cab driver some money and asked him to take me home.

"Be safe," he said as he opened the cab door for me.

I sat in the cab and was proud of the fact that for maybe half an hour, I had not thought of Deep and was grateful for the kind gesture of the cab. I turned around to look back and he was still waiting there. I smiled at him.

"Didi, how did it go?" my sister asked when I got home.

"It was nice," I replied. "I'm glad I went."

"That makes me happy, Didi. Really happy."

Pushpa came to pick me up the next day.

"You know what they say, the best way to get over someone is to get under someone, and Hiten is into you. He could have anyone, literally anyone; the family are absolutely loaded and he wants you. I wouldn't say no but he's my brother's best friend, and you know, you can't do things to mess with family."

"I think he's arrogant."

"I'd say *confident*. Used to getting his own way. So, what shall I tell him? Will you see him again?"

"No. Nothing is going to get in the way of my studies."

"Of course it's not," Pushpa replied.

Hiten came to surprise me one day after work. You see, in those days there was no congestion charge and he came to pick me up in his red Ford Cortina.

"Sexy legs," he shouted.

I looked around and saw him. He had his elbow leaning out of the window and was smoking a cigarette.

"Please go away," I replied.

"I am not going anywhere." He started following me slowly in his car.

"Just go. Somebody might see us."

"I don't care. I will follow you all the way home if I have to."

I kept walking, embarrassed but slightly flattered by his determination.

"You don't know me, but I promise, I will follow you at this speed all the way home if I have to."

So I got into his car and the only reason I did this was because I cared about what people thought and I didn't want him to make a scene in case any of my colleagues saw me. ABBA was playing and he started singing to me. He had a good voice; I had noticed this before.

I sat there, not looking at him.

"Not your song? Don't worry. I will find it."

He changed the cassette. I was resolutely not interested.

"You can drop me off here. Thank you for the lift."

The next day he did the same and the day after that, playing song after song. Asking me to join in. I did not, but every day, I allowed him to drop me a little nearer home.

I wonder if, had there been the congestion charge back then, we would be together because he must have made at least twenty trips before I started talking to him properly.

"I don't know why you keep doing this because this cannot go anywhere. Just because I wore a miniskirt to a bowling alley does not mean I will have sex with you."

"I know," he laughed. "As I keep telling you, I am going to marry you."

"Don't you have work to do?"

"I am my own boss and at the moment, this is my only task and I won't stop. I know what I want."

I tried to shock him into never picking me up again but before I opened my mouth, I thought for a moment how I might miss his humour and his company.

"Listen, it is never going to happen because: one, we are not from the same caste; two, my mother killed herself – so technically, I am defective goods; three, we are poor and my family have nothing to offer you."

"Bhanu, sing with me." He turned up the volume to 'Don't Go Breaking My Heart'.

"Did you just hear what I said?"

"Yes, and I don't care. I am just certain that I want to be with you for the rest of my life."

"But you don't know me."

"I will if you give me a chance."

"Please drop me here."

As I got out of the car, I stopped and turned around. "Do you know anything about poetry?"

"*To be or not to be?*" He gestured.

I rolled my eyes. "Are you into the stars and the workings of the universe?"

"No, but I am happy to take you to the planetarium. Why so Sirius with all the questions?"

He made me laugh. Deep had fooled me with his intensity. What you saw was pretty much what you got with Hiten.

"The song that you play that I like the most is 'Stayin' Alive'."

He was funny, he didn't take life too seriously, which was good for me, and he was charming. It had been five months since Deep's telegram. Not a single word had come back. Perhaps Deep was already married.

I told my sister about Hiten.

"He sounds amazing, Didi. At least give him a chance?"

And I did.

The next day when he picked me up, he was playing "Stayin' Alive".

"So, is it our song, Bhanu?"

I looked at him and smiled. That one look was all it took for him to lean over and kiss me.

"I won't do anything else," I declared. "No heavy petting."

"I know," he replied.

"And if you want to continue this, you must marry me."

Back in those days, if you were caught with a boy in a back alley or sitting innocently in a restaurant, your reputation would be ruined, so I just said it not really meaning it or if I did, I didn't expect him to say, "Yes. No problem."

"It was a joke," I added quickly.

"No, it wasn't, Bhanu. I am going to marry you. I told you that when we first met."

His certainty made him even more attractive and I knew he would fight for me no matter what. He got out of the car, opened my door and helped me out, and then he got down on the pavement on one knee, like in the English films.

"Bhanu, will you marry me?"

"Ask my parents and if they agree, then I will."

"Come on, you can do better than that."

"If they like you, I will. Family is everything to me."

My heart did not explode with happiness, or any other real sentiment. There was possibly a quiet murmur of discontent that I chose not to feel; it was telling me to wait, to get to know him properly and that it was too early.

Was I in love with Hiten? No. Did I want to escape from my house and the strangers in it? Of course I did. Was I on the rebound? Yes. Could he provide me with security and stability? Yes, therapist, the need to feel safe and secure has guided many of the major decisions in my life but more than this, a man like him thought I was worthy, worthy of chasing for months and months. He wanted me. I also had feelings for him. It wasn't a passionate love affair but I definitely had feelings towards him and in any case, passionate feelings of love lead nowhere.

He wanted to come to the house to ask my parents for their permission. If the house didn't put him off, nothing would. The dilapidated house in which we had the luxury of two rooms where the other occupants envied our space. He ignored the people falling out from every room, the suitcases piled high on top of the cupboards, the thick dirty curtains and carpets. He walked into my parents' bedroom, which they had temporarily converted into a sitting room for his arrival. My mother tried to decorate the room with her saris in an attempt to hide the peeling paint and the damp walls.

My father did his best to conceal his awkwardness at the state of the room.

"It is not for long," he mumbled.

"I have heard so much about you, Uncle," Hiten said, ignoring my father's comment. He greeted my mother. "That's a lovely sari, Aunty."

She swooned at his compliment.

My sister brought up a tea tray and an array of Indian sweets that my father had made. They were so elegant that they looked like they did not belong in the room.

"This is my sister, Gauri." I introduced them.

"Ah, Gauri, I have heard so many good things about you."

I was wondering when exactly this was. I didn't remember talking that much about her. Instead of commanding attention, my sister just smiled at him. How the year had matured us, I thought, and I felt proud of her.

Hiten pretended not to notice the surroundings and focused instead on the sweets.

"Not only beautiful but they are delicious," he said, taking another piece.

My mother kept feeding him more and sighing in admiration at his sharp suit.

"You are indeed an amazing cook," he told her.

"Bapa made them," I corrected.

My father tried not to look embarrassed.

"Yes, of course. Bhanu told me. How could I forget? What a great talent."

"It's just something very simple." My father gestured. "Bhanu told me about your plans for a business. I would like to help you."

My father shook his head. "Thank you but no need. Please just take care of Bhanu and allow her to finish her education."

"I will. Uncle, Aunty," he continued, "soon, we will be family and I would like to help you and it's not even help. You have such a talent. Think of it as a business investment."

"Taking care of our daughter is all we want."

"And that is all I want to do," he replied, "but if there is anything you need—"

"We are fine," my father repeated proudly.

My mother could not stop admiring him, her mouth remaining half open – that was, until she decided to ask a question.

"Have you spoken to your parents yet?"

"No. I wanted to ask your permission first."

"You have our blessing. You are a very lucky man; you will never find anyone like Bhanu," my father stated.

"I know," Hiten replied.

I caught my sister's eye and it was a genuine look of happiness.

Hiten left me at the front door. All the inquisitive eyes that had appeared for his arrival were there for his departure.

"I respect you and your family even more. It makes me love you more."

Love, love, I thought. It sounded strange when he stated it. It had never entered the equation for me. Love was not there for Ba but she grew to love her husband; love was not there when my aunt and uncle married. He had seen her just the day before and look how much they loved each other now. Love, at this point, for me, did not need to be in the equation. Love could remain in poetry books and in films. Stability was what things that were made to last were built on.

I went back to my family, who were elated.

"Didi, see, something good always happens from something bad." My sister squeezed me.

"Don't neglect your studies," my father smiled.

I told Pushpa that Hiten had come to ask my parents if he could marry me.

"As long as you don't sleep with him, you'll make it to the wedding. That and getting his mum on side. All I'm saying is don't celebrate too soon. No one has made it past her."

I was unable to sleep that night, thinking about what Deep's mother had done and began to worry.

The next day, Hiten came to pick me up from work. My colleague Mary, who was normally the first to leave, waited behind so she could meet him. After she had left us, I told Hiten about my concerns.

"Let's go, then."

"Go where?" I asked.

"Let's call her up now. What time is it? She will still be awake."

We squeezed into a telephone box near Euston, laughing at the tightness of the space. I was so anxious but excited by his certainty that she would approve of me. It was a lot of money just to say a few sentences.

"Yes, Mummy, she has a very good job."

"Tell her after I go to university, I will be a teacher," I interrupted.

"Shh, Bhanu, I can't hear. Yes, Mummy, she is a great cook... Yes, yes, she is good at cleaning." And then he paused and looked at me. "She is very, very pretty."

Then the pips went, the money ran out, he put down the phone and he said she sounded very happy and it would be fine. I should have worked out the dynamic of the relationship by the number of times he said "yes" and known back then that it would not be fine.

They also have their CIA community network in India, which did the normal investigations and checks that are performed before any marriages are sanctioned. A telegram came back straight away, saying:

RED ALERT. RED ALERT. DO NOT MARRY HER. WE REPEAT, DO NOT MARRY HER. SHE IS FROM A LOW CASTE. REPEAT LOW CASTE. LOW. LOW CASTE. DO NOT PROCEED. MOTHER DEAD – SUICIDE REPEAT SUICIDE. FATHER'S WHEREABOUTS UNKNOWN.

He didn't have to show me the telegram. So I gave him a way out.

"If they are not happy, please, let us not do this. Family and community are everything; let us not upset them."

"I don't care what they think. Bhanu, I will look after you no matter what. Once they meet you, they will understand."

The stars were fated in such a way that we were destined to collide. His need to find a way of detaching from his mother and proving himself. My desire to forget Deep and move on.

The poet Rumi says, "There is a voice that doesn't use words. Listen."

There was indeed a voice inside me that whispered to do a course correction but I chose to ignore it. The fear that I would never again meet anyone was greater, or perhaps the fear of falling truly in love with someone else and losing control as I had done with Deep was even greater than this.

When my mother asked for his mother's details to begin wedding formalities, Hiten told her that due to illness, she would be unable to participate as he had hoped but we could formalise the engagement, perhaps not in its entirety.

The ritual of formalising the engagement consists of various ceremonies between the two families. The first one is Chandlo Matli, where the father of the bride along with four male family members visits the groom's house, place a red vermillion mark on his forehead and give token sum of money, a "shagun". They then set the date for the wedding. My father gathered four male acquaintances and went to one of Hiten's brother's houses to do this. They set the wedding date for the most auspicious time, a year later, and when I heard this, I felt relieved.

The next part of the ceremony is Gor Dhana, which translates as "jaggery and coriander seeds". This is where the bride and her family go to the groom's home bearing sweets and savouries. Five married women from each side bless the couple and then both families bond over a meal. This part of the ritual would be bypassed and without consulting me; Hiten celebrated this in his own way by taking my family to tea at the Dorchester.

My family were excited as they got ready. Hiten came to pick us up in his new car. I don't remember the details of that high tea – what we ate, drank, or what it actually felt like. I was in a parallel world in my imagination, observing it from a distance like a guest, sipping tea and with a ringside view of this Indian family who looked somewhat out of place. At the same time, I pretended to be present, laughing and joking. And then, somewhere towards the end, Hiten presented me with an engagement ring and an envelope for my father.

The part of me who had split off to be the guest observed Hiten's rudeness to the attentive waiter and his roving eye as a pretty, blonde waitress passed him. His constant interruptions as the older gentleman tried to explain the history of the Dorchester and the fact that during the war it was considered to be one of the safest buildings. The guest observed no curiosity on Hiten's part to learn more, no sense of appreciation at the trays of sandwiches and delicacies placed in front of him. She noted the woman to his side, who, when handed her engagement ring, had tears in her eyes that did not appear to be tears of happiness; the woman seemed to fake a smile of delight.

The guest wanted to go up to the woman, shake her and persuade her to leave but right at that moment, the man grabbed her hand, ordered a bottle of champagne and handed the older gentleman an envelope. The gentleman kept the envelope to one side and continued the conversation.

"Open it!" Hiten encouraged.

My father reluctantly opened it. Inside was a cheque for £10,000 to start his sweet business. My father was very touched but refused the money and gave it straight back to Hiten. After much insistence and toing and froing of the envelope, my father finally relented.

"I will pay you every penny back," he promised, accepting it. "Thank you."

"We are family now," Hiten responded.

"I have doubts," I confessed to my sister when we got home. "Huge doubts."

"Everyone has doubts. It's normal," she replied. "I would be worried if you didn't."

"I was sitting at the table today and I suddenly had a feeling that Deep was not married. The first ever words he spoke to me were 'quantum entanglement'; it's basically if two particles are separated, they would both feel the changes to the other. I don't feel he is married. I feel he is looking for me."

"What utter rubbish! Don't be fooled again by his nonsense, Didi. You've come this far and Hiten is amazing. You have made Mummy and Daddy so proud. You really have. It is the best thing that you can do."

Back then, given all the options, I thought it was. My family were invested in the marriage and the new dream of starting again. My father put down a deposit on a commercial property he had found and we began preparing for the move out of the overcrowded house and into the spacious flat above the commercial premises. My sister gave up her job at the post office to help my mother and father run their new business.

I took the suitcases down from the top of the cupboard. Ba's wedding sari that she had left for me, carefully wrapped in muslin cloth, was in one of them. I unwrapped it, smelling it, and carefully unfolded it. When I first arrived in England, I would sleep with it under my pillow and fall asleep imagining myself draped in this sari, marrying Deep. In the morning, I would hide it in my pillow. Every night, I did this, until I found out he was marrying someone else.

What would you have thought to all of this, Ba? I thought about her second husband's persistence, his desire to protect her – she said it wasn't love in the beginning. I carefully folded the sari and put it back; it would be wrong to marry Hiten wearing it. As it transpired, it was a decision that I would not have to make. Then I took Deep's letters, which I kept in a shoebox at the back of the cupboard, and looked at them. Desperate to read them, I resisted.

"I'm so sorry, Deep."

I went into the backyard, lit a small fire and watched the letters burn, asking the fire god Agni to take them away. I fought back the tears, watching them disintegrate.

Perhaps because I am ruled by the planet Mars, I have an affinity with fire. Fires have always given me the strength and opportunity to rise again. A month later, I got married.

yard three

"Your heart knows the way.
Run in that direction."
— Rumi

Hiten said he had a surprise for me. He asked me to take the morning off work and to make sure I wore something nice. At first, I refused as I never took even a few hours off, not even to go to the doctor's, but he was persuasive.

"Just for me, this once; you will understand later."

Dressed in a smart navy suit, Hiten picked me up from the house. It was a warm September day and I wore a long pink and green maxi dress. He had a Polaroid camera in the back of his car.

"Where are we going?" I was excited. "The planetarium?" We were heading towards Baker Street and I had commented earlier that week that I missed seeing the night sky in Tanzania.

"You'll see, *meri jaan* Bhanu."

He parked the car in Marylebone.

"Can you please tell me now?"

"Bhanu, I can't wait any more. They had a free slot and we are getting married." He smiled.

I should have said no. I should have stopped him.

"But my family! I can't do this to them."

"This is just the civil wedding. We will have a big wedding when Mummy sees how happy you make me. I promise you, we will do this properly."

We had to get two witnesses (a man and a woman) from a café nearby. They appeared bemused as they watched us get married and accompanied us as we walked out to "Stayin' Alive", which the registrar hastily put on. Hiten gave the registrar the camera and invited the strangers to come into the photo. It all seemed wrong – very wrong. There was no ritual, no ceremony.

My husband handed them £5 each, a lot of money in those days. They wished us well and quickly walked off. Hiten had booked a hotel room for us. We formalised the marriage. It was all a bit of a shock for me. I went back to work in the afternoon feeling a deep discomfort in the pit of my stomach but pretending that it would all be fine.

My office colleagues wondered where I had gone as I never took any time off work.

"Where were you, Banoo?" asked Mary from accounts.

"I got married."

They almost fell off their chairs.

"To that charming, handsome man that I met?"

I nodded, not allowing the full implications of what I had done to sink in.

Then one of my office colleagues said he had to pop out and he came back with some Babycham and some cake and they celebrated for me.

"What was his name again?"

"Hiten."

"To Bhanu and Hiten, may your lives together be filled with health, happiness and laughter."

It would be fine, I reassured myself, lifting my glass.

"So, what are you doing back here, Banoo? You should be on your honeymoon," Mary said, grabbing my shoulder.

No, there was no honeymoon or honeymoon period – just the mother-in-law who descended on us. The first time I met his mother was a few months after we got married. We had just moved into our first home, which Hiten had bought for us.

"Close your eyes, *meri* Bhanu," he said, gifting me the keys.

"What are they for?"

We got into the car and he told me to keep my eyes shut.

"Still keep them closed." He helped me out of the car and held my hand as we stood in front of a gate. It began raining heavily.

"Open them."

I couldn't believe it: a house of our own with no one else sleeping in unoccupied spaces. He opened the door and he showed me around.

"Of course, it needs work, but I got it at a good price. Like it?" he asked excitedly.

"I love it," I replied.

He held me. "Believe me, Bhanu, when I tell you that I will always take care of you."

I wanted to cry. I believed him.

"I managed to get a bed from my cousin." He smiled.

Of course that would be the first thing he would have got.

"Want to try it?"

Hiten asked me to stop work and to stop studying before his mother's visit so I could get the house ready; he didn't want her to think that I was one of those modern women who did not want to look after him.

"Please, Bhanu, just do this one thing for me."

"But I love my job."

"You know you don't have to work and I will pay for you to go to college during the day. *Meri* Bhanu, I just want this visit to be right so we can get married properly. I know if she gets to know you, she will love you. It's so important to me that the two of you get along."

"Great strategy for bagging him," Pushpa said when I told her that I would be leaving night school.

"There was no strategy," I replied.

"Bhanu, you're talking to me. Acting all cool and not giving anything away and I mean *anything*. Men like him go crazy for that. Hiten has always been all about the chase."

"What do you mean?"

"Play hard to get, drive them wild. Don't get me wrong, I'm happy you got what you wanted."

One simple thing I have learned: if your friends are at first annoying, they will always be annoying, even if they have a generous heart. Sometimes, they really shouldn't be your friends. However, the bonds of familiarity are strong and when you try to break them, you remember all the things they did for you when you needed help and you tell yourself that nobody is perfect.

"I knew you weren't going to stay, Banoo. Who would after winning the lottery and marrying a man like that?" sobbed Mary.

They bought me a fountain pen as a gift.

"I will treasure this and my time with you," I said, holding back my tears.

I threw myself into making a home for us and making the house right for my mother-in-law. I had compromised but if it meant getting her approval and getting married properly, it would be worth it.

A few weeks before she came, Hiten surprised me with a gift. It was a portable colour television set for the bedroom. I thought it was a bit of an odd gift as I preferred to read but he said he liked watching television in bed and in the early months of our marriage he had been too distracted to purchase one due to our bedroom activities. He also bought a huge television for downstairs, a VHS recorder and a stack of Bollywood movies for his mother.

We were one of the first owners of this technology in the community and as such, all the relatives and members of the community who did not previously want to have anything to do with us (due to belonging to different castes) descended in their hordes as if they were visiting a holy shrine. They took off their shoes and gasped as they entered the sitting room, paying respects to the large colour television and the attached VHS recorder. Part of me was pleased that we were becoming "respectable" even if it was through that VHS. Each Bollywood film was recorded on three video cassettes and cost roughly £30, a fortune in those days.

They would bring their families and sit for hours and hours, transfixed by Bollywood films. The one that they wanted to see over and over again was *Kabhi Kabhie*, which I couldn't bring myself to watch. So, to their delight, I would produce an endless supply of Indian snacks, sweets and cups of tea.

"She is nothing like they said," Community Member A commented while munching a samosa.

"Always has a smile," Community Member B added, reaching for another.

"Good at cooking even if the samosas are a bit too salty for me. I have high blood pressure," Member C would add.

That was the way we were slowly accepted back into the community. This is an example of a wider deal – open-door policy for worship of 22-inch colour television and unlimited snacks and beverages, provided in exchange for acceptance.

I grew to like the colour television upstairs and Hiten and I got into the habit of drinking tea and watching comedy shows like *Some Mothers Do 'Ave 'Em*, *George and Mildred*, *Fawlty Towers*. We would sit there holding hands and laugh so much. Hiten could do an excellent Frank Spencer impersonation. Occasionally, I would force him to watch a nature programme but he would joke through it, making voices for the animals. This routine all changed with my mother-in-law's arrival.

Hiten had gone to pick her up from Heathrow Airport. I thought carefully about what jewellery to wear and was about to get dressed in a beautiful pink organza sari, gifted to me by my husband for the occasion. "Mummy will love this one," he'd said enthusiastically as he picked it out. Suddenly, the car horn sounded three times. *How did they get here so quickly?* I must have put on that sari in less than three minutes and felt proud that I had taken control of it and the situation in such a short space of time. Nervous but very excited, I ran out to greet her.

Her hair was dyed jet-black and it was in a very large bun. She was dressed in a white cotton sari and she sat in the back of the car like the Pope. I rushed over and opened the car door for her. She held out her hand and I kissed her ring. She got out of the car. I touched her feet but she did not signal for me to get up.

"What took you so long?" she asked.

"So long for what?"

"You are slow as well as stupid."

Perhaps my husband didn't hear but if he did, he said nothing.

"Do you see this?" She pointed at her sari.

"I am so sorry, Mummy. Who died?"

"You," she said, looking at something she had found on her shoe, "you have married my son."

Hiten said nothing. He laughed a nervous laugh.

I wanted to cry.

"He could have married anyone. Anyone, and I can't understand it. Why you?" She turned to him. "And she is very dusky. You said she was fair."

As if reading from a CV, my husband pointed out my people skills, my aptitude for work and my culinary expertise.

"Bhanu is an expert at making sweets, Mummy. She has made you your favourite pistachio cake. Bhanu, show Mummy inside." He went to get her suitcases from the car.

"Where is this cake?"

I led her to the sitting room.

"Sit down, Mummy. It has been a long flight and I am sure that you are tired. I will get it for you. Would you like some tea?"

"Are you telling me I can't walk around freely in my son's house?"

"No. I thought you would like to rest after a long flight."

She got up and made her way into the kitchen. I followed her and watched her as she took the cake from the fridge.

"You will never be welcome in my family," she said as she dropped it on the floor.

Just then my husband walked in.

"I am so sorry, son. I accidentally dropped it." She looked at me.

"Don't worry, Mummy," my husband said. "Bhanu can make you another one."

I cleared up the mess as she watched me. Hiten brought in the rest of her suitcases.

Although I was desperate to say something, I understood how she was an equally important component to my ecosystem and I knew in that instant that I had to find a way of not letting her see that she affected me, so I decided to pretend that we were in a nature programme, and she was the dominant female pack leader hunting for prey. I would let her believe that she had outwitted me.

She sat down on the sofa, took out her compact, studied her face and dabbed powder on the pigmented areas of her skin. Had Botox and fillers been around, she would have had them and put herself down as a natural beauty. It subsequently transpired that she groomed herself quite frequently, just like a hyena, and the weeks she spent with us revealed that she did indeed have much in common with the hyena:

1. She certainly marked her territory using her anal glands – sitting at every opportunity in other people's chairs, sofas and beds.
2. She could produce some very loud, vocal sounds.
3. Female hyenas have "pseudo male genitals" due to high levels of testosterone and rank higher and dominate the males in the clan.

I wasn't sure about the state of her genitals, but my husband seemed to have lost his in her presence.

"I have got you a gift," she hollered at me after I finished cleaning up.

It is customary for the husband's side of the family to welcome the bride into the family with a sari. The kind of sari offered is a symbol of the bride's worth, which is a lot to put on five to nine yards of material, but the sari is able to fulfil its promise with the colours, fabric, weight and choice of embroidery. The sari gift says so much about the dynamic of the future relationship.

She pointed at her suitcase. "Hiten, my son, open up this one."

"That is so nice of Mummy. Isn't it, Bhanu?" he said enthusiastically, cutting off all the strings attached around the suitcase.

She unwrapped an old newspaper and pulled out a coarse, brown sari and opened it out in front of me. I wasn't even sure what material it was; it had holes in it and looked as if had been discarded by one of her servants.

"Go, put it on!"

I stared at Hiten, who nodded and smiled at me awkwardly.

"Thank you, Mummy," I said, taking it.

It was a very ugly sari but I was determined not to let her think she had got to me, that she had trodden on my feelings of inadequacy and so, as Ba had taught me, I gathered up the layers quickly and in spite of these feelings, put the sari on in just a few minutes. She hadn't expected me to be so quick and was talking about me to my husband as I stood there like a tree.

"She is very dusky; you said she was fair, and she doesn't seem clever. This is what happens when you marry low-caste people."

"Mummy, once you get to know Bhanu, you will see how smart she is."

"I am ashamed to even invite my friends here. What will they think when they see such a low-class girl?"

At this point, I wanted to inform her that they had all been round to worship the colour television and had consumed copious amounts of snacks, cakes and beverages.

"It is very lovely sari," I exclaimed instead. "Thank you."

Later that evening, when we were in bed, I tried to have a conversation with my husband about it.

"Didn't you hear any of the comments she made? Why didn't you say anything?"

"That's just her way, my Bhanu. You will get used to each other and it will all be fine." He switched on the television. "Nature programme?"

We were watching the life cycle of the seahorse and their mating process when suddenly, the handle of our bedroom door turned. My mother-in-law walked in with two cups of tea and a sandwich. "Your favourite, my son: tomato, cucumber and pickle."

I was unsure of what to do as I was in my nightie and it felt very strange. She walked over to his side of the bed, placed the tray down on the bedside table and indicated to him to make space for her, which he did. I glared at him. He made this strange face back at me. She signalled for a pillow to lean against and he gave it to her. I stared at my husband again, but he said nothing.

I was unable to follow what happened to the male seahorse after the female deposited her eggs into the male's pouch as I was confused and too absorbed by the life cycle of the male next to me and the sequence of events that had led to his mother depositing herself into our bed. My first thought was, *Is this normal?* If you ever find yourself asking this question, please know that whatever you are asking about is *not* normal.

I wanted to scream at him, *Get her out of our bed!* However, I was so shocked at his ease, his lack of discomfort at her ruffling his hair, that I began questioning if this was normal. She handed him the sandwich and looked at me.

"Not enough bread for you."

"It's okay, Mummy. I don't eat sandwiches at night," was all I could pathetically manage. What I wanted to say was, *Are you serious? Get out of the bed, you crazy bitch.*

But there was a mother-in-law to win over, the need for acceptance and a proper wedding ceremony, so I looked at my husband once more.

She passed him his tea and watched the seahorse carry the eggs until the young were released into the sea. She didn't see the seahorse go off again to find a new mate as she had fallen asleep.

"What is this?" I whispered.

"Oh, Mummy and I have this childhood ritual."

"I don't think this is normal. We have to move her," I replied.

"Every family has its rituals," he retorted.

She began snoring and I wasn't sure if she was pretending.

"Let her sleep, Bhanu."

"I'm going to the sitting room," I mumbled.

He didn't say, *I'm just coming* or *Please don't do that.*

All he said was, "Okay, Bhanu," like it was the most natural thing in the world.

If there was Google back then, I would have searched, *Is it normal for a mother to sleep with her son aged 26?*

And I would have left had I read the responses. But the internet didn't exist so I took a pillow and blanket and went downstairs to sleep on the sofa.

I have subsequently read a similar post by "anonymous" on an Asian advice site: *My husband sleeps with his mother every time we have an argument. Is this normal?*

I wanted to scream *NO!* (Insert screaming face)

Instead, I posted two GIFs:

1. A huge red siren.
2. A pair of legs running very fast.

Very early the next morning, she was clattering the cutlery. Hyenas also make lots of noise to tell you that they are awake.

"I'm preparing toast for him," she shouted. "I have found more bread. My poor boy will waste away with you. He tells me you don't make it quite right – not enough butter. He's already looking very thin. And don't worry, you go back to sleep because I see you don't have anything to do all day."

"Thank you, Mummy." He smirked as she handed him his breakfast on a tray.

She rummaged through our cupboard and began laying out his clothes. "Shall I make your favourite for dinner?"

Hiten saw me on the landing and smiled as if nothing had happened. "Sleep okay, Bhanu?"

Alarm bells started ringing – well, it was a siren. I went to the phone box. I thought momentarily of calling Pushpa but Pushpa would probably make a few jokes about it and then use the information in years to come.

I called my sister.

"Do you think this is normal, Gauri?"

"Well, I think it is quite cute, as you know what they say... You can tell so much about a man by the way he treats his mother and he clearly loves her very much."

So, it continued. I asked him to lock the bedroom door but he refused.

"Tell her that it is not okay, it has to stop."

"Bhanu, she is only here for three weeks."

"But you are in the same bed with her and that's not normal!"

"What are you saying? She is my mother."

"It's just very strange. How would you feel if I slept with Bapa?"

"But he is not your father."

I should have packed my bags and left but Gauri made me believe that I was overreacting and that it was common for all mothers-in-law to behave in such a way.

I asked my mother how it was for her with Ba, but she didn't say very much except to give me a metaphor about an apple tree. "You may have had the good fortune to have a shiny apple fall into your lap but you have to understand who nurtured the tree, fed it daily, tended and cared for it."

I debated whether to tell her that the apple was still being tended to by the tree. Indeed, it was nestled in the bosom of the tree.

"Please invite her once again," my mother said as I was leaving.

I couldn't bring myself to tell her that she didn't want to see them.

"Why would you want to make me associate with low-class people?" she sobbed into Hiten's shoulder. "Isn't it enough you make me endure this?"

I was unsure what exactly she was enduring as my mother-in-law would sit on that sofa marking her territory and watching her Bollywood films from morning until evening. Sometimes, she would go shopping for clothes or go out to see her friends but would be back in time just before my husband came home and look busy in the kitchen, then tell him what a hard day she'd had.

The torture escalated as Hiten came to his senses and decided to ditch that childhood goodnight. She had observed that I had an asthmatic reaction to an excessive amount of dust and then she got off her backside and began dusting and hoovering.

"My son likes a clean house." She waved the duster in my direction. "And you clearly don't keep it clean." She then shook the contents of the hoover bag into the bin in front of me, watching me wheeze. "You are not of strong stock, are you?"

One day, I came back from the doctor to find Pushpa sitting, having tea, chatting and laughing with her.

"Aunty and I were just sharing stories from when Hiten and I were young."

"He should have married you," she cried. "Why didn't he marry you? You always got on so well and I thought one day..."

Pushpa looked awkwardly at me. "Aunty, I'll tell Mummy and Daddy that you will come for dinner, then." She got up.

His mother looked at me. "Come any time," she said to Pushpa.

"I know that she is not easy," Pushpa said as she was leaving.

"I can handle her."

"Anyway, I came to share some exciting news with you."

"You're pregnant?" I asked.

A few weeks after Hiten and I got married, Pushpa agreed to an arranged marriage to a wealthy businessman.

"No! Ketan surprised me with a microwave. You'll have to come around for dinner, Bhanu. The microwave is amazing. It gets the cooking done in minutes."

It wasn't the moment to tell her that I was pregnant. I decided to keep the news to myself for a while because I didn't want his mother to put a curse on me and also, I wasn't sure if I could stay in the marriage.

Negative people have the power to swallow you into their own black hole just by their proximity to you. Hiten managed to escape by working late and when he was at home, I had no respect for the little boy he turned into. She knew the power she held over him; he was constantly seeking her approval and she never fully gave it to him, and so it went on. It was their equal deal and on some level they seemed to enjoy it.

"Bhanu," she said one evening. "You are looking very tired. I have run you a bath."

I was caught off guard. For one moment, I thought I saw a flicker of kindness. I went upstairs to the bathroom; she had overfilled it and water was dripping everywhere. She watched as I rushed to turn the taps off.

"Make sure you don't drown in it. Was it a drowning?"

"Go," I screamed. "Get out of here, you evil cow."

My husband walked in at that moment.

"Bhanu!"

"Now you see who you have really married, son," she sobbed. "I can't stay."

"Please, Mummy! Bhanu, how could you? Whatever she has done, you will never speak to her like that again. Do you hear me?"

I wanted to leave. Instead, she packed her belongings and left wearing my pink organza sari. Her parting words were, "I have been to the astrologer and this is a marriage that has not been blessed by God and so it will not last and when it doesn't, don't think you will get a penny from us, you filthy gold-digger."

My husband swiftly followed behind, saying he had some business to sort out for her in India.

"I am leaving him, Gauri."

"Didi, you can't. Think of what it will do to Bapa and to Mama. Mama has already had one heart attack. It would kill her. They won't be able to hold their heads up in the community. What will people say? No one will buy sweets from Bapa. What will happen to them? To us? And what will you do with a baby?"

"I will find a way. Not once did he stand up for me."

"Yes, but he loves you. He doesn't hit you, he doesn't really drink excessively and look at all the things he buys for you and she doesn't even live with you."

"I made a mistake. I know that I made a mistake."

"You didn't, Didi. All marriages are like this in the beginning. Remember what Mummy said when she first saw Bapa and look how happy they are now. They are just tests. This is just a test. You made the best decision marrying Hiten, you really did."

I betrayed myself long before anyone else betrayed me because I knew back then that she would be too big a thorn in our marriage. Even though she didn't live with us, I knew the profound influence she had on his life and it was something I could not handle. I also knew that if I didn't leave, that I would never leave. It is only now I realise that many of the things that happen to us, good or bad, are of our own making. Instead, I forgave my husband for his weakness and then two months later, my world stopped spinning. I bumped into *him*.

"Bhanu, I told her that you are the most important person to me," my husband declared when he came back from his trip. Foolishly, I believed him because I wanted to believe him.

"Nature programme?" he asked, smiling at me. "I won't interrupt."

We took out one of the cassettes of *Wildlife on One* that I had recorded and we sat on the sofa in the sitting room, holding hands, reclaiming the space that she had invaded.

We watched the orangutans in the jungles of Borneo. Female orangutans breastfeed their children until they are six or seven and have extraordinary bonds with their mothers. The females seek out their mother long after they have left home and visit them.

I began to cry.

"What is it, Bhanu? What is it?"

"I hope our son or daughter will always find their way back home if they need us."

"You're pregnant?"

I nodded.

A smile spread across his face and then he laughed. "I'm going to be a father."

Hiten pulled me close towards him and wrapped his arms around me. "Thank you. Thank you, Bhanu."

Our relationship went back to being how it was before his mother arrived. He was once again attentive and when I mentioned that our bed was slightly uncomfortable, he got the keys to the car and told me to come with him; we were going to purchase a new one.

"Right now? I can't just drop everything and go like this!" My hair was untied and I was wearing a long khaki kaftan.

"Just come, Bhanu. You could wear a tent and still look beautiful."

Indeed, I was wearing something very similar.

"Okay. Well, now *is* the summer of my discount tent," I joked.

My husband didn't understand. We drove to the furniture shop.

Hiten began trying out beds and was making me laugh by doing his impersonation of Frank Spencer and rolling off the beds. I think we were making a lot of noise, so I turned around to see if we were disturbing anyone. It was then that I saw him.

It was unmistakably him. Lean, muscular, that mop of jet-black hair. I stopped laughing. My heart stopped and if I had let my instinct take over, I would have run towards him because every part of me wanted to run towards him.

It was Deep. My Deep. What was he doing here? I was about to tell my husband that I needed to go to the bathroom so I could figure out what to do but as if sensing my presence, Deep turned around. His face changed and he abandoned the customers he was serving and ran, racing towards me.

"Tara, I knew I would find you. I knew..."

My eyes darted towards my husband.

Deep would know what to do. He always knew. My heart began to beat faster and I almost wished I would pass out to avoid the horror of the situation.

My husband stared at him. "She is not Tara. Bhanu, do you know this man?"

I should have said, *Yes, yes, I do*, and told him that he was an old friend from back home but I couldn't speak, I couldn't get any of the words out so I shook my head.

"So sorry, ma'am, I have mistaken you for someone else. You look just like an old friend of mine."

"It's okay," I said as I held back the tears. I glanced at his fingers. There was no ring. No wedding ring. Deep would be a man who would wear his wedding band and what did he mean he knew he would find me?

"So how may I help you both?" Deep asked nervously.

"A bed. We are looking for a bed," my husband replied rudely. "And it has to be comfortable for my wife."

There, he'd said it. The words I was dreading he would say. Deep looked as if someone had punched him hard. I willed for my husband not to mention the baby. *Please don't tell him about the baby before I get a chance to speak to him.*

Deep swallowed. "Absolutely, sir."

"And sturdy," my husband instructed. "If you understand what I mean." My husband laughed a Benny Hill sort of laugh.

"How is this one, sir? Simple but beautiful," he said, looking at me. "'A thing of beauty is a joy forever'. You want it to last forever."

Keats, I wanted to say. *That's Keats. I haven't forgotten.* Instead, I dug my nails into my hand to stop myself from crying. Why now?

"What nonsense. Come, Bhanu, test it out, lie with me."

Then Hiten began bouncing up and down as I lay there beside him. I felt sick and tried to avoid eye contact with Deep by staring at the ceiling. There were no shooting stars above us, just luminous tube lights. Hiten made a joke about something. I'm not sure what it was. I didn't laugh.

"It's not for me. Come, Bhanu, let's go." He gestured.

No, we couldn't just go. I needed to find a way to speak to Deep and so I uttered the first thing that came into my head.

"What happened? ... I have been waiting for a bed like this."

"No, Bhanu. It's cheap. The mattress is uncomfortable. I want to find you a better bed."

"Maybe I could write down the model number in case you don't find another one you like?" Deep suggested. Hiten was eager to leave.

"Please let him," I urged.

On a piece of paper, Deep wrote down his number and I quickly took it.

My husband took my hand and led me out of the store. I couldn't bring myself to look back at Deep's face.

"It wasn't bad but I wasn't going to buy a bed from him," my husband stated. "Fresh off the boat. You can tell: no class, uneducated, over-familiar. Trying that 'you remind me of my friend' routine. They see us and they think we are all family. Next he'll be asking if he can move in with us and bring his entire family. I've seen his type a thousand times before."

Deep was nothing like that. He would do anything he could to help you, I thought. I contained my emotions and held the number tightly in my hand, planning the moment that I could call.

"I will do whatever it takes to come to you," Deep had said that night as he clung to me, not letting me go. "Just promise you will wait for me."

"Of course I will wait for you."

But then he got married, didn't he? It didn't make any sense.

As soon as we got home, I told Hiten that I needed to get some groceries. It started to rain and he grabbed the car keys to take me. I insisted that I needed to walk as we had been in the car most of the day. He looked out at the rain and said he would walk with me. I couldn't think of what else to say, so we walked together in the rain. He held up an umbrella for me. All I could think of was Deep.

We walked back home having purchased groceries that we didn't need and as soon as we got to the front door, I told him that I had forgotten garlic and said I would only be a few minutes and before he had time to say anything, I left him on the doorstep, running off in the rain, heading for a phone box. My heart was pounding. There was somebody in there and as I waited, the rain seemed to get heavier and heavier.

Seeing me soaking wet in my tent, the lady took pity on me, hurried her call and got out of the phone box. I took out the piece of paper Deep had given me and dialled the number.

"Not one explanation," I shouted.

"Why did you get married? You said you would wait for me," he interrupted.

"What? What do you mean? Why did you get married?"

"I didn't. I came looking for you. Three hundred and seventy-eight days, I have been looking for you. You didn't write."

"I did, I did. My sister said you married a dentist."

"Tara, Tara, listen to me. I am not married."

The pips went. I searched for more coins. Of course he was married. She told me he'd got married. No more coins.

"Tara," he said, "I came to find you. I promised you that—"

The money ran out. I let go of the receiver and began to scream and scream. A man opened the telephone box and asked if I was okay. Tears streamed down my face as I nodded. I placed the receiver down correctly and went to buy garlic.

My husband was there, waiting outside the shop in his car. I dried my tears quickly.

"What is it, Bhanu? Can I do something for you? Tell me."

How could I even begin to explain that I loved another man and if I could, I would go back to him?

"It's just sickness. I was feeling sick and I needed some air."

"Look at you, you are all wet. You need to take care of yourself and of the baby."

Unable to sleep, I spent all night not wanting to believe that Gauri would have lied to me; she wouldn't have written a letter pretending to be her friend. She had picked me up off the floor and comforted me, slept next to me for nights on end making sure that I was okay. She gave me the money she had saved up so I could go out. She was the first person I confided in when I found out I was pregnant. As I looked back, perhaps it was guilt that made her pick me up off the floor, guilt that motivated her many actions; or perhaps, and this was harder for me to accept, some people are just cruel, they have a malicious poison in them that festers and the only way to express it is to passive-aggressively attack.

The slow loris is a cute teddy bear-like animal with large, beautiful eyes, a round head and small ears. It remains in a ball for most of the day, resting. If you see one, your instinct is to pick it up and rescue it. It is, however, a vicious, venomous animal and if it feels threatened, it can mix toxins into its saliva and fur and cause irreparable damage.

My sister had caused irreparable damage.

My mother and father were in the shop and my sister was upstairs trying on clothes she had just bought. She would buy them, try them all and return them, having worn one or two of the items. She didn't need to do this as my parents gave her money but it was more the thrill of seeing what she could get away with.

"What do you think of this one?" she said, trying on a fuchsia blouse with enormous shoulder pads.

"Does it matter what I think? You're going to return it anyway."

She threw me a look, knowing that something was wrong, that I had crossed the line of our deal by not putting up with her shit or pandering to her.

"Deep is not married." I tried to sound matter-of-fact so she would be caught off guard. She looked unfazed but I caught the flicker in her eye; she knew exactly what I meant.

I wanted to scream at her but dug my fingernail into my thumb so I could remain calm. "You read out a letter from your friend Shoba saying that he got married."

"Really? He's not married? But that's what she wrote, Didi. You saw it. I don't know why she would write that if he wasn't married?"

"The letters I wrote and gave to you to send never reached him and he never sent that telegram."

She adjusted the collar on her blouse and I could see her perspiring. "I don't know what you are talking about." She couldn't bring herself to turn and look at me properly.

"Did you write that letter?"

"I did not."

"I'm going to give you one last chance to tell me the truth, Gauri, and God help me if you don't."

"Didi, I don't know what you are talking about. Whatever it is, you need to calm down. Think of the baby."

"Tell me," I screamed.

Gauri did not forward the letters I had given to her to send to Deep. She had faked sending the telegrams and the letter from her friend. Why? Because she thought I could do better. *No, tell the bloody truth.* "You were jealous. You have always been jealous of me. Ever since I came into the house, you really didn't want me there."

"No, Didi, it wasn't like that. I was looking after you."

"Looking after me? You watched me wait, you watched me starve myself, you watched me cut my hair off."

"I encouraged you to go to the party and I gave you money for it and look how well you married."

"Well?"

"Yes, you married well," she shouted. "You came from nothing. I did that for you. I encouraged you to marry Hiten. That's the thing with you, you never appreciate the things people do for you. You always make out that you are some kind of saint. Well, let me tell you, Mama and Bapa did not have to take you in and my life would have been different if they hadn't. You think it was easy always being compared to you? And anyway, I saw him first and you had to take him too."

And there it was. I wanted to tell her what she had done to me, that she had changed the course of my life but I took a deep breath and headed towards the door.

"That's right, you walk away. Never face the things that you have done to other people. You made us leave the farm; it's your fault we came to this miserable shithole. You could have kept your mouth shut but no, you had to interfere and open that mouth of yours. Don't you look so innocent and surprised. Why do you think we got thrown out of the farm? It was because of you. Bapa had to start again because of you and not even a sorry. Your mother-in-law is right, you play the victim really well."

I wanted to run towards her and beat her but I stopped myself. I didn't want to give her the satisfaction of knowing that she had broken my heart.

I have replayed and forensically dissected this conversation over the years. Events happen, and then there are our versions of events – stories we tell ourselves that shape the narrative of our lives, sometimes true, but some re-remembered incorrectly. It has only occurred to me recently that it is all a question of perspective, that we might be the villain in someone else's story and that someone is sitting on a therapist's couch somewhere because of us.

Deep and I arranged to meet at the other side of London at the Croydon multiplex. I asked him if we could pretend just for that afternoon that we had found each other and had moved to York and were visiting the cinema there for the first time. It took me half the morning deciding what to wear and I chose a purple dress with a yellow belt. He liked it when my hair was untied and so I left it out.

On the way there my stomach was churning and I felt sick. I had told my husband that morning that I was going shopping with my sister. I was certain that she wouldn't call or come to the house as we hadn't spoken. Hiten gave me some money for the "shopping trip". I felt hugely guilty but I needed this one last day with Deep, a day when I could find an ending to our story.

"Spend it all," he urged me. "I know what you are like; you will come back with what I gave you."

Before he left to go to work, I had this fleeting thought that perhaps I would not return home to cook his dinner, that I would risk it all and be pulled by my heart.

I looked at my husband. "I want to thank you for—"

"Bhanu, what is this thanking business. It's not even that much. Imagine if I bought you a car; straight to the bedroom then." He laughed. He could make things sound vulgar without meaning to. "Thank me later," he replied, "you know exactly how." He made a gesture with his hand and laughed. He killed any guilt or heartfelt goodbye because at that moment, I imagined him as a pervert popping out of a garden bush.

After I got dressed, I took one last look at the kitchen; it was spotless and then I left. On the Tube journey, I saw a couple holding hands and I imagined how long they had been together. I glanced at my wedding ring. My fingers felt slightly swollen so I took it off and tied it to the thin gold chain around my neck. I pretended that this day was day one of my imaginary life with Deep and we were just like them, out on a sunny Thursday afternoon. He had taken the day off work for our anniversary and shortly, I would tell him that I was expecting a baby. I imagined him lifting me in the air and then not knowing what to do next as he would be filled with such excitement.

As soon as Deep saw me, he ran towards me and hugged me, lifting me off the ground. He wouldn't let go. When he finally put me down, he said, "You look even more beautiful than I remember and believe me, I have remembered you almost every minute of every day for the last year and a half."

I studied his face. His beautiful lips that I was desperate to kiss, his eyes. I could not look directly into them, so I had to look away.

He broke the intensity, pointing to my dress. "No tent today then?"

I laughed. "Don't make fun of it. It's the summer of my discount tent."

"Made glorious by this sun of York," he replied.

Of course he would have understood the reference.

"And all the clouds that lour'd upon our house," I continued.

"Tara, I don't know the next line."

I smiled. "I have been studying, you know, while you have been away."

"I knew one day you would beat me at this game. I hope you are still studying to be a word doctor?"

I didn't want to tell him that currently, I had given up on that particular dream. "I'm still working on it, reading when I can."

"And what do you think of the magnificent York cathedral here?" He pointed to the roof of the shopping centre.

"It is majestic," I replied. "Deep," I began.

"Not now, Tara. Let's do what we said we would do; I have bought us tickets."

As soon as Deep's father was better, he left Tanzania. He didn't get to complete his exams. He was worried; my letters had stopped so abruptly that he borrowed money from a friend to come looking for me. At first, he went to the address on one of the letters and met the old woman there, who said she had never heard of us. Then he went to the post office; they had no forwarding address. He stayed near the post office, asking in every shop where we might have moved to, but nobody seemed to know. He lived just four miles away from the sweet shop, working three different jobs so he could send money home and stay and find me. We could have bumped into each other on any number of occasions, but we didn't. If he had come just a month earlier, we would still have been at the address he had gone to and our story would have turned out differently.

"I didn't expect England to be so cold and unwelcoming and I thought that..."

"There would be rolling hills and people dressed immaculately, drinking tea and discussing poetry," I continued.

"Yes." He laughed. "Well, here in York there are rolling hills." He pointed at the escalators.

"I miss the wildlife and nature, Deep. I sit for hours watching nature programmes just to touch that corner of the world. I miss the smell of cloves, cardamom, jasmine and eucalyptus, even humble ugali. I miss sunsets and sunrises, the blue skies and rustling. Who would have thought that I would miss the sound of animals rustling in the bushes?"

"We can go back," he replied.

"The place that we want to go back to doesn't exist any more, Deep."

"Come, Tara." He took my hand. We ran into the cinema.

The film we had chosen was *Kabhi Kabhie*; it had already started, and people were annoyed that we had arrived late and were disturbing them to get to our seats. He held down my seat so I could sit down first, he then sat down and we continued holding hands like it was the most normal thing in the world.

I cried throughout that film, remembering the first time we had watched it in Tanzania, remembering his words that we would watch the film together in another time and place and I would laugh at the absurdity of my tears.

Why didn't I believe in him? In us?

I began to sob uncontrollably, not caring that I was disturbing other people.

He held me. The film ended. Some cinema-goers glared at us, some muttered obscenities, but we remained in our own world, unable to leave.

We sat there until the cinema was empty and all that was left were discarded popcorn packets and cans. We sat there still holding hands, watching a blank screen. One of us knowing that this was one last moment for us and neither of us wanting it to end. He reached over to kiss me and every part of me wanted to kiss him back, but I couldn't. If I kissed him, I would leave with him and so I turned my cheek and couldn't stop crying.

He held my face in his hands.

"I'm so sorry, Deep. I'm sorry I didn't believe in us."

He put his fingers on my lips as if to savour that moment, as if he knew that he was creating a memory that would last a lifetime. My tears would not stop falling. He wiped them away.

"Remember, Tara, I said we would watch the film again. We can still change the story and watch it again and again until we are old. Come with me."

And for one moment, just one moment, it was a possibility.

I turned to look away from him.

"I'm pregnant."

He paused and I knew exactly what he would say.

"It doesn't matter. I will look after you, and after the baby like it was mine."

"Of course it matters. I can't do that to my family, not after all they have done for me, to my husband. What would the community say?"

"I don't care about what other people think."

"I care, Deep. I can't do it. My husband, he's a good man."

"He is rude, Tara. Does he understand you? Does he see all the possibilities that lie within you? Because it is not about duty and responsibility, or repaying a debt to your family."

I imagined never returning to the spotless kitchen and felt a flicker of joy. I immediately squashed it by thinking of my unborn child; I couldn't deny the baby a home with its real father. I thought about the shame I would bring upon my family, the community gossiping and ostracising them, Hiten asking for his debt to be repaid and my father with no means to repay him. I couldn't do that to them.

"I love my husband," I whispered. "I do."

"Why did you come? Why?"

"To say goodbye. I wanted to see you properly and say goodbye and to say that I am sorry." I began to cry again. "Sorry for not waiting, for not truly believing that I was worthy of you."

I got up and began walking away. He followed after me.

"Please, Deep. Don't."

"Tara," he said. "'Lovers don't finally meet somewhere. They're in each other all along'." He paused. "It's Rumi," he said. "I am reading Rumi."

I turned and continued walking. Unable to dry my tears, I did not look back.

My sister was waiting back at the house. Had she told Hiten? I felt a surge of relief. There was no more hiding. Perhaps Hiten would understand; perhaps he would let me go. My husband looked anxious. "Bhanu, please try to stay calm." It was then I saw Gauri's tears.

"You need to come, Bhanu. Mummy is in the hospital; she has had another heart attack."

Bapa clung to me when he saw me and then when I held him, he sobbed in my arms. She had passed away. Gauri began screaming. Mama was lying in bed and as I walked towards her, I did not recognise her; her soul had already left her body and she looked vacant. I went to touch her feet and held my body straight so I would not collapse with the grief that I felt at that moment. I took a very deep breath and recited a prayer.

As I knew with Ba, normally it is the men in the family that conduct the last rites. But my father asked me to do this for her and so my sister and I washed my mother's body, dressed her and prepared her for her final journey. Gauri chose the journeying sari; it was a red crepe silk with twelve blossoms in the most vibrant colours. Bapa had bought it for her when he found out she was expecting Gauri. They had waited a long time for her.

"It's so beautiful but you should have waited until after the baby was born," Mama had apparently said to him.

"We are going to enjoy and worship this baby now," he had replied. "Nothing will take away the happiness I feel."

They named her after a goddess.

As we wrapped my mother in her sari, I understood how difficult it must have been for Gauri to have me come along and share what she had always taken for granted. I understood the hurt, not necessarily the actions that stemmed from that hurt, but I could understand why. Gauri joined in the mantra as I began chanting. We adorned our mother with a garland of flowers and placed a red vermillion mark on her forehead. Then as we finished, I reached over and touched Gauri.

"I'm sorry, Didi. I really am," she whispered.

After the ceremony, Hiten, Bapa, Gauri and I gathered to witness the cremation. Neither my father nor my sister wanted to push the button that set off the machine, so I pushed it as they cried. I watched the flames engulf the coffin until I could no longer see it. My sister began wailing; Hiten whispered that it was time to go. I wasn't ready and sensed that Bapa also needed a few more moments so I asked Hiten to help take my sister out.

Bapa came and stood next to me. I remembered being a little girl, standing with Ba, allowing the flames to witness my pain. Once again, I attempted to gather the broken pieces that I carried, held them out to the hands of the fire god and released them into the roaring flames. I thought of all of it: the sadness of not having witnessed Ba's cremation, the guilt of losing our home, our country, moving to a foreign land, my sister's betrayal, losing Mama and Deep. I said goodbye to the future that I'd built with Deep and that I would never have with him. Tears rolled down my face as I watched it all burn and then the tears turned into sobs. Bapa held me.

"It's time to go, Bhanu. Please think of the baby," he whispered.

It was because I was thinking of the baby that I wanted it all to burn. I wanted the fire god to take it from me, to purify everything, for it to be a new start for us all.

"One more minute," I replied.

I watched Agni's flames burn. Mesmerised, I felt the presence of Ba. She was telling me that it would be okay and that the sun would rise again for me, for us. I squeezed my father's hand.

"It will be okay, Bapa. We will make it so."

I sought out Rumi's poetry and read his wisdom over and over to my unborn daughter. "'Every hardship passes away. All despair is followed by hope; all darkness is followed by sunshine'." They were like Ba's words. I held on to each word on every page, healing, reconciling with my sister; I put every ounce of energy I had into helping my father get back on his feet and just as Rumi had said, five months later, the sunshine arrived.

My husband and I could not have been happier. I had my own family now and it was time to think of them. As we packed to move to a bigger house, I decided that there was no more space for poetry and placed the books in a box in the attic. All the words that I needed were, in any case, etched in my mind. This was a new start for us.

Looking back, it was a very happy time. I remember there being a lot of music in the house. I was fully present in my marriage. Hiten and I laughed a lot together and he would come home early from work; our daughter brought such joy. Everything I did not have as a small child, I gave to her. It was easy loving her. I know every mother says this, but my daughter was beautiful. All our friends called her *Chaya* or shadow, because she was my shadow. Whenever I wore a sari, she would hang on to the pallu and follow me and if I sat down, she would wrap herself up with it, firmly attaching herself, and as she got older, she would weave in and out of the material, laughing and playing.

"Is it your house, Anita?"

"Yes, Mummy. I love it. It's so beautiful."

"When you are a bit older, Mummy is going to teach you to put it on. Come, sit, Mummy is going to tell you the story of this one."

I would sometimes leave her with Bapa, who adored her; she gave him a new lease of life and he would play with her for hours and take her to the shop where she would eat all the sweets she wanted.

"Don't feed her so much, Bapa. She won't eat her dinner."

"Grandfather's prerogative." He would smile. "The baobab fruit coated in chocolate are her favourites," he would say, taking out a few that he kept in a plastic bag in his pocket.

"No, Bapa, I think the jelabis are her favourite. Which do you love more, Anita? Bapa's sweets or Funny Masi's sweets?" Gauri would ask.

She was also loved by my mother-in-law. My relationship with her was still incredibly difficult but, in some respects, our own cold war had begun to thaw after Anita's arrival. I left her to lay out my husband's and daughter's clothes and there was no more hopping into our bed. In the grand scheme of things, it was only one month of the year and so we had our own version of glasnost for the sake of Anita. Having said that, she could also still manage to plant an undetected bomb somewhere.

The initial stand-off to test the new dynamic was around a ceremony known as tonsure. This is when the baby's head is shaved and is a ritual for purification of past lives and removing any negativity that the baby might have carried with them into this life. In my grandmother's house it was not practised, and instead a haircut would be given around the eleventh month. My mother-in-law screamed and beat her chest, saying the baby would be as cursed as I was. My husband, however, stood by me and as she witnessed the changing alliance and understood the terms of the new treaty, she backed down and settled for a lock of Anita's hair.

Anita was five and I was eight months pregnant with Hari when she paid us her annual visit. Back then, she used to come for three months in the summer and was distributed fairly evenly amongst her three sons. It was a hot sunny day in August and my mother-in-law needed to get some shopping but couldn't walk to the shops, so she asked me to take her in my husband's car, which was parked outside. I was enormous and felt very uncomfortable so told her that my husband suggested I didn't drive unless it was an emergency.

She said it was an emergency; she needed some aubergines. I was about to ask her to walk but it was too late as she had made her way out of the front door and was standing by the car. I reluctantly got the car keys and opened the door for her. She got into the passenger seat.

"Happy now?" I asked as I manoeuvred my front seat even further back. I switched on the cassette player. She didn't like the cassette that was playing and made a strange sound. It was Jennifer Rush's "The Power of Love". If I were driving somewhere by myself, I would roll up the windows, put it on full blast and sing it as loudly as I could. She made her weird, disapproving sound again.

I had had enough and told her to change the tape if she didn't like the music. She reached for the glove compartment and opened and closed it quickly.

"What's the matter?" I asked.

"Nothing."

Her response was too quick. I asked her what she had seen in the glove compartment.

"Handkerchief?" she responded.

She never sounded uncertain, so I reached over her, put my hand in the glove compartment and pulled out a pair of cheap red satin panties. She looked at me. In that instant, I knew, and she knew, that I was going to file for divorce.

Family name and standing in the community was absolutely everything to her and even though she hated me, she would have done anything not to have a divorce in the family.

"I will kill myself!" she screeched.

Of course, I knew she wouldn't kill herself. She loves herself too much and she throws the words around like Smarties. Car doesn't start – suicide. Zee TV not working – suicide. Toilet not flushing properly – suicide.

His lover was my good friend Renuka. I'd met her at nursery pick-up time. She was divorced with one kid and nobody else would speak to her. All the other mothers would talk about her. My daughter and her daughter, Bijal, were best friends. Anita had accidently taken Bijal's coat home once. It was around Easter time and perhaps her daughter would need the coat during the holidays, so I got her address from the school and we went to her flat to return it. It was in a very poor neighbourhood. Renuka asked us in. I declined at first – I am not one to get into other people's business – but she insisted.

The flat was damp and smelly; it was filled with second-hand, broken furniture. It took me back to where I had started when I first came to London but at least I'd had my family. I felt sorry for her having to take in sewing and do other jobs to make things work for her and Bijal. So I gave her work even though I could sew and then I invited her round whenever we had family parties or friends around so she could make friends and grow her business. I packed her food every week.

I knew the wider community were gossiping about her and possibly about me, but on this occasion, I didn't care; I wanted to do something for her. I looked after Bijal so she could do more work. I'm not exactly sure at what point she began having sex with my husband. She was probably with him when I was looking after her daughter – they were probably laughing at me.

There is no excuse for having sex with someone else when your wife is pregnant. Men will tell you about being neglected, feeling left out, feeling the weight of responsibility. Don't buy that bullshit – you are making a baby, sometimes throwing up twenty times a day, carrying their child and so what if you are tired and can't have sex like you used to?

After I found out, my daughter had to stop playing with little Bijal.

"Why, Mummy? Can't she come and play?" Anita cried.

What do you say? What can you say? I said the first thing that came into my head. "She has got dirty fingernails and is a dirty, dirty girl."

Anita started screaming, "Daddy, Daddy, Mummy says Bijal can't play any more because of her dirty fingernails."

"Never mind, *beta*. Ten more Sindy dolls, Mindy dolls, whatever."

Money has always been the solution for him.

When I initially confronted him, he said he needed a cloth to wipe the car and he took the first thing he saw from the laundry pile.

"But they are not my panties," I said, waving the cheap, disgusting knickers at him.

"Really? Mummy's?"

"Yes, your mother walks around with hookers' panties." I threw them at him.

He has always thought I was stupid.

"I don't know, then, Bhanu. I really don't know," he said, sounding semi-convincing.

"I lent the car to Vishan. Perhaps... perhaps Vishan is having an affair?"

It seemed possible. I wanted it to be true of his friend rather than him.

There was no 1471 back then, itemised billing or mobile phones so there was no evidence apart from the knickers. He kept denying it and I needed to talk to someone. I know we are meant to keep these things to ourselves but it was driving me mad. I thought momentarily of telling Pushpa but Pushpa would trivialise this information at some point. I could just imagine her saying:

"What was that song you loved in 1984 – oh, what was it? Remember, you were eight months pregnant. It was around the time you found out Hiten was having an affair. 'The Power of Love' – that was it."

I decided to confide in Renuka, little Bijal's mother. She would know what to do. She had left her husband.

I hadn't been there for a while as Renuka was having some work done and so, for many nights, Bijal stayed with us to avoid the paint fumes.

She opened the door and seemed happy to see me.

"Come in. Come in." She gestured.

I couldn't contain my tears.

"Oh, Bhanu, what has happened?"

I sat on her sofa and cried.

"Please don't make yourself upset – the baby," she said, touching my stomach. "Whatever it is, we can sort it out."

"Hiten," I said.

"What, tell me?"

"I think he is having an affair."

"Are you sure?"

"No. I don't know."

"Oh, Bhanu, it is the hormones." She hugged me.

It was then I noticed a similar pair of cheap red satin panties hanging on her drying stand. I pulled myself away from her.

"Come, let's have some tea." She gestured, making her way to the kitchenette.

"You want something to eat?" She was good – I even began doubting myself until I saw the new kettle and then I noticed all the other appliances. Like in *The Generation Game*, she had amassed a new television, a hi-fi, a brand-new toaster, a big cuddly toy for the child and a similar microwave to us. Hiten loved appliances; he had left his fingerprints all over her flat.

"Anita has the same teddy bear," I managed.

"I know. Bijal wanted the same one. You know children," she replied, as cool as anything. "I got a big bonus from one of my clients."

I wanted to scream at her, call her a fucking whore, to confront her but my words seemed to fail me. There was a crack in my voice and if I stayed any longer, I would fall down that crack and not re-emerge, drowning in tears.

"Coffee, then? Decorators haven't finished. They come for one day and then you don't see them for weeks," she said, reaching for the coffee cup.

I was unable to throw a grenade and detonate it as I would have wanted, or slap her or swear at her or do something. A lump formed in my throat; hot angry tears began to rise. I needed to get out of there.

"I'm not feeling very well. I need to go home," I said, steadying myself on her table.

"Let me come with you."

"No. It's fine. I can manage."

"But Bhanu..."

"With the new baby, I don't think I can have Bijal any more," was all I could say.

I got into the car and screamed all the way home.

My husband was waiting for me.

"Bhanu. Please, I am really worried about you."

I walked past him and went into his office and pulled out his folders. He kept everything meticulously, so it didn't take me long to find the folder with his receipts.

"Bhanu, please," he pleaded, watching me from the doorway.

And there it was, his spending over the course of the months: a TV, hi-fi and microwave from Dixons, two teddy bears from Woolworths – one for Anita, one for Bijal.

"How long?" I screamed at him. "How long?"

He knew he was wading in knee-high shit.

"Six months. Bhanu, it was nothing. You need to calm down and think of the children. Think of the baby. Anita might hear all this."

I threw the folders to the floor.

"Bhanu, listen to me," my husband pleaded. "She was flirting with me, I resisted her, and then..."

"Don't tell me – it's all her fault. Don't bury yourself in a hole. Do you know what I sacrificed for you?"

I should have continued. I should have told him that I only married him to escape the pain of losing Deep and then I found myself in a story that I didn't want to be in and there was no way out but this, this was my way out.

"Bhanu. I'm sorry. Don't go. Please. I am nobody without you. You are my whole life. I'm not sure how I can go on. Please." He started sobbing, clutching me.

"Let me go!" I shouted.

At first, his mother watched as the drama unfolded. Now she had finally got what she had always wanted, she didn't seem to want it. She began wailing and beating her chest, asking God what she had done to deserve all this.

"Do something, Hiten!" she hollered.

I dragged my daughter out of bed and left the house. Anita was screaming. Screaming as I had done all those years ago after my mother fought with my father and left the house. "No, Mummy. I don't want to go!" Anita cried as we left the house. I couldn't think straight. What was I going to do with a five-year-old and a baby on the way?

"It's a game, Anita. We are playing hide and seek in the dark. You have to be very quiet. Come, Mummy will carry you." We snuck into an alley as I knew Hiten would be looking for us. When she fell asleep in my arms, I made my way to the phone box to call Deep.

"What is it, Tara? Do you need my help?"

His voice was comforting. I could finally breathe.

"Deep."

What I wanted to say was, *Deep. I am ready. I'm sorry it took me so long. Please come and get me.* Instead, I asked how he was.

"Good. I completed my postgraduate and... and I got married. How are you?"

He got married. He got married. Of course, why wouldn't he? What was I thinking? Married. Stupid, stupid me.

"Fine. It's nice to hear your voice. You sound very happy."

"I am," he said.

That was it.

"I'm glad." I hung up the receiver.

Anita woke up.

Desperate, I called Bapa.

"Bapa, I need to come home. Hiten is..."

"Is he okay? Has something happened to him?"

"He has been having an affair," I cried.

"Bhanu," he said firmly, "all marriages go through problems. You need to work through it, and you need to put the children first."

"Please, Bapa, just for a few days."

"You will thank me later, Bhanu."

"Please... I have never asked you for anything. You taught us never to compromise our soul. Remember, Bapa, Faust?"

"No, Bhanu – you have responsibilities. There are children involved. You will see it is for the best."

I didn't know who else to call.

As I stepped out of the phone box, my husband was waiting for me in the car.

"Daddy, Daddy," my daughter screamed.

"Bhanu, please," he pleaded, looking at our daughter.

I should not have got into the car, but I didn't know what else to do. I shouldn't have gone back into the house but I was thinking about the children. *Do what is right for the children.*

We got home and his mother was waiting for us. She had begun cooking, acting as if nothing had happened. I went up to put Anita to bed.

"Mummy. I didn't like that game."

"I'm so sorry. We won't do that again."

"Promise?"

"I promise, my little one."

My mother-in-law appeared.

"Please, you need to be calm. Bhanu, think of the baby." She pointed at my pregnant stomach.

Strangely, she would have done anything to keep our marriage together. Maybe it was for the children or because of the importance of her social standing in the community. Whatever it was, she offered to pay off the mortgage and most of the debt to give us security. She was making her deal – stay in this marriage and, materially, you will always be taken care of. She also promised that she would never move in with us or interfere in our marriage again. And yes, I am ashamed to say it, like Faust, I made a pact with the Devil, exchanging my freedom for stability. I took it and kept quiet and actually have kept quiet ever since. All I can say is, there have been many affairs.

Hiten stood at the bedroom door. "It was a mistake, Bhanu. It will never happen again. I promise you. I will do whatever it takes to make up for it. Please," he begged.

There are many times when you come to a new chapter and things can turn out differently. Maybe I should have told him about Deep but my need to feel hurt, angry and betrayed was much, much stronger. Do we steer ourselves to feelings that we are familiar with? Maybe, because for some of us, the saddest of emotions are the ones that feel the safest.

I looked at him, wanting to say something but was unable to speak; the pain of his betrayal felt too much. I just wanted for that moment to close my eyes and be somewhere else.

Close your eyes. Fall in love. Stay there, Rumi says.

I closed my eyes and imagined Deep. We were lying in a field in the middle of nowhere, watching the stars and laughing. These same stars would watch us travel the world and grow old together.

His hands were tracing the shape of my lips and then he kissed me, unbuttoning my blouse. I can still feel his touch.

"'Touch has a memory'," he said.

"Auden?" I asked.

"No, it's Keats." He laughed. As if foreseeing all the events that were to come between us, he whispered, "I will remember this moment for the rest of my life."

Tears streamed down my face.

My son was born in the middle of the night. I knew that his premature arrival was caused by the stress. I watched him helplessly in the incubator, struggling to breathe, unsure whether he would make it. I made a pact with God that if he made it, I would do whatever it took to protect him, to protect both my children. My son made it, but my promise was somewhat hard to keep.

Hari was an especially sensitive baby and he cried and screamed a lot. He wanted to be held, constantly needing reassurance that I wouldn't leave him alone, not even for five minutes. It felt like I was in a black hole. My daughter stayed away from me, sensing my vacancy, and preferred to follow her grandmother or my sister around the house. Gauri had been staying at the house and looking after Anita while I was at the hospital. After I arrived home, I asked her to stay for a few more days but she said she had things to take care of.

"Bhanu, I wanted to tell you first. Bapa has decided to leave me the shop. You know, you have Hiten to take care of things and I suppose he was just thinking of me and who would take care of me after, after you know, he goes." It was an odd conversation that had come out of nowhere and it made me feel really uncomfortable.

"And I don't think it was right how you put Bapa under pressure like that. It was just one mistake Hiten made. Bapa couldn't sleep for days. You don't want to make him ill as well?"

"I needed help, Gauri; I need help."

She chose not to hear me and continued: "I also wanted to say that if you have ever blamed yourself for Mummy's death, it wasn't your fault. Don't ever blame yourself; you couldn't have known that she heard everything."

I was speechless. Had she waited for the moment that I was at my most vulnerable so that she could strike?

"Gauri, are you blaming me?"

"Not at all, Didi. Only God knows what caused her heartbreak." Her eyes fixed firmly upon me. "Anyway, I wanted you to hear it from me that Bapa has left me the shop." In effect, what she was telling me was that there was no way out of my marriage; there would be nowhere to go. It would be a while before I really heard her words. When they did finally sink in, I made a decision to keep contact as limited as I could.

"Just call me if you need anything," Gauri said loudly as she headed towards the front door. Anita ran after her. "Funny Masi has to go home now but we'll play together soon."

Anita began to cry.

"Come here, sweetheart," I said.

"No, you make people go away!" she shouted.

Gauri closed the door behind her.

I was tired and drowning. Drowning in inadequacy, in loneliness, grief, in feelings of betrayal and abandonment but unable to express any of it. Instead, I painted my face, put on a false smile and attended to my son, to the endless stream of visitors, pretending to be happy, pretending to be a woman who could look after the children perfectly, cook and entertain, hiding away any signs of brokenness with laughter. I told everyone that the baby had a bit of gas and it was fine. The truth was I was unable to look after him.

As if sensing his imminent abandonment, my son cried even louder, screaming and screaming and I couldn't make him stop. When he was about four weeks old,

I left him screaming in his cot. I climbed up to the attic, put a pillow to my face and began to scream and scream. If I could have just kept the pillow there and smothered my face, I would have. The pain would finally stop.

Anita came up to find me. She climbed the ladder by herself and she sat next to me and held my hand. Tears rolled down my face.

"Are you going to go away, Mummy?"

What I wanted to say was, *I am thinking about it because it all feels too big.* Instead, I looked at her face and reassured her.

"No, my baby. I am not going anywhere."

"Did you pack all these boxes to go away?"

"No. They were here already from when we moved."

"Don't be sad, Mummy. We can play together." She got up and hugged me.

I dried my tears. "Wait here." I went back down to check on Hari. He was asleep in my mother-in-law's arms. I climbed back to the attic.

"Shall we see what are in these boxes?" I asked Anita.

I opened the box that I knew held all my poetry books.

"Look, Anita. These are my favourite books. They have poems in them."

"What's a poem?"

"Let me read you one."

I looked for Byron's "She Walks in Beauty" because I wanted to feel that young girl I used to be – the one that Deep saw, I wanted to feel she was still somewhere inside of me. I wanted to relive the memory of sitting with Ba and reading it to her and feeling possibility; of her telling me not to fear the darkness and that it would be okay.

I knew Anita wouldn't understand the poem, but it didn't matter, I read it slowly to her. I imagined Deep in the sweet shop, handing me the book. I saw the smile that came across Ba's face when she heard the words for the first time. I remembered reading it over and over again.

"Read it again, Mama," Anita said.

"'She walks in beauty, like the night / Of cloudless climes and starry skies; And all that's best of dark and bright / Meet in her aspect and her eyes: Thus mellow'd to that tender light / Which heaven to gaudy day denies'."

"Mama, there is a pattern and it rhymes."

"What, sweetheart?" I asked, as she brought me back to the present. "What a clever girl you are. It is a pattern: ABA BAB and then again. Shall I read you another one?"

She nodded.

"I love the patterns, Mama, and I love your poems," she said, handing me a life raft.

"Me too," I replied.

Everything in life has a pattern – our own lives are filled with patterns. Patterns give us a feeling of familiarity and safety, even when they are wrong for us. Perhaps we repeat the patterns we seek to avoid, that somewhere in the universe, there is a trail of past memories that pull us back for resolution. If only we could step outside of them, observe the sequence and stop repeating them. Perhaps only the truth enables us to escape the patterns we have created. It was time to create a new sequence, to focus on the children and to simply love them. We carefully made our way back downstairs. I picked up my sleeping son and crawled into bed. "Come, Anita." We lay there, just holding each other, and this was enough.

I brought all the poetry books down from the loft and organised them on the shelves alongside Anita's books. I made sure we always found time to read together and we also read poetry out loud. This was what we did; it was our bond.

As she grew a little older, she would dissect each line as if it were a mathematical equation. "See, Mummy, if you look at this line, you will see the length of the sentence can be divided by the number of words, which is exactly the same as the next sentence."

It was true. Each word was so elegantly precise. We did this for every poem we read, not reading for meaning but for the precision, listening how each word formed a perfect equation. She was a very clever girl.

My son would crawl around beating his drum and Anita would read the words out loud for him so he could have something to beat to. She would then show him how to beat it with rhythm. He loved her, following her around wherever she went, and she was a great big sister to him. Life slipped back into nearly a routine and I kept my side of the pact by doing everything I could to create stability for my children.

Even on the days I didn't feel like it, I could pretend and bake cakes and sweets I didn't want to, entertain them with songs I didn't really like singing and then, one day, I didn't have to pretend any more. I caught myself in this moment; we had fed the ducks, Hari had his blue wellington boots on – he never took those boots off – and the three of us began jumping in puddles.

"Jump higher, Mummy, jump higher," he screamed excitedly. "Like this!"

And it was as if I were outside of myself and I watched this woman who couldn't stop laughing at her son and daughter covered in mud. The woman tried to jump higher. The children laughed at her attempt and then she scooped them both up, dirtying herself; her heart felt content.

I didn't have to pretend any more because I grew into my role as a mother, carer and homemaker; I was the centre of their universe and they were the centre of mine and I gave up the search for whatever else was out there, and any parallel life that I created was for and with my children. We would spend hours together making up our own world.

"Tell us again, Mummy, how you got that scar on your hand?"

"Well, I was being chased by Narosa, the fiercest tiger in the forest. He terrorised everyone so much that they were afraid to go out." I held out my wooden spoon and enacted the scene. "'Stop!' I shouted. 'I am not going to be scared of you any more!' I turned around to face the tiger. He growled at me; his teeth were enormous." Anita would gasp and Hari would giggle. "Then suddenly, Narosa came lunging towards me; his paw clawed the side of my hand. Unafraid, I stood firm and placed the stick I held in my hand in his mouth."

Although my daughter had heard different versions of the story a hundred times, she sat mesmerised. My son rolled around like the tiger, attacking me.

"Another one, Mummy! Another one!"

I told them all kinds of stories and through them I reinvented parts of my childhood with parents out of fairy tales and a world where anything was possible.

If Hiten was at home, he would join us. "That's right, Mummy fearlessly put the stick in the tiger's mouth but then a rhino came charging out from nowhere." He would turn into the rhino and my son would need to ride on him. Together, they would chase Anita and me around the kitchen and then into the living room. Once they had caught us, they would wrestle us to the sofa, the children laughing hysterically. "The rhino never wanted to harm Mummy. It only ever wanted to play with her because it knew how brave she was." He would wink at me, at which point, I would kiss the rhino and his son on the head; the rhino was a big child at heart, and I believed him when he said he'd never intended to hurt me.

For anyone peering into the windows of our home, they would have thought we were the Indian version of the Walton family. Huge friends and family gatherings at the weekend, the house overflowing with parties, laughter, music, acceptance from the community and no interference from his mother. This period was a happy one.

School altered things: we didn't send Anita to the local primary school. Instead, she went to the private school so we could avoid bumping into Hiten's ex-lover and her daughter. Anita was also exceptionally bright and got a scholarship. The effect of being in this school was that Anita didn't want to embrace her culture. Unlike the primary school, the private school was predominantly white and in a very affluent area. Anita began to change. When she was about ten, she shaved off her black bushy eyebrows and filled them in with yellow felt tip pens. Unsure of why she had done such a thing, I shouted at her.

"I want to be like all the other girls," she cried.

I tried to reassure her that she was beautiful as she was.

"No, Mummy, I am not."

We should have just taken her out of the school but thought about all the opportunities she would have. Instead, I tried to reinforce the importance of culture, taking her to celebrations and dances, telling her stories and cooking with her. It only worked for so long. As time went by, Anita didn't like Indian food because "everything smells". She wouldn't eat with her hands, responded to me in English when I spoke to her in Gujarati and she no longer wanted to go to my father's shop. The Navaratri dances she used to accompany me to as a small child became "really boring", and the saris unfashionable. The more I enforced the notion of culture and roots, the more she pulled away.

I consulted Pushpa – not that she was a childcare expert, and her children were younger than mine, but she was my go-to cultural attaché and occasionally, could put things into perspective.

"Relax, Bhanu, you are too serious. It's the beginning of the teenage phase. They pick up on your vibe. The more you push, the more they rebel. Try to engage with them on their level, talk about their interests and don't look at them directly when you are talking to them."

It was, for me, counterintuitive. I wanted to control and at times when Anita rolled her eyes or answered back, I felt a surge of anger rising within me at the ingratitude and lack of respect. At that moment, I could have slapped her. Instead, I breathed deeply or walked away; with every year that passed, the distance grew even wider. The answers Anita required from me needed to be shorter. She had a mathematical brain. Things were either right or wrong, just a simple "yes" or a "no". No further explanation required of how it was when I was a child: "I know, you said, back in the olden days when you were younger..."

I tried out Pushpa's method.

"Yes, it was very different back then, Anita." I glanced at her sideways as I folded the clothes. "A-ha are a great band, aren't they?"

"Really, Mum? Really!"

I think I might have tried too hard when I should have let go. It didn't need to be perfect; it was, in fact, far from it.

Hari took a lot of coaxing to go to school. He didn't like it; he just wanted to spend his time playing or cooking in the kitchen with me. Hari was very delayed in his communication and just pointed to things and made grunting sounds. We thought there might be some problem and took him to a speech therapist, but it was just laziness and as soon as we didn't give him the things he pointed to and Anita stopped translating for him, he started talking. We should have also learned from that lesson.

Hiten was away a lot and whenever he came back from his trips, he bought the children something big and expensive. From a young age, Hari had an interest in music so on one of his trips my husband bought him an electric guitar. He was six. He had musical talent but never stuck at one thing long enough to develop it. Instead of being firm with him, we gave in. By the age of ten, he had an array of musical instruments and had learned that whatever he wanted, he would get.

The move from being the centre of your children's universe to being designated to the status of Pluto is not something that happens overnight but it certainly feels like it. Learning that your parents are human, cannot fend off tigers single-handedly, and that they make mistakes, is probably a similar process to discovering that Father Christmas is not real. The mechanics don't make sense – heavy man through narrow chimney, or no chimney at all. Presents to roughly about a billion children in a night in that hot, sweaty outfit – no, something definitely not adding up here but never mind, there are presents to unwrap, so we'll push those anomalies to the side. Then, one year, the game is over and before you know it, you are a declassified planet.

It is a similar scenario to discovering your husband is a serial adulterer. Hold on a minute: slightly overweight, jovial man goes on many business trips, brings back presents for all. Let's ignore the smell of alcohol, cheap perfume and his unending enthusiasm, as it all seems to be functioning, all the planets are still in orbit. I will concur with everyone who thinks he is a wonderful man. It's not that I ignored all the signs, it's just I wasn't ready to see them.

I performed the required wifely duties three or four times a year and sometimes on special occasions. Not because I wanted to, but it was keeping up my side of the unspoken deal. It was for me an extension of the housework, like having to wash the outside windows – something that needed to be done but could wait until absolutely necessary.

"Bhanu. I love you. Shall we do it?"

This was my husband's mating call.

To be completely honest, sex with Hiten has never done anything for me. The first time we "made love" was straight after the registry office. It was on an iron "vintage" bed in a hastily booked hotel around the corner. I have often wondered if we got married swiftly because he couldn't wait any longer to have sex. As soon as we got into the room, Hiten untied my maxi dress, threw off his suit and tie and speedily unbuttoned his shirt. He grabbed my hair and pulled me towards him. I was scared, excited and nervous. He was an incredibly attractive man; there was a lot of chemistry between us. He was on top of me, jumping up and down – that was it. Over, very quickly. I thought, *Is this it?* I tried my best to bypass this thought as he panted heavily and rolled over.

"That was amazing, wasn't it, Bhanu?"

"It was," I pretended, disorientated.

On many occasions, Pushpa has tried to elicit details of our sex life, perhaps only to tell me how great hers is. Pushpa says sex is utterly amazing, "like landing on the moon and you are floating". If you look at her husband, there is no evidence of weightlessness. There is no chemistry between them, no out-of-this-world radioactive glow.

What nonsense! I wanted to say. I have had passionate sex with another man, and it was still slightly uncomfortable. Okay, maybe it was only twice; the first time it was uncomfortable and with practice it could have been different, but I never got to find out – but floating? I don't think so. Anyway, how do we know that the moon landing was real? They could have all been pretending in a TV studio. *That's right, Neil. Jump a bit higher next time and stick the flag in that spot over there.*

The G-spot, we will probably discover, like most things, is an invention made up by the man in marketing to make women feel inadequate.

Believe me, people pretend. People pretend for various reasons. Stop and think. Who is going to say I married someone thinking it was going to be fireworks in the bedroom and for forty years I didn't even really get a sparkler? Maybe with Deep it might have been different. Bangers and rockets out into the stratosphere? Who knows?

yard four

"Go find yourself first so you can find me."
— Rumi

I found out about my husband's second "official" affair as I was sorting through the laundry. Well, to my knowledge it was his second affair; it could have been his fiftieth. He was probably the Indian version of Hugh Hefner with his party house on the hill and I wouldn't have wanted to see it. I had probably sorted through a thousand loads of laundry, missing the lipstick marks. As the saying goes, *When the student is ready, the master will appear.* In this case, when the housewife is ready to see the adulterer, the Y-fronts will manifest.

It was like any other preparation for a white cotton wash on a forty-degree cycle. I was separating out whites from colours when I spotted red lipstick marks on his white Y-fronts. With a pincer motion, I picked them up and looked in disgust at the Y-fronts. Like a forensic scientist, I inspected the lipstick marks carefully to ascertain the type of lips the woman would have, and the brand of lipstick she chose to wear. Upon inspection, there were no further clues.

In a state of shock or denial, I loaded up the machine and, as I poured the liquid into the compartment, did an assessment of what this could potentially mean to the family: confrontation = breakup, drama and consequences for the children, such as no arranged marriage for Anita should she go down that route. Other consequences: Hari failing his exams, becoming even more insecure about his intellectual ability. Then, the standard finger-pointing, judgement and ostracisation from the community towards a divorcee of my generation, elderly father dying of shame and me being blamed for another death in the family, thus fulfilling the Mars effect defect legacy. Option two: pretend and continue in marriage = keeping the family together and fulfilling my pact of protecting the children.

I left the dirty Y-fronts on top of the mop handle in the en-suite bathroom. It might have looked like a white flag of surrender but when Hiten came home in the evening, I asked him to move out of the bedroom under the pretext of him snoring too much. I had noted that the Y-fronts were thrown back hastily in the empty wash bin. There was no disagreement from him.

This was our new deal, renegotiated without any real need for words. There was no screaming, no chest-beating, no drama.

Go and do what you want to do. Relinquish me from servicing your needs and let me do what I have to do. We can still make this look good on the outside.

I sealed it with the following words over breakfast: "I am going to get a window cleaner to do the outside windows."

"No problem, Bhanu," he replied, not looking up from his paper.

"I'm going out for the day tomorrow, leaving early, so you will have to sort out dinner for the children as I will probably be back late."

"No problem."

The thing that I most wanted to say but could not was, *I'm leaving you, Hiten. Life is so short and there must be more to it than all this pretending.*

The children did not notice when I moved all his things into the spare room. They were teenagers, so there could have been an earthquake measuring eight on the Richter scale that hit the house and caused mass devastation and they wouldn't have noticed.

Despite being thirteen, my son still had difficulty speaking in proper sentences, preferring the rhyming couplet, and my daughter never left her room. I stayed mostly for the children, and also, by then, was too vested in the image of the happy family we had fought so hard to create, the respect we had from the community, and yes, all the material comforts, which included a detached property that provided a false sense of security. I stayed because I was too scared of leaving.

My reaction to his affair was to go into our garden, scream as loudly as I could, desperate to escape somewhere. I calmly watered the flowers and thought about purchasing a day return to York.

I had thought of Deep over the years, especially when things were difficult, but they were fleeting thoughts – wondering where he was, and if he was happy. If I concentrated really hard and listened, my intuition would tell me that he was still in London and that he often thought of me too. If I caught my mind escaping to past memories, I would force myself to think different thoughts; I was married to someone else and so was Deep. After the discovery of the Y-fronts, I thought, *It doesn't matter now; think about him all you want and if you want to bring Deep and York into your reality, do it, get a ticket and go to York.*

I carefully chose what to wear and opted for a light grey dress with a yellow cardigan. I hadn't worn a dress in years and decided against wearing a belt as my stomach had slightly expanded. My hair was cut short in a bob and I wondered what Deep would make of it. In my imagination, I wasn't a forty-something-year-old woman, but in my early twenties. I had waited for him, not marrying Hiten, and he had found me in London, working one Saturday in my father's shop.

The shop bell went; I was in the kitchen when I heard his voice, asking my sister if we sold almond barfis. My sister laughed complicitly because in this scenario, she was kind. I dropped the tray that I was carrying and ran out to greet him, embracing him in front of everyone.

"Deep, you came!"

He hoisted me in the air. "Did you even doubt for a moment that I would?"

"Bapa, Mama, this is Deep. He's, he's my…"

"With your permission, sir, I would like to marry your daughter."

In this version, I married Deep wearing the red wedding sari Ba had given me in a religious ceremony with all my family present.

I nervously boarded the train at King's Cross and walked towards the carriage, where I imagined Deep would be waiting for me. I found two empty seats, sat in one of them and closed my eyes and began to immerse myself in a world that I had wanted to recreate for so many years. "Tara, Tara." I heard his voice. It was unmistakably Deep.

"'The minute I heard my first love story / I started looking for you, not knowing / How blind that was. Lovers don't meet somewhere. They're in each other all along'," I whispered.

"Rumi," he replied.

My first love story was Ba telling me how her brother-in-law had come to find her. She was living in one small room with her two children. He gave her some money, which at first she refused, but he insisted that she take it for the children. Although he lived far away from the town that she moved to, he would stop by every week with gifts and food for the children. Ba tried everything to dissuade him from coming, sometimes not answering the door. He would leave the gifts for them on the step and return the following week. "He saw me, Tara, he really saw me, and he said he didn't care how long it took for me to believe him; he would wait," Ba reminisced.

"What is your favourite Rumi quote, Tara?" I heard Deep ask.

"'What you are seeking is also seeking you'. It sums up perfectly what we believe in – the pull of the universe. Can I have two?"

"Two what?" he asked

"Quotes."

"Hmmm, let me check. Today, there appears to be no ration on Rumi quotes."

His jet-black hair was shorter, his lips were still full and those eyes, still warm, intense and tender.

"The other one is, 'the wound is the place where the light enters you'. Let me guess yours."

Suddenly, the passenger seat next to me felt as if it had been hit by a boulder. I quickly opened my eyes.

"I'm very sorry, sir, but this seat is taken," I informed the man.

He huffed. As soon as he got up, I put my handbag on the seat and closed my eyes again.

Deep had finished his degree, qualified as a civil engineer, and I was a teacher. One day, he came home and said, "Let's go, Tara, let's do it. If we don't go now when we have no real responsibilities, we will never do it." He placed the tickets for York on the kitchen table.

The food trolley came, and I ordered two teas. The large man who wanted Deep's seat stared at me as I set each of them down. The man watched me and shook his head. I closed my eyes again. Deep nodded at me reassuringly and took my hand. We sat there in silence. I savoured the touch of his hand. It was firm yet very gentle.

Deep and I got off at York station, and we walked around the city centre on a warm day in August holding hands and eating ice cream. First, we visited the cathedral and, like a knowledgeable tour guide, he spoke enthusiastically about the history of York Minster. We stopped and stood in front of a huge stained glass window.

"The Heart of Yorkshire window. What do you feel, Tara?"

"Safe. I feel safe and full of possibility. It is so beautiful, so majestic."

"You know, according to legend, couples that kiss under this heart will stay together forever?"

I was aware that all of this was in my imagination, but I hesitated because if I kissed him, even in my imagination, it would mean something. I closed my eyes and allowed imaginary Deep to kiss me and I felt it, tender, loving, and part of me knew that when the time was right, we would find each other again.

We continued walking along the cobbled streets and admired houses that, one day, we might live in.

"Come, I want to take you to Auden's birthplace. It is around the corner from here."

It was then that I had to stop because I believed that he would actually be waiting for me there. In some parallel universe, he had also taken the decision to take a trip to York that day and we would meet. I was scared.

"Deep, I have changed so much. I am not sure how you would feel about me now. I don't think you would be proud of me. I question things like the moon landing."

I could hear him laugh.

"I have been hardened by life. Disconnected. I don't trust it. I don't actually like the person I have become."

"There is nothing you could become that would not make me love you," he replied.

"Deep, I am going to leave you here, and when the time is right, we will visit Auden's birthplace together, but it is not right now."

"Tara," I heard him whisper. I left him on the street, in front of a beautiful Georgian house with a red door.

Alone, sad, unable to cope with my feelings, I sat in a café thinking about home. What was I thinking? There were things to deal with. How could I make things work? Hari was struggling with his schoolwork, he was playing up, and in spite of endless tutors, there was no interest there. Anita was leaving for university soon and that would probably be it, no more daughter at home, and I didn't have the relationship I had imagined with her. I had to make things better for both of them. She wanted a party at the house, which I had previously said no to. I said no because she wanted a marquee in the garden, waiters to serve the food, and us to stay overnight in a hotel.

"No problem," my husband said.

The thing is, you want your children to appreciate the value of things. I suggested that she could have friends around, and I was happy to cook for them all and leave them to it.

"Don't worry about it, Mum."

Parenting should come with a manual. Turn to Chapter 14. What to do when your daughter wants an expensive party, but you don't want to create an entitled brat who, later, has no clue about what happens in the real world. If I took that thought further, who will bail them out when we are dead, and they run out of money and become destitute and poor? Fear. Most of my thoughts that guided my parenting were based in fear. Fear that if Hari did not study hard enough, he would have no job, no home, be unable to look after his family; all outcomes for them led to destitution, poverty and heartache.

I thought about what my cultural attaché Pushpa would do. She had managed to become friends with her children, so she would probably be at the party, wearing a tight-fitting spandex outfit, drinking champagne with them. I had never managed to become their friend. I thought about what she would do for Hari.

On the way back to the train station, I found an HMV and asked the assistant if he could point out the section where I could find rap music. I spent two hours in there, listening to various songs, and then I found two rappers and got very excited. On the journey back home, I began writing down the lyrics from the sleeve and making notes, counting the syllables, highlighting the iambic pentameter and comparing the raps to Shakespeare's sonnets.

I entered the house through the kitchen door as if I had never escaped, took off my coat, put down my bag and saw the stacked-up empty pizza boxes that my husband had ordered for dinner and resisted the automatic urge to tidy.

I ran up the stairs and knocked on my son's door and gave him the Shakespeare book.

"He was one of the original rappers," I said excitedly. "Listen to his words, how they are formed, and now put them next to LL Cool J." I took the sleeve off the CD cover and began reading.

"Don't do that," he groaned.

"That took some thought, Mum," Anita said as she walked by.

"I hate Shakespeare and I hate reading," Hari added.

"What can I do to make it easier for you?"

"Stop trying so hard," he said, closing his door shut.

My inner urge was to break down the door, take off my slipper and beat him with it – I took a deep breath.

"Mum, don't worry about it. By the way, you look really nice."

"Today I went to York, Anita."

"Wow, what's in York?" She seemed interested.

"Auden's birthplace. Come, sit down with me and I will tell you about it."

"I'd love to, but I have to hand this in tomorrow."

I tried not to look disappointed and instead replied, "You can have your party."

"Thanks, Mum. You're the best."

She hugged me tightly. I just wanted to cling on to her and cry, but I was acutely aware not to appear needy or lonely or sad.

"I will tell you about York another day."

I threw myself onto the bed in the bedroom that I had once shared with my husband and I cried. The day had been overwhelming. As I looked up, I noticed that my husband had purchased a television set for me with a built-in DVD player. On the side were a stack of new wildlife DVDs. A stuffed cuddly monkey wearing a black beret was hanging from the television. He had taken the old television into the spare room. Marriage is complicated. Our deal had been renegotiated without the need for words. There was still a great fondness for each other there. Was it love? Perhaps, or perhaps it was more a familiarity and an understanding, and breaking away from the familiar at this point in time seemed too monumental. There was my son to think about, or that is what I told myself.

The crime scene had been cleared up; the Y-fronts with the lipstick marks had been laundered, ironed and put away. At the weekend, I cooked a huge feast and we entertained our friends. Nobody would have suspected a thing; the show went on. Hiten and I joked that we finished each other's sentences.

"You two are like mind readers," Pushpa's husband commented at one point.

"Derren Brown," Pushpa added, pointing at my husband.

Hiten laughed heartily and touched my hand. "*Mere* Debbie McGee."

Technically, Debbie McGee is a magician's assistant and not a mind reader, but I didn't correct him, as it would spoil the illusion. Also, his choice of Debbie McGee was right in some ways – if only he knew that if I could do my own disappearing act, I would. I was simply waiting for my son to leave home.

Deep became more than just a visitor in my thoughts when my daughter left to go to university. I really missed her. I missed her presence, her sitting at the kitchen table doing homework, chopping vegetables awkwardly with me. I even missed her silence. That's when Deep took up more of a permanent residence in my imagination. Hiten and Hari were in and out of the house most evenings, so we probably only ate together once or twice a week. Food was always cooked for them both and left out, so all they had to do was heat it up. The dirty dishes would be left in the sink for the following morning, but I didn't mind; I would go to bed early and talk to Deep.

In my parallel life, Deep and I had moved to York, to the Georgian house with the red front door on the cobbled street next to Auden's birthplace. The home that we had set up wasn't full of electrical gadgets, drum kits, decks and records, but filled with books, and had an attic with a skylight where we could see the stars. In the evenings, we would sit and talk. Deep and I spoke mostly about poetry. I would take out either Rumi or one of the Romantics and read to him, and in my imagination, he was there sitting next to me on the bed, listening. Sometimes, we would have whole discussions about what the poems meant. Other times, we would sit and watch nature programmes uninterrupted, and talk about all the people we knew back home, and what we would do when we went back to visit.

At first, I felt no guilt in doing this because I imagined Hiten being serviced elsewhere; and although I was planning to leave once Hari left for university, there was still some kind of feeling towards him – perhaps it was fondness? There was definitely humour.

When Hari was around seventeen, he announced that he was going to spend the weekend away at a tennis tournament. This was a source of much amusement to us because he hadn't picked up a racket in years; he was probably going away with his girlfriend who we knew nothing about.

"You'll need your balls," I said to Hari when he came into the kitchen with his overnight bag. I glanced at my husband, who I knew was trying not to giggle.

"What?" Hari was confused.

"They are in the cupboard under the stairs, Hari." My husband turned his back to me, and I knew he was trying to contain his laughter.

"Oh right – yeah, thanks," he replied.

Then, when Hari left the kitchen, Hiten exploded into a fit of laughter; he had tears in his eyes.

"Advantage Bhanu." I smiled, high fiving him.

"No," Hiten replied, unable to get the words out, "mini-break." His laughter set me off.

"No, no, no – love."

It was in these moments I resolved to think of Deep less; there was definitely some kind of love between us. There was also a shifty look when a text message came through, and the ghost of my past love would swiftly return.

A year later, my son sped off in his silver Golf GTI to take up his place at University of Southampton. At the time, we didn't know that there wasn't a course there, and that we were just funding his lifestyle for four years.

Fifteen years later, we are still waiting to go to his graduation ceremony. Every year there was some excuse. "Mum, Mum, Mum... there was a fire, innit, and all the paperwork got burnt in the office, so they need time to work it all out. Mum, Mum, Mum, I forgot to pay the fee for the diploma, so we've got to wait until next year."

Bloody nonsense but I believed him. Anyway, when your children leave home, if you are able to, it is a good time to leave yourself. If you miss this window, there is a strong probability that you will never leave.

My husband and I stood on the driveway waving him off and then Hiten said he had to go to the accountant's, so I went inside the empty house on my own. I sat on the sofa, looking at the family pictures. Anita holding Hari as a baby, her first day at school. Hari with his face smeared with chocolate cake on his fifth birthday. Hiten and me at our twentieth anniversary party; that was taken shortly after I discovered the Y-fronts. We were standing in front of a cake, holding hands, smiling, not one crack in my foundation. The children have left home, all the unspoken contracts have been fulfilled, the cage door is wide open, but I am unable to leave.

Rumi asks, "Why do you stay in prison, when the door is so wide open?"

It's a good question.

Perhaps I am used to it?

Or I am scared that there is nothing on the outside for me.

The next line is, "Move outside the tangle of fear-thinking. The entrance door to the sanctuary is inside you."

Maybe I don't like the person who is inside.

I got up and went upstairs to clean my son's room. While picking one of his dirty mugs off the floor, my back went. It was agony.

"I give up!" I screamed. "I give up. I am asking you for help. Please." In excruciating pain, I began to sob uncontrollably. "Please just show me a way forward."

After I dried my tears, I felt foolish for asking for divine intervention, so I crawled to the bathroom to get some painkillers. I lay on the bathroom floor for half an hour and crawled to the phone and managed to get an appointment to see the GP. It was in the olden days when all you had to do was to call and not wait three weeks to be seen. Desperate, I called up Pushpa, who said she could give me a lift to the surgery, but she couldn't stay as she had to see her son off to Oxford. Pushpa's son was studying to be a doctor.

"One day he will be able to operate on you, Bhanu," Pushpa said as she left me at the surgery. LOL was not around in those days.

Yes, I will make sure to leave my body for him and the advancement of medical science, I wanted to say.

"Yes, that would be great," I replied instead.

Pushpa's daughter wanted to be a dentist. Pushpa will have all her medical requirements covered.

"Anita still undecided if she wants to be a maths teacher?" Pushpa asked casually.

Anita had completed her maths degree and she was on a gap year working in a wildlife sanctuary in Kerala.

My husband gifted her the £7,000 required for the year to look after Rani the elephant.

"Yes. Undecided." I have learned to keep sentences short. There is nothing to pull or extract from a short sentence. Pushpa looked at her watch and said she had better get going. She handed me over to the receptionist and drove off. The receptionist, taking pity that I had been dumped in the surgery, kindly walked me to a seat and helped me sit down.

I nodded at the other patients and was going to ask the receptionist if she could kindly hand me *Woman & Home*, when I spotted a book on the chair next to me. It appeared to have no owner. I picked it up and flicked the page to the attached Post-it note. Out of curiosity, I read the highlighted paragraph.

The author described people not really living their life but sleepwalking through it on autopilot, pretending to be happy, not realising the extent of their misery, boredom or death, even. Then something unexpectedly meets them on their path; it could be a book, a song, a person or something else. Many people don't recognise whatever has been sent and continue along their journey with their eyes half shut – but for others, it saves them.

I looked around the surgery; it was as if this paragraph were written for me. I checked again that no one was looking and put the book in my handbag. I have to say, I have never stolen anything and at a later stage I returned the book when I got my own copy, but right then, it gave me such a thrill to take it and the thought of reading more of the author's words filled me with such excitement that I forgot about my back pain. So, when I was called, I almost skipped into the consulting room.

The doctor gave me an injection and I took a taxi back home, pain free. I made the floor of my bedroom comfortable, got changed, and took Anaïs Nin out of my bag. I sat down on the floor and said a prayer of thanks before opening the book. I laid my head down on the pillow, opened the book carefully, and began reading. Although she was a French-American lady who died in the year before I came to the UK – 1977 – she was writing for me.

She spoke of the two women who lived inside her, one of them drowning, and the other an actress who hid what she really felt and presented someone who she thought the world would accept.

That was me. She was writing about me. For the endless gatherings with friends at weekends, I would paint my face and be dressed in the brightest sari ready for the moment I was required to perform.

"Bhanu, tell us another story."

I sold my stories for acceptance and laughter. Leaping up off the sofa and performing whenever required. Parts of my life were rewritten for their entertainment and sometimes, I would enlist Hiten's help. We made a good double act. Nobody would have any idea that ten minutes before, we weren't even speaking. We had become experts at concealing all the imperfections in ourselves and in our marriage and when the party was over, we would tidy up and retreat into our own rooms, slowly degenerating from the boredom. But Hiten, obviously, was being regenerated elsewhere, and I was too.

I read on: she talked about ways to be free and one of them was escaping reality through the imagination. I sat up.

As I have tried to do, Anaïs. This is what I do. In my imagination, I am living a life with Deep.

I turned back to Anaïs Nin's diary. Every page spoke to me. You could say that we only ever see the things that are relevant to us but as I lay there reading her words, I cried. I cried because I felt that there was someone who understood me, who was with me. I cried, remembering Ba, who hugged me beneath the stars, telling me that I was worth something and that the universe was on my side. Ba and Deep made me believe that constellations of stars would reorganise themselves for me, that I was not just a star amongst many, but special, fated for good things. Maybe it was true, and I had got in my own way by trying to control and cling to safety – by not truly believing that I was worthy of such a feat of universal generosity.

This time, it felt as though the universe had listened to a prayer that I had put out and had conspired with me to find this book. Imagine if for one nanosecond, the universe had decided to take a quick glimpse at my life and wanted to help me. For the first time in over twenty-five years, since the birth of my daughter, I had a feeling of overwhelming joy, a feeling that a door had opened for me and all I had to do was walk through it.

I highlighted one more section; it was about finding peace and loving myself as I was.

I recited this section over and over until I was back on my feet.

For the last twenty years, I had held on to Rumi, chanting his words like a mantra when I felt I needed them. It wasn't that I was letting him go, it was just that there were other worlds to explore. The pain in my back went away in less than a week and as soon as I could, I got out of the house to explore the poetry section in the library. It wasn't very big, so I travelled further out.

A hearing-impaired librarian helped me find the complete works of Anaïs Nin, which I did not take out but read religiously every day at the library. Anaïs made even the most boring things sound magical and she made me want to live my life to the fullest. I was there for about three months when the librarian, who I now knew was called Martin, introduced me to an even bigger world with the works of Sylvia Plath and her style of confessional poetry. Her life was such a tragic waste.

You are down, Sylvia, but get up! I wanted to shout when I read about her husband's affair. *Things happen. Get up, Sylvia, get up!*

I wish there was a parallel universe where we could speak to people from the past and give them strength to endure so they are able to change their destinies. I suppose, sometimes, people are too broken. The wound is too big and the thought of light entering is inconceivable. Sylvia put her head in the oven and gassed herself while her two children were sleeping in the next room. Like my mother and like so many women before, she killed herself because it was all too much. What if we are able to heal the brokenness in others through words, through food, through touch; and perhaps through this act of service we are able to heal our own broken hearts?

I allowed this thought to stay with me and expand until, one day, I overheard that there was an opening in the library for an assistant librarian and although it was something I could only ever dream of, it felt like a calling – I was meant to apply.

Don't ever ask anyone's permission to go for your dream because they can rob you of your enthusiasm even before you start.

"Bhanu! My uncle's niece's cousin once worked in a library and it was the most boring job ever. Who wants to be all day with musty, dusty books?" Pushpa knows everyone who has done everything. "Anyway, why do you want to work – Hiten not looking after you properly? Are you having financial difficulties?"

Not at all. I have found my vocation. I also want to escape my lover's ghost, who is following me around this big house. He has made his way downstairs and is ever-present now the children have left. Also, I want to stop pretending, I want to stop having superficial, rubbish conversations like the ones we have.

I didn't say this. Although Pushpa and I have known each other for years, it is all very superficial. Our relationship is like the Little Pig's house made out of sticks: one big blow and I think it will be gone.

Anita laughed when I called her at the wildlife sanctuary when she was on a break from feeding Rani the elephant.

"But Mum, you are not very patient with people and you know it is a library so you can't talk."

My son was more encouraging. "Mum, Mum, Mum, people find all kinds of answers when they look inside but they hide – hesitating, procrastinating, no decision-making. Lots of people communicating but faking so go ahead and do it, Mum. You go and get some fun. You got a thumbs up – from me." He motioned a thumbs up.

Good God, I thought. It was quite good until "go and get some fun". I was so delighted that he was on his computer degree and seemed to be enjoying it (this was obviously before I knew that he was faking it). Perhaps some new talents would emerge.

"Thank you for your support, Hari. It is much appreciated."

"You don't need to work, Bhanu. If you need more money, just ask me." My husband tried to get me to change my mind. "Anyway, what will other people think? What will Mummy say if she hears that you are working?"

Forty-six-year-old adult male with mummy issues seeks... seeks no resolution.

And just for that reason, I was determined to get the job.

The job requisites were to have a love of books. "Tick", as they say. To have some clerical experience – "tick". Some previous library experience – no tick, but there was some diversity/disability quota, which I could clearly tick on account of my ethnicity, giving me some extra points.

I asked Martin if he wouldn't mind helping me fill in the application form and in exchange, I packed him a tiffin with some Indian sweets, which he seemed grateful for. I then went to hand the completed form to Mr David, the library director. His secretary said he was out, and she would be happy to take it, but I decided to wait for him. He took hours but when I saw him, I pounced on him with my completed form.

"Mr David, sir, I don't think I have wanted something quite as much as I have wanted this. I know you might get hundreds of applications and I may not be as experienced or qualified as most of them, but I will learn, I will do everything it takes to learn so please consider it."

"Thank you," he replied, slightly baffled.

A week later, he called me in for an interview.

Mr David began asking me about my favourite books and I could see he was impressed as I quoted Shakespeare, shared my love of poetry with him and told him that I had recently read the entire works of Anaïs Nin and Sylvia Plath.

He asked me if I had any previous experience of working in a library. I told him apart from being a visitor, I had none but I enjoyed putting books back where they belonged, even if I hadn't taken them out. I was generally very orderly and added that I had great respect for librarians. "Philip Larkin worked all his life as a librarian and look what he produced," I said enthusiastically.

"So, you are also familiar with the works of Larkin?"

I nodded, and, in my imagination, I was transported to a stage and handed a microphone to participate in a poetry slam. It was the moment that I had been waiting for, a moment to grab hold of. I looked at him and began reciting "This Be the Verse", one of Larkin's poems I felt passionate about – the one about parents fucking up their children.

I would like to say that Mr David was mesmerised by my recital but it was more that he was unsure of what to say, having forgotten his next question. He hesitated. "And are you familiar with the Dewey Decimal system, Bhanu?"

"No, but I am familiar with many other systems: the caste system, the marriage system, the solar system, so I don't think it will be difficult to acquaint myself with another system."

I could tell he wanted to laugh. This was my territory. All I had to do was to make him laugh.

"Humour can always get you out of a situation – it's also a very good system," I added.

"Quite right. So, no prior experience of working with library systems," he noted.

"No, but I am a very fast learner. Once you show me something, you don't have to explain it twice. I also have an elephant's memory. I don't forget a thing. 1979 – Death of Lord Mountbatten. 1981 – Lady Diana got married."

He stopped me there.

I could have continued to the present day as I have linked all the queen's major events with my own timeline:

1982 – Prince William born – Anita's first birthday.

1984 – Birth of Prince Harry – Husband's affair. Hari born.

1992 – Annus horribilis. Fire at Windsor Castle – House burglary. Mother-in-law tries to extend one month to two.

1995 – That *Panorama* interview – we won't even go there but I remember sitting there gripped with a tube of Pringles.

I have always been a fan of the Queen and in spite of the age difference and her love of dogs, I am able to identify with her. She is all about duty, tradition and the family, and keeps whatever feelings she has inside. God alone knows there must have been days when she wanted to make her own exit.

"Okay. Thank you, Bhanu. Have you had any experience of removing a drunken person out of a public place or calming down an agitated person?"

I thought about my drunken father and all the demanding people I have had in my life. "No, but I have experience of dealing with difficult people and very difficult situations."

He wanted me to elaborate but it was not the appropriate place to talk about my family situation, my mother-in-law or indeed my sister. I looked at him and nodded back to him, signalling that it was a terrain that we should not cover. He stared back at me.

"Well, I am unable to give you a concrete example but generally, I just maintain calmness. I am a very calm person. Calm..." I repeated, taking in a deep breath, "and I generally get along with people. I know Martin already and we understand each other perfectly even though he is deaf. I mean, hearing-impaired."

"And why do you want this job?"

"Listen, Mr David, I might not be the most qualified or experienced person but I want to learn. I love words, how they are put together, how they can soothe you. Words have helped me through some of the most difficult times of my life and if I am able to guide people to books that might help them in whatever way they need, then there has been a purpose to all of it."

"Thank you very much, Bhanu, for coming in. We will be in touch."

That ending seemed like a thank you but no thank you. So, imagine, when two days later, he called me to tell me that I had got the job. I thought for a moment about who I could call up and share the news with. I called my son in Southampton, but he was not there. My husband asked me to tell his mother, friends and family that I was volunteering.

"Let's see how long you last, Mum," Anita said from her elephant sanctuary.

Deep – Deep would have been proud of me.

My boss in the adult literature section was Abigail, and Martin was the other librarian I was supposed to be assisting. Hillary, a recent university graduate, was head shelver/receptionist and she sat mostly at the front desk and enjoyed playing solitaire on the computer when she thought nobody was looking. Abigail was highly educated and, like Philip Larkin, she had graduated with a degree in English literature from Oxford. She was how you would imagine a librarian to be – mousey with glasses, and she always wore a cardigan and a pleated skirt covering the knee. Perhaps she had a cat; that turned out to be the one thing I found out in the sixteen years I worked there since she avoided any personal questions.

Never have I been unable to find out at least a few details about someone, but she was like an impenetrable fortress. I'm sure the community would also fail miserably in gaining access to the drawbridge. All

I knew was that she would bring in sad, soggy tuna sandwiches and, on a Friday, she would buy a Marks & Spencer microwavable pasta meal, heat it up and read a book. Abigail appeared to have a particular interest in plants and herbs. I once offered her a methi paratha, telling her about the healing properties of methi but she seemed uninterested and declined politely. She probably thought that she would need to return the favour. No deals emotional or otherwise to be struck with Abigail.

"The Dewey Decimal system is a classification system used to arrange books via subject. Each book is issued a shelf mark number – see here." Abigail pointed to the book. "It's found on the spine of the book and arranged in numerical order."

It did not take long for me to grasp. I have a very methodical mind that has shelved events and facts in the correct compartments for years. It is second nature to me; I don't process. I just note and shelve. Husband's fourth affair = Affair/Hus/4, Family & Friends' Betrayal = Bet/FF/18, Mother-in-law's Meddling = MED/MIL/346, Daughter's Eye Roll = ER/Dau/478 and so forth...

Then there was training on how to deal with clients. You don't speak to them unless there is a fire. You wait for them to come and speak to you. There are non-verbal signs you give to stop noise. First the head rotation, looking in the direction of the noisy perpetrator; then there is the eyebrow-raising. If this doesn't work, the fingers go to the lips. This too is easy for me. I am used to non-verbal communication from HUS & DAU. MIL can be quite dramatic and vocal. The next step is a "Shhhhh" with finger raised to the mouth and the last resort is expulsion of the culprit.

Abigail gave me first-hand experience of this as she shhhed me often. I found the first few months of not being able to talk extremely difficult and I wanted to leave as I couldn't escape my thoughts, but three things happened to change everything. They let me help reorganise the poetry section, Martin began teaching me how to sign so we could have proper conversations in silence, and I discovered that non-verbal communication could be incredibly funny.

Martin and I sat together every day on our lunch break. I would bring lunch for the two of us and he would teach me to sign. It was a slow process and it took me about a year to become fluent but what a world it was I discovered. As Rumi said, "Silence is the language of God. All else is poor translation."

Martin and I could discuss books and poetry without disturbing anyone. He introduced me to Greek mythology, which was his passion. Greek mythology and Indian mythology were not that far away from each other; you have a god for everything in both Greek and Indian mythology. Zeus and Indra sounded like very similar characters (both king of gods, both gods of Rain, both had the same weapons) and the Trojan War was close to the Ramayana – both fought on account of a woman. The cultures were very similar.

One day I was asked to cover the front desk for Hillary. The amount of times a librarian hears, "I'm looking for a book; I have forgotten the name, but it has a blue cover. Do you know which one it is?" On the front desk that day, I must have heard it a hundred times; I understood why Hillary escaped with solitaire. After the fiftieth request, I took a trolley and filled it up with blue books. When Hillary came back, she saw the books and couldn't stop laughing. All I need is someone who understands my humour just a little bit and off we go.

"Hillary, be careful, you were about to bump you head on that shelf."

"Okay. Thanks, Bhanu."

"You need to be a bit more shelf-aware."

She stopped and then she laughed. Abigail looked across at us sternly.

"The thing with Abigail is that she is too shelf-conscious," she replied.

There were countless ways we tried to make each other laugh. Hillary knew about my love for wildlife and one day, she came in wearing a monkey hat. All you could see behind the front desk was a monkey's face. Abigail was not impressed and asked her to remove it.

"This is a place of work and you are behaving like children in a playground."

We found ways to get around this. Martin, Hillary and I had "spine conversations" – this was when we arranged books with their titles on top of each other.

What's Inside? (Book placed by me.)
Uranus. (Hillary.)
A Black Hole. (Martin.)
Get Back to Work. (Placed by Abigail.)
It's Not Funny. (Placed again by Abigail.)

If there was a house for my soul, it was the library and for the first time in a long, long time, I felt like me. I began to like myself again and I felt useful assisting other people in finding words that might touch them in some way. Words are healing. Work with them all day and they can't help but soothe you. Perhaps I was assisting them; perhaps I was helping myself – it didn't matter. Whenever I was asked by clients which poetry they should begin with and also when I wasn't asked, I guided all who came to Rumi. I would leave Post-it notes in the relevant sections of his work for them. *For anxiety, For hope, For a broken heart, For grief...* Abigail did not say anything about the notes and so I continued.

"Deep, do you remember what I said? I have finally become a word doctor," I would tell him as I sat on my bed.

"I didn't doubt it for one minute," he replied.

Most evenings, I would tell him about my day as we sat together.

One day, I knew I would tell him in person. One day, I knew we would meet and, as Auden said, it would be a "real occasion"; but until then, I would slip into the gap of these two worlds and make the most of this wonderful job that life had presented me with.

My husband, sensing the change in me and perhaps feeling my joy, began making efforts in our relationship. He arrived home from work early to have dinner, and he bought me flowers.

"Why is he buying you flowers? Was there a discount at the petrol station?" Pushpa asked. "And is it all still working down there? Not suffering from leakage? Remember the pelvic floor exercise. Even when you are rolling chapattis you can do them."

Pushpa, with too much time on her hands, had moved from cultural attaché to sexual health attaché. Good God, this is probably what happens when your children have left and you stay at home. You start worrying about other people's sexual activity and incontinence problems.

"Remember, when you are chewing food, try to chew it evenly on both sides. I think you are mostly using the right side; that is why the left side is sagging so much. It will be the menopause soon," Pushpa added. "That's not going to be easy, so follow my advice. Vaseline to start with."

One day on my way back from the library, I got a text message. Back in those days text messages were rare.

Put on some lacy panties.

It was from my husband.

The onset of the mobile revolutionised the way my husband conducted affairs. I texted back, *I think you have sent this to the wrong person.*

No, Bhanu. It is meant for you.

Have you lost your mind? I replied quickly. Or, had I known what 'laugh out loud' was back then, I would have just texted *LOL*.

I want us to try again.

Lacy panties will not do it.

What will, Bhanu?

He came home and suggested he might move back into the bedroom, or perhaps visit one evening.

"Bhanu, the children have left home. It is now time for us. What do you say?" Then he slowly took off his jacket, tie and other garments, and began singing Rod Stewart's 'Da Ya Think I'm Sexy?'.

He could still make me laugh.

"Do you think you might be a sex addict?" I asked, glancing up from rolling the parathas.

He thought I was joking and continued singing and removing his clothing.

I put down the rolling pin and gave him my full attention. "I am being serious. We have never talked about it – all your women – but if we are going to make it work, we have to."

He stopped dancing. He was standing in his Y-fronts in the middle of the kitchen in silence. And in that moment, there was nothing more I wanted to say.

"There was never anyone but you." He had tears in his eyes.

Like The Beautiful South's 'Song For Whoever', I wanted to reel off a list of women's names, adding a few Indian ones in there, but I resisted and let him continue.

"I will stop it all. You have my word."

He sat down at the kitchen table and broke down. I put down the rolling pin and sat with him. He said none of them meant anything, it was just the excitement, the escape from routine and responsibility. Perhaps I should have told him about Deep.

"Please forgive me, Bhanu."

He held out his hand. I took it.

I could say I took it because we had come this far, because I cared about what the community thought, because very few women of my generation in my culture got divorced. It was probably all of this, and that I still had some feelings for this man who sat before me. What if I became fully engaged in my life with him?

I told Hiten that I liked the separate rooms but he could come and visit and we could take things slowly, and, well, if he could too, it might work. It is a strange thing that the moment you take your attention off everything that is not working and put your energy and attention back in yourself, things rearrange themselves in an order that you could not have possibly designed. I am not going to lie and say that the sex was stratospheric or that I located the G-spot, but there was genuine affection there. These were happy years for me; my job gave me purpose and security, the relationship with my husband evolved once again and my children were finding their own way in the world. I did not yearn for anything, not even Deep. There were no more full-blown conversations with Deep, just occasional fleeting thoughts.

My father passed away peacefully in his sleep a few months before I turned fifty and more out of obligation, I began to invite my sister Gauri into the family. She came to my fiftieth bringing a wilting pot plant.

"Happy birthday, Didi," she said, holding out a tired-looking orchid that had been dyed blue.

"Thank you," I said. It needed immediate watering but Hiten and the kids were eager for me to open their present.

It was a number plate – 8HANU – and then they took me outside to a black Mercedes.

"Happy birthday, Bhanu." He kissed me on the cheek.

"Yeah, you're the best ever mum. You are number one," my son added.

"Hope you enjoy it, Mum." My daughter kissed me on both cheeks. She had completed an MBA in France and had got a job as an investment banker in the City.

"I don't know what to say." I genuinely didn't know what to say.

"Come on, get in," my husband instructed, handing me the keys.

They all got in the car with me. My children were squashed in the back with Gauri and I took them for a drive. I could sense my daughter's anxiety; she doesn't like getting in the car with me; she thinks I am not a safe driver just because I failed my driving test five times and every time she gets into the car with me, she does a calculation of the probability of having an accident and always asks if we have updated our insurance.

"You need to update the insurance policy," she instructed.

"And off we go," I replied, smiling.

It was a smooth drive in spite of the nervous tension in the car. Then, as I drove along an empty street, I decided to apply the emergency brake. I checked the rear-view mirror and I slammed down the brakes. I slammed down the brakes because it was the first moment in my entire marriage that I felt truly liberated. They were all in that car with me and I wanted them to see a part of me that I had kept hidden.

"Really, Mum! Really? You could have caused an accident!" my daughter said, exasperated.

"No. I checked the rear-view mirror before braking."

Though I was feeling liberated, I work within the parameters of safety.

My husband started to laugh and then he couldn't stop.

"Mum, you kicked it with that brakin' and left everyone shakin'." My son did a flicking motion with his hand. He had finished university and said he had got a part-time job in Southampton. I wished someone would employ him on a more permanent basis. That was my only real worry in life, and I was grateful that this was it! My sister was unsure of what comment the situation required and clutched the pot plant tightly. I wasn't entirely sure why she had brought it into the car with her but then again, most things she did baffled me.

As soon as we got inside, Anita asked my husband for the insurance papers and checked them while we served cake. She is very thorough. Before she left, she printed off new forms for better cover and left them on the kitchen table.

"Will we see you next weekend, Anita?"

"Sorry, Mum, I've got a lot of work on." She was very busy in her new job. It was an important job as she seemed to be in a lot of meetings.

"Do you want me to come by the flat next Sunday?" I asked. She had bought (well, put down a deposit for) a flat in Marylebone with her signing bonus and also our help, and when she was very busy, I would send her food for the week.

"I'm fine, Mum. Hope you had a lovely day." She kissed me on both cheeks.

"I really did, *beta*," I replied. "Thank you!"

"Got to head too, Mum." Hari hugged me tightly. I gave them both their respective food parcels.

Gauri got up too. I was going to invite her to stay for longer, but then changed my mind.

"Happy birthday, Didi."

"Thank you." I gave her a food parcel, hugged her and saw them all out.

As I began clearing the table, Hiten came in.

"Sit down, Bhanu. It's your birthday today. I will do that."

Appreciating his gesture, I sat down and glanced at the insurance forms that Anita had left on the table. "Please indicate if you have had an accident in the last year," I read out loud.

Hiten stood in the middle of the kitchen with the dirty dishes in one hand and his right hand extended.

"What are you doing?" I asked.

"Indicating," he replied.

I started to laugh.

"After this is done, let's watch something together?" he suggested. "Maybe we could watch a comedy? Remember how it used to be, Bhanu; you go up. I will bring you some tea."

We sat together watching television in my room. He reached for my hand and I took it. It was a nice end to a fiftieth birthday.

Hari moved back in with us a few years later and once again the dynamics changed. He didn't make it onto the housing ladder, given the fact that by the time he got to the first rung, he got tired of climbing and left his job. He would leave work every six months.

I suggested that his ladder might be against the wrong wall.

"Well, of course it is. Work is just a construct of capitalism, it's elitism, there ain't no realism. People being controlled by the system. I just wanna do my music."

"We have never stopped you, Hari."

"Yeah, but you've never made it easy, have you?"

I think perhaps we made it too easy.

When Hari turned thirty and there were still no signs of him moving out and my husband wanted to give him the deposit like we had done for Anita, I vetoed it because I didn't want us to pay for his mortgage every time he was out of work.

"I'll just rent it out, Mum, and live here."

I wanted him to appreciate the value of things. "When you can stay in a job for a year, we will think about it."

He never managed to.

This too is my fault as property now has become unaffordable for the youth – well, he is no longer a youth but anyway, the current housing crisis is down to me. "Yes, of course I control the global economy, like I control everything else. Climate change: yes, that's down to me too – cooking too many chapattis on the gas ring. We gave you a good education. Go and use it."

"You don't get it, do you, Mum. It's about control. You control when I get a flat. You control what I do."

"I don't control anything. Work hard and you can achieve anything."

"Don't you get it? I can't."

"You can't work hard?"

"I can't leave home."

"Well, that's not my fault, is it?"

I didn't really hear his words. It is only looking back that I understand what they meant. All our even deals, tiptoeing around him to protect him and making him feel safe have created an adult who is scared of being independent. What he was trying to say was that his own cage door was open, but he couldn't fly anywhere.

There were other things that concerned me; money and jewellery went missing. Then, the twenty-four-carat gold carriage clock gifted for our thirtieth anniversary disappeared, as did a painting that I wanted to get valued on *Antiques Roadshow*. I discussed it with Hiten but he was distracted. I suspected that maybe he was back to his philandering ways but I didn't want to see it. I told myself we needed to get Hari back on track and our marriage issues could wait and then, by some miracle, Sarah came into our lives. We all had dinner together and then she disappeared.

I had just sat down to watch a downloaded episode of *Blue Planet* when the doorbell rang. The takeaway drivers always confused our address with the house on the top of the street, so I went to redirect them. Standing there was Sarah. I hadn't seen her in months, since the dinner. This time, she was dressed in yoga wear. I was slightly embarrassed by my outfit as I was wearing a T-shirt and elasticated tracksuit bottoms. Had I peered out of the window to check who it was, I would have made time to put on a sari for the occasion.

"I know Hari's playing football, Banoo, but I have just come to drop off his phone charger. He left it at the flat." In those few seconds, I managed to find out that she was in a flatshare with three other girls and he sometimes went around for a sleepover. Even though I didn't have a brassiere on, I was desperate to invite her in. "Come in, come in, Sarah." You don't leave your future daughter-in-law on the doorstep, no matter how badly dressed you are.

"I don't want to disturb you."

"No disturbance. I was just about to watch *Blue Planet*."

"That's my absolute favourite programme. Did you see the one with the polar bears?" she asked.

"That's the one that I am about to watch," I replied.

It was fate. She was meant to be here, and I was supposed to make the most of this opportunity.

"Tea? Masala tea?" I tried not to sound too excited by her presence. My children used to be embarrassed when they were teenagers and I used to make masala tea for their English friends but now, it is very popular. "Or turmeric latte? Or fennel tea?" Again, previously ridiculed but now in vogue.

"Whatever is easy, Banoo."

I thought I would impress her and make a fresh cardamom and ginger tea, which I served in a Royal Doulton teapot reserved for special occasions, alongside a silver tray with a selection of Indian sweets that I had made.

"Wow! This looks amazing. You've gone to so much trouble."

"No trouble at all. They are homemade – organic."

I was so overcome with excitement at having an unexpected visitor and that it was Sarah, that I was at a loss for what to say.

"Hiten has gone to play bridge." Well, that's what he'd said; he had gone out with a poker face.

"This is so gorgeous," she enthused, sampling the coconut barfis. "I would really love to learn how to make them."

Oh, Bhagvan! Someone in the family finally wants to learn how to make sweets from me. Anita had never wanted to as she said they were too greasy. "I will teach you," I replied hastily and quickly realised the speed at which I had answered. I have been reminded by Anita to give people space, so I added, "if you ever want to learn."

"I'd love to," she replied.

I wanted to get out my diary and confirm a time and date but had to resist.

"You just let me know when you are ready."

I found out a little bit more about her. Her mother had passed away when she was very young (cancer) and her father had never remarried; they had a very close relationship. Sarah had met Hari in a club on a hen do (not ideal but better than Tinder). He had walked up to the hen party and said he had never seen anyone as beautiful and that he would do whatever it took to have one dance with her. (We have heard that before; the apple does not fall far from the tree, as they say.) She chose to stay and dance with her friends but he wrote a rap/poem for her on a piece of paper (I dare not ask) and left his number. I did some PR for him, adding that Hari was very creative, imaginative and bold (he could be).

They had been dating each other for nearly two years. *Two years?* What more did they need to know about each other that they didn't know already? Time was ticking; he wasn't getting any younger.

Sarah was a Montessori nursery teacher. Apparently, the Montessori ethos is to teach children independence from a young age. Perhaps my son would have turned out a little differently had he been taught the method in his formative years. Never mind, now Sarah was here, she could put him straight. Sarah was also training to be a yoga teacher and her instructor had recommended a class which was near to where we lived (hence popping in after the class with the charger). She was efficient and as she was talking, my heart leaped at the thought of my future grandchildren; independent, yoga-loving, Indian sweet eating, appreciative children. Thinking about what they might look like, I had lost the thread of the conversation.

I thought we might be still on the yoga subject so I said, "I would love to do yoga but I have a bad back."

"Banoo, you know that there are some great positions to stretch the back out. Let me show you." Before I knew it, she had left the dining room table and was on the other side of the room where she had found a space. "Come on, Banoo."

I became acutely aware of her fit body and my sagging breasts that would be dangling in my T-shirt. So, I made a joke: "Na, maste here."

"Pardon?"

"Namaste here," I repeated. "I will find it a bit of a stretch."

She laughed and she could not stop laughing and in that moment my world was complete. My future daughter-in-law not only loved *Blue Planet*, wanted to make sweets with me but she got my jokes.

"Oh my God, that is brilliant. I can see where Hari gets his humour from."

"Sarah, can I be honest with you? My breasts will be jiggling everywhere. I am not wearing a brassiere."

"Brassiere? I've never heard anyone call them brassieres." She laughed again and came towards the table with an outstretched hand.

We did downward dog together, cat, cow and a few other animal positions, and during that time with her, I felt no back pain. At the end of it, I said, "Sarah, there is something I want to tell you and please don't be embarrassed."

She stopped smiling and I was worried that I would offend her, but I wanted to be honest with her. "My name is Bhanu. Bhanu. Think of walking into a barn and stopping in your tracks because you are surprised by the size of the cow: Barn – ooh! Now put those two words together very quickly!"

She didn't appear offended at all and, instead, repeated my name correctly.

And then without much thinking, I said, "Or if you like the name Tara better, you can call me Tara."

"Tara's a lovely name." Sarah smiled.

"It means 'star'."

"And you are," she replied.

She called me a star. How graceful she was; she took feedback and turned it into something positive. I wasn't used to such a reaction. Ecstatic, I could have done a round of sun salutations. Then, not only that, she asked for my help.

"Now, Tara, you can also teach me how to pronounce some of the yoga postures correctly."

I wanted to cry. Everything I could have dreamed of, presented right here in front of me. I thought of all the sleepless nights worrying about Hari, if he would be okay. Who would have thought him capable of finding a girl like Sarah?

"They are in Sanskrit, but we can google them together."

She arranged to come around the following Wednesday after her yoga class to learn how to make

Indian sweets and we would google Sanskrit words together.

As soon as she left, I was bursting with joy; it felt like I had won the lottery of daughters-in-law and I wanted to call everyone I could think of and tell them.

Now I understand why people take out a full-page advertisement in the newspaper to announce forthcoming weddings but then I thought, *Bhanu, contain yourself, don't get too excited and no need to announce it to the world yet. Contain your happiness and when the time is right, you can get out the tannoy.* Instead, I ran upstairs to my airing cupboard/temple and gave thanks for her, promising I would overwrite any genetic Indian mother-in-law codes of conduct and always treat her well.

Even though I played down Sarah's visits, Hari wasn't impressed.

"Mum, why is she calling you Tara now?"

"It's what my grandmother used to call me."

"And that makes sense because…? I don't want you getting over-familiar with her. It feels like pressure. No pressure, Mum."

"Yes, you told me. You are just going out."

After making his coffee, he did not put the milk back in the fridge. There would only be a limit to which Sarah would put up with his absentmindedness and general untidiness, so I made a mental note to have a proper conversation about it with him later. I didn't want him to connect the two things. There were definitely a few of his habits he would need to change, like not making his bed, not putting the toilet seat down after use, leaving coffee cups around, throwing wet bath towels on the bathroom floor and a few other things that we would need to work on to make the relationship divorce-proof.

I began to worry how he would bring up those lovely children without a stable career.

"You can always work with Dad in one of the shops; you know, jewellery can be a very creative career. Lots of interacting with people; you are so personable."

"Listen, Mum, I'm in project management; why would I want to sell jewellery?"

"It's just you seemed to have gone part-time and you are out most nights."

"Like I've told you before, I'm doing my music."

I wanted to tell him that women like Sarah rarely came along, that he had to up his game in order not to mess it up.

"Please put the milk back in the fridge and wash up your cup," I asked politely.

He stared at me as if I had asked him to perform a set at Glastonbury with no prior warning. I tried to talk to my husband about it. I caught Hiten by surprise; he was on his laptop. Startled, he closed the laptop quickly.

"We need to stop making things easy for Hari. You need to stop giving him money. Couldn't you take him into one of the shops, tell him there is a big problem with project management?"

Hiten did not look directly at me. "Don't worry, I will speak to him."

I suspected that he had discovered online dating but pushed these thoughts to the back of my head.

Nearly every Wednesday, the Royal Doulton tea set would be brought out; Sarah would come to visit after her yoga class. I would share stories about Ba and recipes learned from my father and we would make Indian sweets and savoury snacks together. She taught me how to make a vegan shepherd's pie. Sarah couldn't believe that in forty years I hadn't gone back to Tanzania. How could I explain that I kept it alive in my memory, that a large part of my life was spent living in my imagination with these memories and if I went back, I would have nothing left. Part of me wanted to tell her about Deep; he had recently re-entered my imagination and once again taken up residency in the room upstairs. It was best not to draw Sarah into my parallel life. Instead, when I was sitting on my bed, I would relay the conversations I'd had with her to Deep.

"Deep, she told me about losing her mother when she was eight. I couldn't control my tears and we sat and cried together. I wanted to tell her about mine but couldn't. Deep, you would love her; she's kind and gentle. There's a child who is being dropped off at nursery and he's always shouted at by the dad. Sarah wants to say something to him and asked me what I would do. 'Tell him,' I said. She values my opinion."

Sarah invited me into her world, into the nursery to teach the children how to cook, and I was aware that our lives were becoming further intertwined but I didn't care. I invited her to come to the annual Navaratri dance with me. Anita, Hugh and Hari never came, and I thought it would be an experience for her.

"You invited her to garba? You've got to be kidding me, Mum. What are you thinking?" Hari asked.

"It doesn't mean anything. It's a cultural experience for her."

"You know that's not true. This is what I mean. I'm always pressured by you, Mum."

"You don't have to come."

"If you keep on like this, I am not going to marry her."

I was momentarily shocked. I'm not sure that I was shocked at the thought of him actually having thoughts about marrying her or shocked that he wouldn't. I decided that after garba, I would back off and perhaps just meet with her monthly, or perhaps fortnightly. I couldn't retract the invitation as Sarah was excited; there was a festivity to celebrate.

Sarah looked amazing in the gargari choli that I had purchased and draped for her. It was blue and red and it set off her eyes. Of course, I was aware that some members of the community were finger-pointing and gossiping. This was a big annual festivity where marriages were brokered; the women in the community would collect further bio datas, swiping right or left for their database of eligible candidates, and she was an anomaly who did not fit into their system.

Community Member A came up to us: "Hari's friend, *che*?"

"Yes, and my friend, Sarah."

Member B followed shortly behind and looked Sarah up and down and then turned to me: "No Hari?"

Clearly, he was not there and then she answered her own question: "DJ-ing?" She said it distastefully as though he were her local MP, who had not bothered to sort out the rubbish problem she was experiencing with her overflowing recycling bins.

"Working late," I stated. It's always best to keep sentences to a minimum so there is nothing to latch on to. That or feign deafness, but Sarah was with me.

"Working?" Member A said to Sarah.

"Yes. He's at work," she repeated politely.

"No," Member A said. "You working?"

"Yes," Sarah said, baffled by the question.

"Teacher," I stated quickly.

"Mother? Father?" Member B asked.

"Yes, they are all teachers too," I said, trying to hurry Sarah along.

Sarah smiled at me.

It would have been harder to make our getaway if Member C was there; Member C would have been on her toes, asking what schools they taught at, if they were private or state-funded, and then attempting to find out if Sarah was planning to have children, if so, how many and would they be going to private school.

Pushpa came over with her daughter-in-law. They were dressed similarly in royal blue.

"Sarah, I have heard so much about you," she said, kissing Sarah's cheeks. "This is Nisha. Nisha is at KPMG. I'll leave you to have a chat."

Pushpa took me aside. "Great girl," she said, "but, Bhanu, don't get your hopes up too high."

Sarah didn't stay to chat to Nisha. "Come, Bhanu, the dancing has started," Sarah said, taking my arm. In that moment, there was no back pain. We began to dance. Occasionally, I would imagine Deep as my partner, recalling the first night we had met and danced; but that evening, I didn't, and I didn't even have to take painkillers for my back as I was elated by Sarah's presence and her enthusiasm. In spite of dancing in a large concentric circle, it felt at times that there was just the two of us there and soon she would formally be part of our family.

The first blow that came was that due to library cuts, I was being made redundant. This news was cushioned by the fact that Anita was pregnant and then, a few days later, Sarah came over with Hari and showed off her engagement ring. My husband had got it for him from one of his jewellery shops, but she didn't have to know that. It had a large blue sapphire with encrusted diamonds around it. I knew Hari was going to propose but I didn't actually believe he would, so when I saw it on her finger, I almost passed out with happiness.

"Welcome to the family, Sarah," my husband and I said proudly. I was too overwhelmed to say much and hugged them both. As we sat down to have lunch, I thought about broaching the subject of having the wedding at The Grove and possible wedding dates, but my husband, sensing this, asked how Hari had proposed, knowing the answer as we had helped him with most of it.

They had gone to the Shard and when dessert came, there was a tray of Sarah's favourite Indian sweets that spelled out "Marry Me?" I wondered if Hari had brought the tray back. Now that they were nearly married, and they would be looking for somewhere to live, Hari would focus on getting a "proper job" and we could help them with a deposit. It had been a bumpy road, but he had finally got there.

"No big wedding, Mum. Registry office will do!" He looked at me. I was obviously disappointed and then he added, "Only joking! We'll have the wedding that Sarah wants."

My mind was racing. I wanted to get out the folder with all the information I had been collecting and start planning with her there and then, but my husband glanced over at me.

"If you need me, Sarah, for anything, I am here," I replied.

"Of course I'm going to need you," she said. "I think it's important for us to have a Hindu wedding ceremony as well."

I wanted to cry. "Are you sure? You know you will be united for at least seven lifetimes?" I joked.

She looked at Hari. "I'm sure," she said.

I don't care what people say but when your children are finally settled, that's when you feel real contentment.

Unfortunately, their engagement only lasted four months.

I was teaching her how to make methi parathas when she asked me if I thought he could change.

Of course he will change, Sarah. He will change because he loves you. Now, don't question any further; please take him. This is what every fibre of my being wanted to tell her. I couldn't bear the thought of losing her, of her not coming around every Wednesday and filling the kitchen with her warmth. I couldn't think of the future without her, or my lovely grandchildren who she would bring round and we would make sweets and laugh together.

Instead, I held back my tears and I said, "'There is a voice that doesn't use words; listen'."

She looked at me, "That is so beautiful. Is it Rumi?"

I nodded. "I can't ever seem to follow his advice; perhaps you will be able to."

She made a swallowing sound and looked away and when she looked back at me, tears were streaming down her face and I knew that she had made her decision.

"Thank you, Tara. You've done so much and have always made me feel welcome."

And that was it; I knew that was the end.

Sarah hugged me. I clung to her, biting my lip, and did not want to let go of her. She was like a lighthouse that had appeared from nowhere and I knew that once I let her go, she would disappear out of sight.

"Tara," she said, untangling herself from me, "Hari needs help. Perhaps some counselling? There's a lot of anger there."

"Yes, maybe that is the way forward now. I am very sorry, Sarah."

"You've got nothing to be sorry for. It's not your fault." She kissed me on the cheek and wrapped her slender arms around me once again. I started to cry.

That was it. Sarah left him. She didn't even have the Princess Diana ring to leave on the table or take with her if she wanted because he had sold it. I sat at the kitchen table and looked around at all the gadgets and utensils. If I had allowed myself to sit there for any longer, I would have felt the prison that it was; I would have felt the disillusionment of my marriage, the wasted years, the anger towards my son, the loss of my job and Sarah and perhaps I would have got up, walked out and kept walking. But the flowers needed watering in the garden and the part of me that needed to keep the show going to confirm that it had all been worth it, connected the hosepipe and stood there watering flowers when the person trapped inside of me wanted to scream, take the shears to them and hack every one of them off.

So when I saw the look that Margaret had when watering her flowers in the garden after the loss of her daughter, I understood it. I wanted to grab her, reach out to the part of her that was also lost. How to set her free? That was the part I was unsure of.

I pretended not to hear this woman inside of me clambering to get out, put away the hosepipe, went back inside and prepared dinner.

After Sarah's departure, Hari left his job and began DJ-ing full time. He would be up all night and sleep during the day and when he woke up, he would start watching programmes like *Antiques Roadshow* and property programmes like *Location, Location, Location*. When he started watching *Homes Under the Hammer*, I hid the deeds of the house and made sure anything valuable was put in the safe. I knew he was gambling; I tried talking to him. He was lying on the sofa, flicking between channels. I took the remote control from him.

"You could have just told her that it would all work out." He fixed his gaze on the television while he spoke to me.

"But it wouldn't. You have a problem."

"The only problem is you, Mum. You could have just said nothing."

I had the biggest urge to take off my sandal and just beat him with it. "My mistake was to make it all easy for you. Take *responsibility*."

He took back the remote control.

I told Hiten; Hiten said he would sort it out.

Only after I was made redundant did I actually see the full extent of his deceit.

Redundancy came as a big shock to me. I thought I could stay in some voluntary capacity, but the library was closing down. Hillary had left a while back but Abigail, Martin and I had been together for sixteen years and we were like a little dysfunctional family.

The news sinking in coincided with Sarah's departure. I cried non-stop for a week and was upstairs most evenings talking to Deep, asking for some guidance. He suggested I spend time with Hari and make sure he got back on track before jumping into volunteering for Help the Aged. When the actual day of my leaving came, I thought Mr Davies would come out and tell me there was a mistake. He came out of his office and thanked me for the many years of service. I thanked him for the opportunity and tried my best not to howl, throw myself on the floor as I had wanted and take him down with me. Instead, I pinched my finger and thumb together and graciously accepted his gift.

I attempted to hug Abigail, but she patted me awkwardly on the back. I got her an indoor herb kit. I thought she would live in a ground-floor flat where her cat would have access to a cat flap, but she would have limited access to a garden of her own.

"And this is for your kitty-cat," I said, handing her a ceramic cat bowl with *Tiger* written across it.

"Charlie. His name is Charlie. That's very thoughtful of you, Bhanu."

She did have a cat. And that is all I ever got to find out about Abigail in all our years together, but then nobody really got to find out about me either – well, only the story that I presented them: happy middle-aged Indian lady, GSOH with love of poetry, seeks knowledge and to share knowledge.

"Bhanu," Abigail said, "that was kind, what you used to do with those notes. I'm sure it touched a lot of people."

I began to sob. It was awkward as Abigail was unsure of what to do. Martin handed me a tissue.

"This is not the end," he signed.

"Yes. We will meet again," I replied.

"Of course we will, Bhanu. What I meant is that there is a big adventure waiting for you."

There would be no adventure. My life would shrink back to how it was before, roaming the rooms of the detached house with Deep, escaping reality. My daughter was pregnant so things might be different? There was the baby to look forward to, another beginning. Perhaps she would need my help, though knowing my daughter, perhaps not.

I smiled at Martin and gave him a present that was wrapped awkwardly because of its shape. It was a colourful tiffin carrier. I unwrapped the gift that they had bought me. It was a T-shirt that read: *I will Dewey Decimate you.*

I began to laugh.

It is a T-shirt that means a lot. I wore it the first time I held Leyla. I wore it when the loan shark came around to collect the debt my son owed him. And I was wearing it when I finally met Deep again.

Pushpa kept reading the words on the T-shirt, trying to make sense of it.

"Is it meant to read 'Desi-mate'?"

For the non-Indian people, Desi is a term for all things Indian. She read it again. "I will Dewey Desi-mate you? But what does it mean? I will convert you into an Indian? Or Dewey, I will be your Indian friend? Who is Dewey?"

"It's a library system. Ask your son. He will know. He knows most things."

"Bhanu, I have noticed that since leaving that library, you are very sharp with me. Did you try the hormonal patches like I told you?"

"No, I haven't. I'm going to see if I can control it with my diet."

"You need more than diet. I can feel that hormonal rage, Bhanu. You are very angry. I know you are upset with Sarah leaving; I did try to prepare you for that. Is everything okay with Hiten?"

"He is a serial adulterer," I said calmly.

I said the words half-expecting her to be shocked but she responded in a matter-of-fact way that I should really have anticipated.

"I know that, but is everything else okay? You are not in any major financial crisis, are you?"

"No," I replied.

"Not worth wasting your anger on that, Bhanu. You knew what you were getting into when you married him and you know he will always come back to you."

I'm not sure if I did know that I was marrying a serial adulterer but yes, I married him to feel safety, not knowing that in exchange, I would give up my freedom.

"If I could, I don't think I would do it again."

"Don't think too much. You just enjoy this phase of life with your grandchild." She hugged me. "Compared to most, you have a very good life."

Hugh called me later that evening to tell me that Anita was in labour. He was away on business. I rushed to the Portland hospital.

"Which room is she in?" I asked the receptionist, with my tiffin carrier in hand. There are certain things you must feed a woman who has just had a baby.

"One minute, madam. I will go and check for you."

Then I spotted Anita walking around the ward – it wasn't really a ward, more like a hotel lobby. She was with a friend.

"Anita." I rushed over to her.

"Please, Mum. I told you not to come. You will spoil the rhythm."

She glanced at the tiffin carrier. "Whatever that is, I don't want it."

Her friend looked uncomfortable and whispered, "Hypnobirthing."

"And please don't wait, Mum. I need to be calm. Calm, Mum. I will call you later."

I waited for hours out of sight. Pushpa was right, Pushpa was always right; the baby would be a new beginning. When Anita called, it only took a few minutes for me to arrive.

I looked at Leyla lying on Anita and I started to cry.

"Here, Mum. You can pick her up."

"Really?"

I held Leyla close to me and we walked towards the window. The sun was rising across London. I wished that she would be totally free. I wished that the thorn that had been in each generation, in my mother, in me, in my daughter, would finally work itself out and with Leyla, there would be nothing to prove to anyone and she could be free.

"She is beautiful, Anita. She looks like you."

"I think that there is something of you in her, Mum."

"No. She's too beautiful to look like me."

"Don't say that."

"I can come and stay if you want? You might need help. You need to sleep, to eat. Having a baby is…"

"It's okay, Mum. Hugh is on his way back and we have hired a night nanny."

A night nanny is a qualified stranger who will bottle-feed the baby in the night so the mother can sleep.

"I understand," I lied. "If you need anything, please just call me."

My daughter had erected a marquee in her garden for Leyla's first birthday party. It was a circus theme and Anita had hired costumes for us. Hiten, Hari and I dressed up as clowns, which was apt; there was quite a bit going on beneath the painted smiling faces and the oversized clothes. Hari had begun working part-time with my husband in one of the jewellery shops. We converted the garage into a studio for him so he could make his music and keep busy spinning decks instead of roulette wheels. I missed Sarah, as I'm sure Hari did, but wasn't allowed to mention her name in the house.

Hiten was online dating; I caught a glimpse of his profile picture on his laptop. He looked at least twenty years younger. I felt resignation. I wasn't going to leave. The familiar, no matter how uncomfortable, seemed the safest option and I told myself that I had a son who needed stability and a daughter and a granddaughter who needed me. Anyway, where would I go? What would I do? And as Pushpa said, compared to most people, it was a great life and whenever I needed to escape, Deep was there.

It was like the circus tent – built on precarious foundations, and all of us bound together keeping the show going, complicit in making it look good on the outside.

Nobody would have ever known what each of us hid.

I had prepared some snacks for the party; my hands were full, so Hiten opened the car door for me. He was dressed in chequered green and yellow trousers and had a curly blue wig on.

"Nice jester!" I joked.

"I'm a great juggler," he replied, taking one of the bags as I got in.

Indeed, he was!

"I've got some big shoes to fill," Hari added as he got in the car.

We all laughed. Mine was a pretend sort of laugh and I suspected Hari's was too.

We collected my mother-in-law from Hiten's brother's house. Her face was unpainted; she wore an orange wig and a white sari. Hiten got out of the car. She cackled when she saw his outfit and then nodded at me to indicate that she wanted to sit in the front. I got out and sat with Hari in the back. She reached out for Hari's hand and touched him as I strapped myself in. En route, my mother-in-law announced that she wasn't happy staying at her son's. She paused and announced that her daughter-in-law was torturing her – cooking all sorts of food she didn't like.

"Nah, Nanima, you don't have to put up with that. Come stay with us," Hari volunteered. I kicked him with my enormous clown shoe.

"I am happy to cook for you and send it to you," I added quickly.

She ignored my offer and turned to my husband. "I know you will make everything okay for me, son," she replied, holding his hand tightly. "You have always looked after me so well." She looked up at the mirror and caught my eye. "You have looked after everyone."

Margaret, Hugh's mother, was dressed as a trapeze artist. I noted that she had great legs, which she had always kept hidden in her trousers. She laughed heartily when she saw us walk in.

"Oh, Banoo, you look marvellous."

"So do you," I replied. "You have wonderful legs."

Her husband Malcolm looked down at her legs as if it was the first time he had seen them. Margaret had been a dancer.

"Banoo, Hit-en." Malcolm extended his arm. He had come as himself, without the bib.

Cynthia, their daughter, was dressed as a ballerina and was holding Leyla.

Leyla cried when she saw us. I took off my nose and she cried louder. "I think it's all a bit overwhelming for her. How are you, Bhanu?" Cynthia asked.

I wish I had sat down and talked to her more because that was the last occasion where we would see her.

Hugh, dressed as a ringmaster, came over to greet us. He was laughing. "Thank you so much for making the effort. Have you got a drink?" He called the waiter over. Anita was also dressed as a ringmaster and was busy circulating and making sure everyone had what they needed. I looked around. There must have been more than a hundred people there. It was all very different from Anita's first birthday when we invited friends and family over and gave Anita her first solid food of rice, ghee and honey. Leyla had fallen asleep.

"Mum, you look amazing!" Anita pinched my red nose.

"I left the snacks on the kitchen table, *beta*."

"Don't worry about that." She gestured at the many trays of food being passed around. "Let me introduce you to a few friends."

I spoke to some mothers from her NCT group. They were talking about the "cry it out" sleep-training and self-soothe methods. I advised against. They were only babies for so long. Time would go quickly; better to enjoy their children and let them know that their parents would always be there. Otherwise, later, when they became parents to adults, as mothers they would be "crying it out" often and being blamed for all the things they didn't do. One of them laughed and asked my opinion on a range of subjects. I have never been asked for parenting advice so stuck to her most of the afternoon.

My mother-in-law was tired; we had to drop her off. Hari stayed behind. My mother-in-law began tearing up as we said goodbye and as Hiten walked her to the door, she began sobbing, adding that her last wish was to die in the home of her favourite son.

"Please don't worry, Mummy. We will do something," he replied.

He got back into the car. "Bhanu. We have to do something for Mummy. I want to invite her to stay with us."

"I don't think that is such a good idea," I replied.

"Bhanu. She is old. We need to take care of her. It's our duty."

We got home. I got changed into my T-shirt and elasticated jogging bottoms and went to the bathroom to take off the make-up. A happy clown's face was staring back at me. I needed to find a way to stop pretending. I couldn't have her stay. I had to tell Hiten straight. What would other people think of me if I didn't take an old woman in? Deep was standing behind me as I began wiping the make-up off.

"What should I do, Deep?"

"You have to find a way to forgive her," I heard him reply, "then your decision will be easy."

The doorbell went and I had to end my conversation with him there; it wouldn't stop ringing. I didn't know where Hiten had disappeared to, so I went downstairs.

It was a loan shark. An enormous, menacing bald man. A loan shark had come to the door and asked for the money that Hari owed him. He was taken aback by my half clown face and then he read my T-shirt. "I will Dewey Decimate you." He smirked. I screamed for Hiten to come downstairs. We paid him quickly so the neighbours wouldn't see and got rid of him.

"I told you he is a gambler!" I shouted at my husband. "I told you and you said you would do something."

"It's a phase, Bhanu. I went through all kinds of phases. I will speak to him."

"No, no more excuses. We need to do something. He is thirty-four!" I continued shouting. "We have allowed this to happen."

A few minutes later, Hari walked casually through the door.

"Mum, Mum, Mum, it's not what it looks like. A friend lent me some money. I forgot to pay it back. He just sent someone round as a mess-about."

"And the twenty thousand pounds you stole from us? The signatures you forged?"

He said nothing.

"Pack your bags," I shouted.

He looked at my husband. "Dad?"

"Bhanu!" my husband urged.

"You are thirty-four. Go and pack your bags."

"Well, I haven't got anywhere to go,"

"Yes, and that's also all *my* fault."

He went upstairs to pack his bags.

"Bhanu, think about this. What will people say? What will *Mummy* say?" my husband pleaded.

"I don't care. This has to stop. All of it. I can't do this any more."

Hari came down the stairs sheepishly. I turned away. My husband gave him some money. Where would he go, anyway? He was also like a homing pigeon. He would go to Anita's house. After a week, she would get fed up of him and he would be right back here.

A few weeks later, he asked if he could come home. He said Anita was paying for him to see a therapist and that he was "really getting his shit together".

That was her unspoken deal she made with him: *Please don't clutter up my house, annoy Hugh with the use of your English language and dirty my white bespoke sofa. If you leave, I will give you some money and pay for counselling.*

Something had changed in the deal between Hari and me. In the sense that he knew that I was no longer prepared to tiptoe around him, put up with his nonsense, and that it was time for him to get a proper job and become a responsible adult. I also knew him well enough to suspect that he would do whatever it took to stop the change. People will do anything to stay with the familiar no matter how uncomfortable. I should know. Something big was coming – I could sense it.

We didn't talk about the counselling. Hari wasn't selling any more of our household items and it looked like he was filling in application forms and going to interviews. Probably also sensing that our deal was changing, my husband put away the laptop and decided to make a commitment and do something big, hence secretly – or not so secretly – arranging the anniversary/vow renewal. Before then, he handed me two tickets.

"I have a surprise for you, Bhanu."

I had heard that forty years earlier.

He handed me two tickets for a fortieth anniversary cruise.

On our Caribbean cruise, the captain made a special announcement and toasted us, but Hiten was too sick to attend. Helga sat next to me, dressed in the Keralan sari that I had tied for her and I raised a glass of orange juice as everyone wished us many more happy years together.

Then Helga and I went to the nightclub on the ship. They were playing all the 1980s dance tracks and for that night I had no back pain and we danced the night away, ending in a duet of George Michael's "Freedom!".

yard five

"Tear off the mask, your face is glorious"
— Rumi

For most of my life, I have been pretending to be the person that I think I should be because I think if I met the person that I really am, I'm not sure that I would like her. The events leading to finally opening the door of my prison were as follows:

1. Meeting Helga on the cruise.
2. Seeing the therapist.
3. Visiting Margaret.
4. My son's letter.
5. Seeing Deep again after thirty-five years.

I will begin with Margaret's visit. Nobody sees the series of defeats that have shaped our lives. If anyone sees us, they might see an older woman. That's it – an older woman beamed down from outer space with no history and nothing much to offer. But I saw the battles Margaret had fought and the final one looked too big to overcome.

Come back, Margaret. Don't lose yourself in the rhododendrons. Call yourself back. It's not too late. Feel your grief, is what I really wanted to shout but I didn't, and I couldn't stop thinking about her, about the series of defeats big and small that I have also allowed to shape me and the stories that I have told myself and believed about them. What would it feel like to be free of all these stories?

And then my son handed me his letter, severing the deepest tie. The bond that I believed kept me in this marriage.

"Read it, Mum."

Perhaps your children express the grief that you are unable to?

I sat and cried on my daughter's white sofa. Helga, in that moment, was the gatekeeper of my thoughts and did not allow me to disappear into my imaginary world with Deep. I looked at the sofa – symbol of my daughter's need for order and cleanliness. It was another reminder of my failure as a mother and not having been braver in my life. I heard Leyla crying and so I quickly dried my tears. She was smiling at me as I went into her bedroom. I picked her up and went downstairs.

We sat on the floor singing nursery rhymes. "One, two, buckle my shoe, three, four, knock on the door." Leyla was laughing.

"Bikit, bikit." She smiled at me.

I reached in my handbag and gave her a biscuit.

Leyla signed at me for another one and I knew I shouldn't have but I gave it to her and then she asked for *agua*. I quickly went into the kitchen to get her beaker and when I came back, I saw the sofa. She had thrown up all over the white sofa. It had gone everywhere. I quickly put Leyla in the high chair, got some Fairy liquid, kitchen towel and water and started clearing it up. My heart beat incredibly fast as I was dabbing. It seemed to spread even more. I took the hair dryer and blow-dried it, but the stain appeared bigger. I put cushions on the sofa but couldn't hide the stain.

My daughter called to check how I was and said that the nanny had collected her prescription from the doctor's and was on her way back home.

"Yes. Everything is fine here," I said, looking at the big stain. I hesitated. "I'm sorry."

"What for?"

"For your OCD behaviour. I'm sorry I did that to you. And for all the other things that I am unaware that I did, like not allowing you to play with your friend without a proper explanation."

"Mum. I know you are upset but can we talk about this another time? Do you want me to send you an Uber to get back home?"

"No. I need to get some shopping. I will catch the train."

The nanny came back.

"*Dios mío!*" she hollered when she saw the stain.

"Biscuit," I said, re-enacting the scene for her.

"Oh! *La señora no va a estar contenta,*" she said, pointing at a picture of my daughter.

"No. *No contenta,*" I replied, imitating her potentially angry face, "but it will be okay. It will all be okay." I touched Concetta's shoulder.

"*Pero, señora...*"

I kissed Leyla goodbye and said "*Adiós*" to Concetta but she was already on WhatsApp talking about the sofa stain to someone.

I boarded the District line with two bags of shopping that I had stopped off to get and was thinking about my son and his letter. My family wouldn't really miss me if I continued on this line. I could take the train to Heathrow airport and pay Helga a visit as promised and escape the dreaded "surprise" fortieth anniversary/vow renewal. Helga would slap her huge thigh with delight. These are promises you make as a formality but neither person expects you to carry it through. But Helga, she would be genuinely happy and then from there I could travel to wherever I wanted.

I would miss Leyla. Really miss her. Well, after my daughter sees that stain, she would probably deny access. I think I would even miss my husband; we fit together, albeit awkwardly – he gets my humour. He might be devastated for a day or two but he'd get over it. And I know I can't look after his mother. My thoughts were veering too dangerously so I began thinking about making something nice for my son to eat – but then, the terms of our deal have been broken. Should I cook for him? How best to approach the conversation with him? The old me would have ignored it and carried on.

I got off at Acton and changed to get the Piccadilly line. The shopping bags were weighing me down, so I stopped. I heard a voice.

"Tara, Tara…"

It was him. Unmistakably him. I have heard this voice so many times in my imagination that I didn't want to turn around and for him not to be there.

"Tara," he said again as he touched my shoulder.

Why now, when I was smelling of baby vomit, had turmeric-stained hands and was wearing blue jogging bottoms with an elasticated waist? This was not how I had imagined it. There was no time even to straighten my straggly hair.

His voice was tender. I turned around slowly, not wanting him to see what I had become. He took my shopping bags and I began to cry, and I couldn't stop crying. He placed them on the floor and held me until I stopped.

Deep didn't say anything. He just looked at me as if he was taking in all the years we had been apart. He had aged too: his hair was completely white, he had deeply etched wrinkles and wasn't the young Deep of my imagination, but he was still there. His eyes were the same as ever.

"There's a Starbucks across the road," he stated, knowing that an Underground station was not worthy of this moment.

Although it was just yesterday, I'm unsure of exactly how we got to Starbucks and I can't remember if he ordered for me or if I had ordered a frothy latte and an almond slice that I would never eat. All I know is I just sat there in disbelief.

It's true what Rumi says, I wanted to shout to all the customers sitting in the café. "*What you are seeking is also seeking you.*" It's true what Deep had said all those years ago, the intensity of our feelings meant that we would always be drawn to be together. I had held on, I'd believed, and he came to me. All these years of waiting and he came, and he came the moment I let go of him. He was here. Deep sat down and he held my hand. It was warm. I put my other hand to hold his and I didn't care who saw us. He was finally, finally here.

"'Touch has a memory'," I said.

I don't think he heard me because he would have said *Keats* and we would have slipped back into our game. I was about to repeat it when he asked, "Where do we begin, Tara?"

Instead of beginning with pleasantries and perhaps because my son's letter was very much on my mind, I began there. I took the letter out from my handbag and read it to him.

He shook his head as I finished but instead of allowing him a moment to offer his opinion, I told him about my husband. Apart from mentioning it to Pushpa, I have never told anyone about my husband. But yesterday, I didn't care, and I talked and I talked without pausing. Not caring if anyone saw us, my hand clutching his, I felt free, like Helga. It was as if a big burden had finally lifted and I was weightless, and for one moment, I believed that Neil Armstrong did land on the moon and there was more for me.

He told me how his wife had died and how he'd looked after her until the end. I imagined him reading her poetry until she slipped away. I was jealous and then felt guilty about feeling jealous towards a dead woman so hid it by quoting Rumi.

"'The world is the playground and death is the night'."

He looked puzzled.

"It's Rumi," I said.

He didn't say anything. Instead, he took a deep breath and said, "Come with me. I have thought about you so often. Especially recently."

Me too, I wanted to say. *Every time I couldn't face what was going on, I escaped to my imaginary world where we have been living happily for forty years. Today, is in fact, day 13,870 of our imaginary life. We have a daughter who will not stop access on discovering a biscuit-stained white sofa and a son who is not a gambling addict.*

And I don't know why – perhaps to test him, I said, "We are not people in a film. We have responsibilities."

"We have fulfilled them," he replied calmly.

"Were you happy in your marriage?" I asked.

"Yes." He nodded.

"That's good," I lied.

"Tara, there are no excuses any more."

Then I got scared. The cage door was finally, finally open, and I was too scared to fly out. It couldn't be this easy.

"I have a nail appointment. My nails need to be manicured."

"Stop it, Tara. Stop pretending," he said, raising his voice.

"What was it all for if I was such a shit mother? That's 13,870 days wasted."

"They weren't wasted."

"Yes, they were. I stayed for them. Was I such a bad mother that he needed to escape from me – that's why he said he gambled: 'I needed to escape from you'."

"He didn't mean it."

"Perhaps I didn't give him space to grow. I wanted to keep him safe, but I was controlling."

"You did your best."

"Did I? He is ashamed of me. My daughter is ashamed of me. I'm ashamed of me."

He wanted to stop me, but it was the truth.

"I am ashamed of myself."

"Tara, listen to me. Today is a new start. We can start again. Come with me."

I reached for my carrier bags. What was I thinking?

"It's my fortieth wedding anniversary tomorrow.

They are having a surprise party. It's a vow renewal – no, it's a *wedding*." I felt sick.

"I don't care. Go and tell your family. Make whatever arrangements you need to make, and I will come for you. Look at me. Look at me, Tara. I see you. I see you. I have always seen you."

I looked at him. Yes, he and Ba were the only people who had really seen me. I thought of the moments I had spent with him, without him really being there. Then I smiled and told him how I had made the trip to York, imagining him there with me. I described the beautiful Georgian house with the red front door on a cobbled street. Finally, we could make the trip together and perhaps stay there.

"York? What's in York?" he asked. "I live in Richmond. My children are in Richmond."

His words landed heavily but, in that moment, I chose not to take in their enormity. "It's Auden's birthplace," I replied slowly.

"Ah yes!" he said. "Of course it is. My memory is not what it was. No, I couldn't move there. I really need to stay close by to my girls and my grandchildren. I have four of them, three girls and a boy. Noah is quite mischievous. A bit like…"

He was not even aware of the huge accident he had caused. It was a multiple pile-up. I was in an utter state of shock. I cut the almond slice he had bought me in half, but not because I wanted to eat it; it was something to do. I offered it to him.

"No, thank you. I'm on insulin." He refused the half and then he listed all the medication he was taking, ending with metformin.

"You can control it with diet," I suggested, trying to find my way out of the wreckage.

"You can help me control it," he replied.

I searched his eyes to find my Deep.

"I need some time to think, Deep. I have an appointment now, but I will call you," I said calmly.

I reached for my shopping bags.

"But, Tara..."

"Deep. Please. Give me some time. It is a big decision. There is lots going on."

"But you haven't even eaten your cake. It was three pounds."

"I'm not really hungry."

He took the almond slice, wrapped it up in a serviette and put it in his pocket. "My grandson will enjoy this."

"I'm sorry but I really need to go. I will call you." I went to grab my bags.

"Let me help you with that," he said, reaching for my bags.

"Thank you." I smiled my stroke victim's fake smile.

"We will talk later," he said.

He did not notice the fact that he had run me over with his words and left me for dead. My Deep, or the Deep of my imagination, would not have bought an almond slice for me. He knew I did not like sweets, he knew that I had stopped eating them after hearing that my mother had drowned. And my Deep would not have reminded me how much it had cost.

Then, as I began to walk away, I stopped. I turned to look at him.

"Deep, 'Lovers don't finally meet somewhere. They're in each other all along'."

He looked confused.

"It's Rumi."

"Ah yes. It is such a long time since I have read any poetry," he said, with no recollection of the words I have clung to for nearly forty years. I smiled back at him and continued walking.

"I will call you, Tara."

Tears streamed down my face and a huge knot began to form in my throat. "Stupid, stupid woman. You are a stupid old woman." I swallowed the lump and made my way to the nail bar because the truth that I had waited for forty years for someone who did not really exist was too much for me to handle right then.

The Chinese girl who was doing my nails was not really interested in speaking to me. "It's my wedding tomorrow," I informed her.

I expected her to look shocked.

She nodded but didn't look up at me. Why would she? I am invisible.

I wanted to get up, stand in the centre of the salon, beat my chest and wail uncontrollably – but I, like Margaret, was resigned to yet another defeat and stayed safely amongst the rhododendrons, pretending it was okay, that it would all be alright; and perhaps this was what this stage of life was about – to slowly disappear, to be grateful for what you have and not want anything more.

I got home and as I unpacked the shopping, I saw the note my son had stuck on the fridge with my recently purchased fridge magnet from the Caribbean.

I'm not coming.

There it was for all to see, in lieu of the finger paintings I had not stuck up in his childhood. I left it there, not hiding it as I might have done before, and stared at it.

My daughter started calling. I did not pick up and then she began texting me.

Really, Mum, biscuits on the sofa?

Then:

HOW MANY TIMES DO I HAVE TO TELL YOU NO BISCUITS!!!

Followed by:

That is not going to come out.

And:

Bespoke sofa – RUINED.

I switched the phone off.

I took out the Auden book of poems from the drawer of the dressing room table. The inscription read, *Tara, the loving one will always be me.* I placed it in the bin and then I took it out again and cried and cried. Huge sobs that nobody would ever hear because

I am invisible. I don't exist. I am a stupid, stupid old woman, who for forty years has lived a parallel life with someone who does not exist. Perhaps I have caused my own invisibility by not fully being present in the life I have.

Rumi asks why we stay in a prison when the door is wide open?

Because it is too late. It's too late.

The next morning, I got up and in the same autopilot way I have lived my life, had a shower and made myself a cup of tea. I sat on the bed and switched on my phone. There were several missed calls and messages from Deep. I didn't listen to or read any of them. There was a message from my daughter apologising for overreacting. Nothing from my son. He had not come home. I finished my tea, wondering whether it was possible to make a run for it. What a ridiculous thought: everything was paid for; friends, family and the community would be arriving soon. My husband and I were friends, we had come this far and we would see out the last chapter of our lives together. That was that.

The thing that was really worrying me was being witnessed by Agni, the fire god. I would close my eyes at that point. Yes, I would just breathe deeply and pretend I was somewhere else – not sure where exactly, as there was no parallel life any more – but I would think of somewhere. I proceeded to get ready even though I had hours, but I thought, *If I'm ready, there is less chance of me changing my mind.*

My husband came striding in and handed me a bunch of flowers and then he opened the jewellery box that was in his hand and took out a sparkling diamond necklace.

"Is this really for me?" I pretended.

"Who else?" he asked, undoing the clasp and touching my neck tenderly. He placed the necklace around my neck, did up the clasp expertly and we stood in front of the mirror.

"It's beautiful. Thank you," I said, touching his hand.

"Like you," he repeated. "Forty years! Remember the start. Now look at us. Not bad, eh, Bhanu?" he said, still laughing, and then I think he said he was going to get his mother.

Ah yes, the sudoku-trolling mother-in-law, who would soon make her visit permanent.

"Don't worry about Hari, he will be coming," Hiten added.

"Don't you want to talk about it? The letter?" I asked.

"Ah, Bhanu, don't take everything so seriously. He was just upset."

Hiten probably sorted out that problem with a couple of thousand pounds.

"And the sofa. I told Anita we would get her a new one."

No surprise there either. She probably called him after the discovery.

"Anita, *beta*, I can't talk now. I am tied up."
"But it's *ruined*!"
"Never mind, *beta*. Ten more bespoke sofas."
"*And* she fed Leyla biscuits. The amount of times—"
"*Beta*. I can't talk now," he would have said.

I finished getting ready and brought out the woman who, as Anaïs Nin says, will shortly be ready to get up on that stage and I looked at her. Layers and layers of foundation accompanied with blusher and lipstick. She looked like a drag queen – a tired drag queen who didn't want to perform any more.

Ignoring the feeling in the pit of my stomach and ignoring cheerleading Helga, who is encouraging me to leave, I got two aspirins from the bathroom cabinet. I went back to the bedroom and stood in front of the mirror practising my surprised face – the one for when I see the stage, the priest, the fire and the room filled with all our friends and family.

Then I got a text message. It was from Pushpa. It was an emoji of a pair of brown running legs. I counted five seconds for the second message; sure enough, another message arrived, but it was from Margaret.

Happy 40th anniversary to a lovely couple. I hope you enjoy many more years together.

There was no follow up *LOL* from Pushpa.

Our lives are made up of a series of events that culminate in the big event. It's not that one day you choose to leave your whole life behind. You hear stories of a man who went to buy a loaf of bread and never came back. There was a build-up to leaving, an inability to communicate what was wrong. We are invisible long before we are invisible, just like we are broken-hearted long before we are broken-hearted. We have betrayed ourselves long before anyone else betrays us.

For forty years, I have been in a story that I didn't really want to be in and the reason I wrote that story was to escape pain, the pain of abandonment; but with each chapter, I have abandoned a part of myself – so now I don't know who I am any more. I created another story to make the one I am living in more acceptable but that story is not real. I don't know who I am any more without all these stories and perhaps I am afraid to find out, because after all the unravelling, maybe the truth is that I am an unlovable, invisible woman with nothing left to offer.

But maybe, maybe I am not...

I reread Margaret's message and thought of the many more years together; the years in front of me were fewer than the years behind me. Like the man at the counter who buys his bread and keeps walking, a doorway appeared in front of me. I quickly began unravelling the sari, pulled out the pins that held my bun together and wiped off the layers of make-up. I looked at the necklace. Forty years. My gift for forty years of service.

I took it off, placed it back in the case. Resisting the urge to tidy, I left the sunrise sari on the floor and quickly got changed into my Dewey Decimate T-shirt and tracksuit, put my trainers on and hastily gathered a few things together, throwing them all into a small case. I hesitated, wondering whether to take the necklace with me, but left it behind.

Keep going, Bhanu, sehr schön! Helga cheered loudly over the doubts and over the fear. I ran down to the kitchen with the case and saw my son's note on the fridge. I took it down and wrote on it, *I am sorry, Hari, I am sorry, Anita*. Sticking it back on the fridge with the Caribbean cruise fridge magnet, I glanced one last time at the kitchen. The car horn sounded three times. My husband and mother-in-law pulled up to the drive. My heart began beating even faster as I closed the back door and walked quickly to the Tube station, looking over my shoulder, hoping they wouldn't notice me and convince me to get back in the car with them.

When I got closer to Heathrow airport, the signal from my phone came back on; there were missed calls and messages from my husband, daughter, son and Deep. I would reply to each of them, explaining. But first, I began with Margaret.

Dear Margaret,
"And the day came when the risk to remain tight in a bud was more painful than the risk it took to blossom." Anaïs Nin.
Fuck polite, Margaret.
Get out of the rhododendrons. There is still everything to play for.
Love
BHANU

author's note

I used to build rockets – metaphorical rockets. Some failed to launch, some exploded mid-air, some lit up the sky and changed my whole world. Then, I stopped building them.

The reason was a series of events in a very short space of time: death, birth, marriage. I decided to keep myself safe. I no longer built rockets. I told myself that dreaming about the adventure was much better than the adventure itself. It was a lie. Safety kept me from taking risks, from disappointment, from failure.

If you are invested in your safety, you will have a heap of broken pieces with no universe to explore. Your world gets smaller and smaller and a part of you starts rusting. Eye rolling, a theatrical exhalation of breath and an inability to appreciate other rocket builders are some of the symptoms of rust.

You join the other side. You know, the ones who say it can't be done. Nobody knows that you have joined the other side as it still all looks good on the outside.

The outside. Keeping the outside looking good requires a lot of work. Especially when you are not feeling like it. Keeping the outside looking good is done for other people.

I met a sixty-two-year-old woman whose outside was pristine. Great family, friends, great life. For some reason, she invited me in. I mean really let me in and showed me the mess. She had hidden it from herself, from others. I sat there and listened to her tell the truth for the very first time. Then I met another woman, and another, all with the same story. Regret, disappointment, the longing for things to be different…

The truth is amazing. It has the power to crack open any carefully constructed façade, to make you want to start again. This is what happened in my interactions with all these women who spoke the truth for the first time. It made them want to change their life. It made me want to be braver in mine.

I wanted to tell this story in the hope that you see that "unravelling" is not a thing to be feared but an opportunity for something else. That just when we think it's all over, it's only just beginning…

Thank you to everyone who has helped me along this journey and to you, reader, for following me this far.

Preethi Nair, September 2024

Thank you to the following authors and publishers who granted permission to use their work:

The Essential Rumi – Translations by Coleman Barks, HarperCollins Publishers Ltd, 1995

The Essential Rumi Quotes: Top 300 Most Inspiring by Shahram Shiva, 2023

"The More Loving One" from *Homage to Clio* by W. H. Auden, published by Random House. Copyright © 1960 W. H. Auden, renewed by the Estate of W. H. Auden. Used by permission of Curtis Brown, Ltd.

"Tear off the mask, your face is glorious" – extract from Ghazal (Ode) 1621. Translated by Azima Melita Kolin and Maryam Mafi, *Rumi: Hidden Music*, Harper-Collins Publishers Ltd, 2001

"Preethi Nair is a one-woman whirlwind"
– HarperCollins

Preethi worked as a management consultant and gave it up to follow her dream and write her first book, *Gypsy Masala*. Having been rejected by most publishers, she set up her own publishing company and PR agency to publish and promote the book all whilst putting on a suit and pretending to go to work. Working under the alias of Pru, Preethi managed to gain substantial coverage and after two years of a roller-coaster journey, she signed a three-book deal with HarperCollins. She won an Asian Women of Achievement Award for her endeavours and "Pru" was also shortlisted as Publicist of the Year for the PPC awards.

Having never acted before (not even at school), Preethi went on to write, act and produce *Sari: The Whole Five Yards*, a sell-out one-woman show in the West End. Preethi adapted this play into the novel *Unravelling*, which has been optioned for television.

Preethi is also visiting professor at various business schools, teaching modules on creativity and journalling for personal leadership.

www.preethinair.com

ALSO BY PREETHI NAIR
100 Shades of White
Gypsy Masala
The Colour of Love

FOR CHILDREN
Anjali's Story: My Magical Lip Balm Adventure